Tranquil
LIGHT

Tranquil LIGHT

a novel

ANITA STANSFIELD

Covenant Communications, Inc.

Published by Covenant Communications, Inc.
American Fork, Utah

Printed in Canada
First Printing: August 2010

16 15 14 13 12 11 10   10 9 8 7 6 5 4 3 2 1

ISBN-13: 978-1-60861-073-0

For my friends.

"The pleasure of a generous friendship is the steadiest joy in the world."
—*Charles Dickens*

CHAPTER ONE

Anaconda, Montana

Chas Leeds heard the baby crying and rolled over in her warm bed, suppressing the urge to groan aloud. Her husband, Jackson, was asleep beside her. Or maybe he too was wanting to groan. Isabelle wasn't yet seven months old, but at the moment she had a nasty flu bug that was making her feverish, nauseous, and cranky. She'd only slept in short spurts through the night after the first signs of illness had hit at bedtime. Since Charles, their two-year-old son, had been afflicted with the same symptoms a few days ago, Chas felt confident that Isabelle would be much better by the end of the day. But right now she just wanted—and needed—some sleep. She thought of the guests at the inn she and her husband ran who were anticipating a lovely breakfast once they arose. When the baby's fussing got louder she heard Jackson sigh loudly, and she knew he was awake.

"I got it," she said and forced herself out of bed. He'd already walked the floor with Isabelle twice during the night, and he'd taken the brunt of dealing with Charles during the night when he'd been sick.

Chas got Isabelle out of her bed, glad at least that her stomach was apparently empty at last and that the vomiting had stopped. She knew the baby likely had a stomachache and was hungry, but she also knew that trying to feed her now would only aggravate the problem. She could only do her best to comfort the baby and ride out the illness. And every step of the way she was hypervigilant about germ control. If either she or Jackson got sick, it would complicate life immensely. She also had to be very careful on behalf of their guests.

Of course she always was, but when dealing with sick children, germ prevention was especially high on her radar.

More than an hour later, Chas had finally coaxed Isabelle back to sleep, but the sun was coming up and she knew if she tried to go back to sleep, she'd end up feeling worse throughout the morning. She'd be better off taking an afternoon nap. Her friend Polly, who came in every day to work in the office of the inn and to help out wherever she was needed, would be more than happy to cover a few extra hours so that Chas and Jackson could get enough rest to be functional.

Chas put Isabelle down in her crib and took the baby monitor with her into the bathroom while she took a shower. She got dressed and peeked in on her husband and both babies to find them still sleeping. She went downstairs and put in a load of laundry, straightened up the kitchen, and ate some toast and juice. She heard Charles on the *other* baby monitor, and hoped he wouldn't wake Jackson before she got upstairs. With two babies in separate rooms, they'd acquired high-quality monitors on different frequencies so that they could always hear the children fuss, even while she and Jackson worked in the inn that was attached to the house.

The inn itself was a restored Victorian mansion that had been functioning as a successful bed-and-breakfast for several years. The attached house was very new and had only been occupied by the family for a matter of weeks. They'd moved in around Thanksgiving, and now they were barely into the new year. They could hear a little chime anywhere in the house if one of the doors to the inn opened or closed, and from their kitchen they could see the office and hallway on a little monitor connected to security cameras. Their new house had a separate front door with a decorative sign that said *Private Entrance,* and by next summer the fenced-in patch of dirt behind the addition would be transformed into the perfect yard for barbecues and a children's play area.

Chas entered Charles's room to see Jackson lifting their son out of his crib. There were still moments when just seeing her husband took her breath away. He was twelve years older than her own midthirties, but their age difference had never been an issue. He looked younger than his years in spite of prematurely gray hair that he wore in a short, almost military style. When Chas had first met him his hair had been salt and pepper; now it was mostly salt with only hints of the fact that it had once been as dark as the hair that both of their children had been born with. Before Chas had met Jackson, she'd been alone for twelve years, except for her grandmother, following the death of her first husband. Jackson was a tremendous blessing in her life, and she loved him beyond description. She couldn't think of anything better that could have happened to her than to be loved by a good man who was willing to share everything with her—even sick babies.

"Good morning," Chas said. "I was hoping to get here before he woke you, and—"

"It's okay," Jackson said. "I need to get up anyway." He kissed Chas in greeting. "Did you get any sleep?"

"A little," she said. "I'm counting on Polly to help cover for me later so I can get a nap."

"Good plan," he said, and Chas greeted her little son as well. "Why don't you go ahead and get started with what you need to do," Jackson added. "I've got the kids covered for the morning shift."

"Okay," she said and kissed him again. "Good luck."

Chas went back downstairs and through the door that joined the kitchen of the house to the kitchen of the inn. According to habit she did a quick walk-through of the main floor, making certain all was in order. Since guests were welcome to get snacks and beverages out of a specific fridge, use the computer in the parlor, or read books and newspapers left in the dining room, she always checked to make certain that nothing had been left out of order. The office and outside doors remained locked when both Chas and Jackson were not actually in the inn. Guests had a key to get in and out of the outside doors. Except for nighttime hours, the signal chime would ring in the house to alert them to anyone coming in.

Chas straightened things up a little, checked some lists in the office for Polly and the room maids, then went to the kitchen and set to work on the specialty breakfast for which her inn was famous. She'd been running the place on her own while caring for her elderly grandmother when Jackson had first come to stay here more than four years earlier. And the rest was history. Now they shared the business, their home, two children, and the same religion. He'd had no interest in her religious beliefs when they'd first come together. But he'd been baptized nearly a year ago. They'd been through a great deal together, and they'd come to a place where life was good and Chas couldn't be happier—barring temporary setbacks like sick children. But even that was just a little inconvenience in contrast to the challenges that many people dealt with. An hour didn't pass without Chas acknowledging how very satisfying her life was and how much she had to be grateful for.

Chas began to feel tired as she neared the completion of serving breakfast to their guests. Polly arrived, and they took a few minutes to catch up as friends while Chas was cleaning the kitchen. Polly had been Chas's right hand at the inn for years; becoming best friends had just made it all the better. Ironically, Polly had married Jackson's best friend not so many months ago. Polly and Elliott lived in a small house about a mile from the inn, and Elliott worked as a security guard for a large corporation in the city of Butte, less than an hour away. Polly had recently discovered that she was pregnant. Since Polly and Elliott were both in their thirties, they were thrilled with the prospect of becoming parents. So far Polly hadn't been too ill with the pregnancy—just tired enough that she often came into work a little later than usual. But the work she did was flexible, so it all worked out well.

Polly went to the office to get started on the usual paperwork. Chas finished up in the kitchen and went into the house to check on Jackson and the children. He was walking the floor with Isabelle, who was fussing, while Charles played nearby in the midst of a vast conglomeration of toys. Chas was grateful for this new addition to the inn where they were able to live with their children and not have to worry about their guests being inconvenienced by the noise or the mess.

"How's it going?" Chas asked, taking the baby from him.

"I think she's doing a little better; she's probably just hungry. But I'm going to let you decide when it's time to try feeding her again."

"Let's try it now," she said, sitting in the rocker to nurse Isabelle.

Jackson took a shower while Chas was with the children. By the time he finished, Isabelle was asleep in her crib, and Chas was picking up toys.

"You know he'll just dump them out again," Jackson said to his wife.

She looked up and smiled. "That's why I'm going to hide *some* of them."

"Good plan," he said and bent over to help her. Since Charles was momentarily enthralled with public television, they managed to get everything picked up without his noticing.

"There now," Chas said while Jackson was putting some toy containers on a high closet shelf. "If I can see the floor at least once a day, I might remain somewhat sane."

Jackson turned to look at his wife, wondering what he'd done to deserve ending up in this life—a life that he'd never even thought to hope for. The very simplicity of what they shared made it all the more wonderful. In contrast to his years in the FBI as a perpetual bachelor, sharing life with Chas was close to heaven. He paused a moment to touch her face and press a hand over her shoulder-length brown hair before he kissed her and said words that he knew he could never say enough. "I love you."

"I love you too," she said.

"Why don't you rest for a while and I'll—"

Polly came in through the kitchen door, which she knew was acceptable during business hours if she needed something. Since the kitchen was part of a large area they called the common room, this was usually where she would find one or the other of them if they were at home. "There's someone here to see you," she said, looking at Jackson.

"Me?" he asked. "Is this someone I know?"

"Apparently," Polly said. "But I've never seen her before. She says she knows *you,* but she wouldn't tell me anything else." Polly stood beside Chas and nudged her with an elbow. "I think *you* should go with him, and I'll watch the kids." She added in a whisper so that Jackson couldn't hear, "She's blond and gorgeous and she wants to see your husband. I think you should go with him."

Chas straightened her hair a little and hurried to follow her husband into the inn. By the time they had turned the corner into the hall, Chas rethought what she was doing. She couldn't think of any logical way to explain following her husband in order to be present during his conversation with this mystery woman. Reverting to a more dignified attitude, she passed by Jackson, speaking softly—

but not so softly that the beautiful blond woman waiting in the hall couldn't hear her. "I've got some calls to make. I'll be in the office." She glanced discreetly at this woman as she passed by, glad that she didn't get caught doing so. She *was* beautiful, well put together, and dressed to perfection. She was slender and had a youthful way about her, but her age showed in her face. Chas guessed her to be middle to late forties, which made her near Jackson's age. She wondered if that was significant to this visit, although Chas couldn't begin to imagine who this woman might be.

Jackson had no idea who to expect. Even when he saw her, it took a long moment for the familiarity to take hold. And when it did he felt instant turmoil. Feelings that he'd believed for years had been laid to rest apparently were not. His heart began to pound and he felt a little clammy. He reminded himself that he was a married man, then he had to acknowledge that what he felt wasn't so much attraction as a sharp rush of memories—some tender and rich, others heartbreaking. Still others made him angry.

"Julie?" he said, needing the intonation of a question to assure himself that it wasn't his imagination turning her familiarity into something it wasn't.

"Hello, Jackson," she said with a smile that intensified the memories. A part of him wanted to hug her tightly—for old time's sake. And a part of him wanted to yell at her and tell her she had a lot of nerve showing up here after what she'd done to him. But it had been about thirty years since she'd broken his heart. That was all in the past. His brain worked hard at convincing his emotions that it truly *was* all in the past.

"How did you find me?" he asked when neither a hug nor anger seemed appropriate.

"I saw your sister in town last week," she said with a thick Southern drawl. "She was always so nice to me."

"Melinda is a very kind person," Jackson said, wondering if he should be angry with his sister for telling his old girlfriend where to find him.

"I hadn't been back home for years," Julie went on. "Then I finally decided to spend Christmas with my dad. And lo and behold I ran into Melinda. The last time I'd talked to her she said she hadn't heard from you since you'd joined the Marines. But now she tells me she connected with you a few years ago, and the two of you are close."

"Yes, that's all true," he said, but he still wanted to know why she'd come all the way to Montana, apparently to find *him*.

Before he could ask, she went on. "Truthfully, she didn't tell me *exactly* where to find you. I confess I did a little detective work. She told me you were running a bed-and-breakfast in a little town about an hour from Butte. The rest was just a process of elimination."

At an obvious pause, Jackson knew she was expecting a reaction. Now that he'd become accustomed to his high-school sweetheart actually standing there, he was thinking that he would have preferred that she stay away. He didn't know why she'd come all this way, but he didn't feel any desire to reconnect with this woman to politely reminisce about days gone by. He doubted they had anything in common anymore, and wondered if they ever had. He had a sick baby to take care of and an inn to run. He was far too busy to waste time chatting with someone he'd spent years trying to forget.

"I have a reservation," she said while he was still trying to think of something to say. "Melinda said this was a great place. I thought I'd stay a couple of nights and see for myself."

That's just great, Jackson thought with a biting sarcasm that he wanted to say aloud but knew wouldn't be polite. "So, it's a vacation you came for," he said.

"Well . . ." she looked flustered, "yes. A vacation is . . . always nice."

"So, you *didn't* come for a vacation," he said. He didn't want to sound rude, but he *did* want to be straightforward about the situation.

"Well . . ." she said again. "Mostly, I came to see you."

Her overt coyness made him angry, but he kept his tone even. Instead he pretended to be utterly surprised and chuckled. "Me? You came all the way to Montana to stay a couple of nights for what? What exactly? If it's a conversation for old-time's sake, you could have called."

"I didn't want to call. I wanted to *see* you."

"So, now you've seen me. I've got work to do. *Mrs.* Leeds is in the office." He motioned with his hand. "She can take care of getting you checked in. Enjoy your stay."

He turned away and she said, "Wait. Is that it? What *about* some conversation for old-time's sake?"

Jackson couldn't deny that his instincts made him feel terribly uneasy about all of this, but he knew that he didn't have just cause to be rude. Feeling the need to soften the moment just a little, Jackson forced a smile and said, "I'll be around." He walked toward the office. "Come along. You can meet my wife."

"I'd love to," she said in a voice that made him wonder if she was lying.

Jackson led the way and stepped into the office ahead of Julie. "Chas," he said, and his wife came to her feet behind the desk, her eyes sparkling with a curiosity that she quickly disguised. "I'd like you to meet Julie . . . uh . . ." It wasn't that he couldn't remember her *original* last name. He just knew she'd been married at least once.

"Oh, those last names don't matter," Julie said. "Just Julie." She stepped forward and held out a hand toward Chas, as if she might be interested in becoming the woman's best friend. "It is *so* wonderful to meet you at last. Did he say *Chas?*"

"That's right," Chas said, alerting Jackson to her ignorance with a discreet glance.

"Uh . . . Chas . . . Julie is . . . from my hometown. We knew each other in high school."

"Now, don't go all bashful on me, Jackson," Julie said, letting go of Chas's hand to playfully slug Jackson in the shoulder. She looked at Chas and said in a stage whisper, "We were high-school sweethearts is what we were. I'm sure he's told you about me."

Jackson instinctively felt the same way that he'd felt in the FBI when he was questioning someone and he knew they were trying to get the upper hand, or trying to throw the authorities off the scent of something they were hiding. He knew Julie's reasons for being here were not to vacation, and he knew she'd been hoping that Jackson *hadn't* told Chas about her, and the comment she'd just made was an effort to cause a rift. But Chas smiled with perfect confidence and said, "Of course. He's told me everything."

Julie looked momentarily deflated, then she began giving Chas the same explanation she'd given Jackson about running into Melinda and her decision to just come here and see what the place was like. It all sounded even more dubious the second time. Jackson interrupted to say, "I should check on the children. Since you have a reservation, Chas can take care of getting you checked in and settled."

"Oh, good," Julie said, something in her eyes indicating great pleasure at being left alone with his wife. Jackson tossed Chas a cautious glance and turned to leave. "Will I see you later?" Julie asked before he could get out the door.

"Um . . . I . . ."

"Why don't you join us for dinner?" Chas enthusiastically interrupted Jackson's stammering, and he fought the urge to glare at her.

"Oh, that would be so great!" Julie said.

"See you then," Jackson said and hurried back to where he'd left Polly watching out for the kids.

"Who is she?" Polly asked immediately.

"It's my high-school girlfriend," Jackson said with intense chagrin.

"Ooh," Polly said, "I detect some disdain."

"I wasn't trying to hide the disdain, Polly," he said. "It doesn't take a lot of effort to *detect* it." He sat down, quickly noting that the baby was still asleep and Charles was playing contentedly on the floor.

"I take it the two of you didn't part well," Polly said.

"No, we didn't. But what bothers me more is the way she's behaving *now*. I have no idea why she's even here." Polly lifted her eyebrows, implying she wanted to hear all the juicy details. Jackson just motioned with his hand and said, "Why don't you go help my wife deal with her so we can get some work done."

"Oh, right," Polly said and hurried away.

Jackson was still sitting there stewing over this ridiculous interruption to his life when he looked up to see Chas standing there.

"You okay?" she asked.

"Beyond feeling annoyed, I'm fine. How are you?"

"I'm fine. Why wouldn't I be?" She chuckled. "She doesn't intimidate me, if that's what you mean."

"I would never expect her to intimidate you. She couldn't hold a candle to you."

"What a nice thing to say, Jackson Leeds. I think I'll keep you."

"Good," he said, and she sat down on the couch beside him. He put his arm around her and kissed the top of her head. "Not many more weeks and you're going to be stuck with me forever."

"I know," she said with delight. "I can't wait."

They were both counting down the days until they would be sealed in the temple—then they would be together forever no matter what. They already had the flights and rooms booked for Washington, DC, for a little Valentine's Day vacation that included a visit to the temple there to be sealed and to have their children sealed to them. They were doing it at the first possible opportunity, which was exactly one year beyond Jackson's baptism, and they had both agreed many times that there was nothing more important in their lives than putting the temple at the center of all they did.

Jackson tightened his arm around his wife and thought as he often did of how much his life had changed since he'd met her. Even when they'd married, he'd never imagined that he might embrace the religion that meant so much to her. It had been a clear agreement between them that he would support her beliefs but he'd had no intention of becoming converted. But Chas had believed that with time and patience he would eventually come around. And so he had. His only real regret was that he hadn't come around sooner. He wished they were sealed already. It wasn't that he was worried about something happening to come between them. He'd just heard so many marvelous things about the blessings of the temple that he wanted to be privy to that experience, and know that it was a part of what he and Chas shared.

"Julie seems nice enough," Chas said, tossing an unpleasant pebble into the serene pond of his thoughts. "A little silly, maybe."

"Yeah, she *seems* nice enough," he said with a hint of sarcasm, "but I want to know what she's doing here."

"You're suspicious?" Chas asked, sitting forward to look at him.

"Yes, I'm suspicious. No one comes this far to stay at an obscure bed-and-breakfast—alone—just for a vacation. No one! She wanted to *see* me, she said. She knows I'm married, but she wanted to *see* me. I would bet she either wants money, or she—"

"Money? You think she would try to finagle money out of you? Has she ever done anything like that before?"

"No, but—"

"Then why do you think she would do something like that now?"

"It just . . . doesn't feel right."

"So you jump to money as her motive? She spent an awful lot on a plane ticket to get here. That doesn't make a lot of sense to me. Has she got any reason to think you're rich?" Chas snorted an indelicate laugh. "'Cause you're sure not."

"No. Really?" He pretended to sound offended, then laughed with her.

"So, I don't think her motive for coming is money. I think that's just . . . silly. Why would you think that?"

Jackson thought about that and said, "Because money is easier to admit to than why I *really* believe she's here."

"Why?" Chas asked, lifting an eyebrow. When he didn't answer she said, "You don't want to say it."

"No, I don't."

"Because you'll look like a fool when you realize she has no motives at all?"

"Oh, I know she has motives beyond a 'vacation.'"

"Is this your FBI gut instinct talking?"

"Yes," he said firmly, and her eyes widened.

"And you think you can profile her and her motives after just a few minutes of conversation?"

"Yes," he said again.

"So, tell me."

"For years she didn't know where to find me. Nobody did. Then she runs into my sister on a rare visit back to our hometown for Christmas. She wouldn't go back there for any reason unless she'd just had some kind of a breakup and she was on her own."

"How do you know that?"

"Melinda told me soon after we got back together. In one of our little brother-sister chats she brought up Julie. She said that she lived in Kansas City, had some kind of career there, and Melinda said the only time she'd been home to visit her father had been between husbands. She didn't say if that had been more than once; I didn't ask. I didn't care. I still don't care."

"She broke your heart."

"Yes, she did. But that was a *very* long time ago. And I have the good sense to know now that the *reasons* she broke my heart indicate a great lack of character. She claimed that she loved me; she said she wanted to spend the rest of her life with me—*until* she realized I was serious about joining the Marines. She didn't love me enough to become a military wife. She said, 'If you join the Marines I won't marry you.' So I joined the Marines, and then she behaved as if the breakup was my fault. I knew it was the right choice for me; I knew it was what I had to do. I knew it would be difficult for her. No one has ever claimed that being a military spouse is easy. But *you* did it. You left all of this," he motioned with his arm, "and your sweet grandmother to support the man you loved . . . because you loved him." He took a deep breath. "You know all of that."

"Yes, but . . . you sound upset that it's been . . . unearthed."

"I'm not upset over Julie. It was so long ago. And I know now that if I *had* married her, I would have just become one of her ex-husbands. Life with you is better than anything I ever could have gotten anywhere else."

"Okay . . . I'm glad. But you're upset."

"I'm upset because she just . . . shows up here out of the blue . . . and she's got motives."

"Motives you haven't actually told me about yet."

"She's hoping to hook up with me again."

Chas was so astonished it took her a moment to catch her breath. Then she laughed at the ridiculousness of it—until she realized that Jackson hadn't even cracked a smile. "You're married. She knows you're married."

"Yes, that's why it feels so suspicious."

"You're serious. You really think your old girlfriend would come all this way and go to all this trouble to . . . what? Break up your marriage?"

Jackson shrugged. "To give her the benefit of the doubt, let's just say she wants to assess the situation. Maybe she thinks if I'm not *happily* married, she could get me back into her life. I don't think she cares whether or not I'm rich or handsome or even a nice person. So don't go thinking that this is some ego trip for me to have my old love showing up. I could care less what she thinks. I believe this is just a game for her—to see what she can or can't get away with."

Chas shook her head and tried to take this information in. "You really got all of this in just a few minutes? I know your instincts are good. I'm not questioning that. But you haven't seen the woman in . . . what . . . thirty years?"

"Something like that."

"I think we need to put assumptions aside and just take her visit at face value. It really doesn't matter, because either way she's going to find a happy marriage."

"Yes, she is. But please be careful with the amount of information you give her. Don't get all chummy with her. You can be polite, but . . . keep it . . . well, treat her like a guest, not like my old friend."

"Okay. I can do that." Chas thought about it a minute. "I don't mean to contend with your theories, Jackson, but I just cannot believe that a person would really *want* to break up someone else's marriage."

Jackson let out a sardonic chuckle. "Your naiveté has always been charming, Chas, but I spent years investigating crimes for a federal agency. You wouldn't *believe* what people will do, the lengths they will go to, all for the sake of attempting to accomplish something that makes absolutely no sense to a reasonable-thinking person. Maybe I'm jumping the gun, but I'd rather err on the side of being too cautious with her. I don't trust her, and I certainly don't like her."

"You once loved her."

"I was a different person then." Jackson stood up. "You'd better get a nap while you can. If you think that *I* am going to cook dinner for Julie, you're sorely mistaken. *You're* the one who invited her."

"I did, didn't I."

"Yep," he said with a chuckle. "I *will* watch the kids while you cook, but I'm *not* in on this project."

"Fair enough," Chas said and went upstairs to the bed that was still unmade. It quickly beckoned her into it, and she fell asleep wondering if it could really be possible that Jackson's theory was right. It felt unnerving to think of having a woman with such motives under their roof. She felt grateful to know that her marriage was strong in ways that this woman could never comprehend.

* * * * *

Chas awoke from a nap and realized she'd been sleeping deeply. A glance at the clock made her realize she should *not* have invited her husband's old girlfriend to dinner. She didn't have nearly enough time to fix anything that would make a good impression, and she felt completely unmotivated and lacking in energy. She hurried downstairs to assess the situation and found Polly on the couch, watching a video of one of her favorite chick flicks, holding a bowl of popcorn. The children were both playing on the floor.

"Oh, hi!" Polly said. "Good nap?"

"A little too good, perhaps," Chas said. "I've got to—"

"That divine chicken mushroom stuff you taught me to make is in the oven. There's a salad and a raspberry cheesecake in the fridge. Jackson made the salad, even though he told me it went against his principles on this whole dinner thing. The table in the formal dining room is set for three with the best stuff. The babies are apparently all over the sick stuff and are happy, as you can see. Elliott is coming here after work to help me watch them, because there's double of all the food so we get some too. I told Jackson that dinner might go more smoothly without the babies, because I know they generally make any meal a circus. He said he didn't *want* it to go smoothly. But I insisted. And before you gush with ridiculous appreciation for my noble gestures, let me remind you that I'm just storing up favors because I'm going to have a baby and I have no idea what I'm doing, and I'll probably fall apart and you'll have to come and save me."

"It's a deal," Chas said and sat down next to her friend, exhaling loudly. "You're the best."

"I know," Polly said and giggled.

"No, I mean . . . really. I'll have to do a lot of saving you to even begin to make up for all the times you've rescued me."

"That's what friends are for," Polly said and held the bowl out toward her. "Popcorn?"

* * * * *

Dinner with Julie present *did* go smoothly. Jackson pitched in and did more to actually get it on the table than Chas did. And he took every possible opportunity to leave the table to get something from the kitchen or check on the kids. When they were finished he insisted that he would clear the table while the ladies visited, and then he served dessert. At this point Julie started teasing him about coddling and spoiling his wife way too much. Jackson just smiled at her and ate his dessert.

During a lull in the conversation, Julie said to Jackson, "So . . . I was hoping we could talk."

"Talk," he said.

Julie glanced discreetly at Chas. "It wouldn't be too much to ask to have a private conversation, would it?"

"There's nothing we need to talk about that my wife shouldn't know."

Julie looked confused and distressed but covered it quickly. "I doubt very much that she'd be interested in hearing us reminisce over all the stupid things we did in high school."

"On the contrary," Chas said, "I'd love to hear about it."

"I thought you'd already told her everything," Julie said to Jackson in a tone that was somewhere between teasing and accusing.

"Everything important," Jackson said, but even as the words came out, he realized that he was being set up. And since he hadn't actually told Chas *everything,* he could be in trouble.

In the months that he'd been initially getting to know Chas, he'd known very quickly that the moral standard she'd lived had been very different from his own. With the way he'd been raised and the associations he'd had through the military and the FBI, it had simply never occurred to him that saving intimacy for marriage might be a good thing. He'd told Chas he'd been in love with Julie, and it had hurt him deeply when she wouldn't commit her life to him. He'd told her that in the following years he'd had some brief and meaningless relationships. He'd certainly implied that there had been physical intimacy in those relationships. Sharing anything more specific than that had never felt necessary, but he had to admit that a part of him had always wondered if his wife should have known more about his past. He'd always been private about many things in his life; not just this.

He'd always told her that she knew everything about him since the day they'd met. And that was true. But in that moment he feared that his omission of certain details of his past was about to come back and bite him. He hadn't told Chas *every*thing about his relationship with Julie. He just hoped that she would forgive him, should this conversation end up going awry.

CHAPTER TWO

Jackson was relieved beyond words when Julie pleaded fatigue, thanked them for a lovely dinner, and went up to her room. He helped Chas clean up, but neither of them had much to say. A part of him wanted to ask what was on her mind, but he didn't want to hear her admit that she might be wondering if there was more to his past with Julie than she knew about. Since it had been thirty years ago, it didn't seem like it should matter. But at the moment, it felt to him like it mattered. And he wished that he hadn't been so stupid.

They found the children in good spirits in the care of Polly and Elliott. The adults all visited a while before the babysitters went home; then Chas and Jackson did the usual evening routine getting the children bathed and put down for the night. They chatted very little beyond saying how grateful they were that the kids were both healthy, and hoping that their family was done with the little flu bug.

Jackson and Chas sat in bed together and read from the scriptures, then they knelt side by side and prayed, all according to their normal routine. Chas went to sleep quickly in spite of her nap. Jackson felt exhausted, but it took him a lot longer to stop thinking about the way his past had come back to haunt him. He finally decided that he just needed to talk to Chas about it, clear the air, and stop fearing that her ignorance of the matter might come between them. He had nothing to hide in their present relationship. His past had been washed clean when he'd been baptized. He just didn't want Julie knowing something that Chas *didn't* know. And he was determined to resolve that problem first thing in the morning.

* * * * *

Chas woke up in the night with a stomachache, knowing she had the virus that had afflicted her children. Within an hour she was in the bathroom throwing up. She got a blanket and pillow and camped out on the bathroom floor in order to save the trips back and forth until the vomiting stopped. Jackson found her there when Isabelle woke up around four to be fed. He opened the bathroom door and said, "There you are. Are you okay?"

"No," she said and moaned.

"You're sick?"

"Yes."

"Do you want me to give the baby a bottle?" he asked, and she reluctantly agreed. She wasn't worried about giving Isabelle her germs since the baby had already been sick. But she wasn't sure she could get through nursing her without needing to throw up.

"Can I get you anything?" Jackson asked with concern.

"No, thank you. If you'll just . . . handle the kids . . . I'll just . . ." She was overcome with a new wave of nausea and motioned her husband out of the bathroom. He closed the door and she threw up again.

By the time daylight arrived, Chas had gotten past the vomiting but she didn't feel motivated to leave her now-comfortable spot on the bathroom floor. She also didn't want to get in bed next to Jackson and contaminate him with her germs. She was relaxed but not asleep when she heard him open the bathroom door, and looking up she saw his concern.

"You okay?"

"Better than I was a few hours ago."

"That's something, I guess."

"How are you?" she asked. "Are you sick?"

"Fine so far; still doing germ control. Why don't you get in bed. I'm up for the day."

"Okay, you talked me into it," she said and came carefully to her feet with Jackson's help. He made sure she was tucked in and had what she needed before she said, "It's Michelle's day off. You're going to have to cover breakfast."

"Not a problem," he said. "How many guests do we have?"

"Just one," she said with a little smirk.

"No," Jackson muttered. "No, no, no, no, no. I do *not* want to serve breakfast to *her.*"

"She's not some kind of alien, Jackson. If you don't want her to see her old boyfriend lowered to serving meals at an inn, then—"

"It's not that at all. I love the work I do here, and I don't care what she thinks of me. I just . . . don't want to interact with her at all."

"Well, I'm afraid you don't have a choice," Chas said. "Polly has a doctor's appointment this morning so she won't be in until later. I can handle watching Isabelle for a little while, especially since she's already had the germ. But you'll have to take Charles with you."

"That part is not the problem."

"Oh, it'll be fine," Chas said. "Quit making such a fuss. Look at it this way; now she'll get that private conversation with you that she wants."

"Precisely! I don't *want* a private conversation with her."

Chas said more seriously, "Maybe you need one. Maybe you need to hear what she has to say and stop all of your speculating. And if your suspicions are correct, maybe you need to let her know where you stand." She glanced at the clock. "Besides, she didn't request breakfast until nine. You've got more than two hours. Her menu request is on the fridge, and most of it's already been prepared."

"I know the breakfast drill, Chas. I don't want to talk to her." He sighed. "But you're probably right. Ignoring her isn't going to make her go away, is it."

"Not likely."

Jackson quickly assessed his feelings and the thoughts that had kept him awake last night. The children were still sleeping. He would never get a better chance than this to say to Chas what needed to be said. He sat on the edge of bed and forced words out that would make it necessary to get it *all* out. "There's something I need to tell you."

"What?" she asked, concerned.

"I don't want Julie being here to cause any tension between us. If she's come here to create a rift between us, I don't want that to happen. I don't want her to have that kind of power over my life."

"Why would she? She has nothing to do with us."

"No, but you're aware that she and I were once very close."

"Yes, of course. You've told me how she broke your heart; you've told me what happened."

"But when Julie said last night that you knew everything, I realized that you don't know *everything*. I don't want her to have knowledge that you don't have. I don't know why she's here, but I don't want her to say or do anything that might blindside you or catch you off guard."

Chas heard what he was saying and considered the guilt in his eyes. She suspected where this was headed, but had to say, "Just tell me and get it over with."

Jackson couldn't look at her when he said it. "Julie and I were . . . intimate."

"Is that supposed to surprise me?" Chas asked and Jackson looked at her. "You've already told me that you were raised without any values. You've told me that having a moral standard in regard to intimacy was something that had never occurred to you before we'd met. Did you think I would believe that excluded a time in your life when you were a hormonal teenager, in love with someone you wanted to marry?"

"And that doesn't bother you?" he asked.

"Of course it bothers me. The only person I've ever been intimate with was my husband, and he's dead. You'll never have to face him. I don't particularly like sitting across the dinner table from a woman who was once intimate with my husband. But that's just my female jealousy talking, Jackson. You've told me many times that I know everything about you from the minute you met me. On top of that, you were baptized. It's all washed away."

Jackson sighed. "You are amazing."

"Am I?"

"If it was the other way around, I'm not sure my *male* jealousy would handle it so well."

Chas smiled at her husband. "As long as she knows that you're mine and you don't let her get away with any flirting, I'll be just fine." She closed her eyes, sleepy after a bad night. "But if she tries to steal you away, I'm going to have to scratch her eyes out."

Jackson chuckled. "No worries. There is nothing or no one in this world that could ever lure me away from you. I have the best of everything right here, Chas. And I love you."

She opened her eyes. "I love you too."

Jackson took care of the children instead of going out for his usual early-morning run so that Chas could rest. He was glad to do what needed to be done to care for his family, but he missed the opportunity to clear his head and get his blood pumping—especially with the prospect of seeing Julie today. He dressed the children and fed them, and Chas kept an eye on them while he showered and got ready for the day. He made certain Chas had what she needed and left Isabelle to play safely near the bed while he took Charles to the inn. He kept his little son with him while he made certain the inn was ready for the day and that everything was in order, then he set Charles free to play with the toys that were now kept in the kitchen in order to entertain him when he needed to be there during work hours.

Jackson washed up and began his simple preparations of Julie's breakfast. He watched the clock closely with the goal of having everything fresh and just right, provided the guest arrived at the dining room at the time she had specified on the menu slip she'd filled out the night before. When several guests were at the inn, they often set out a buffet, but when there were only a few, they stuck to the individual menu method. Jackson would have preferred to be putting out a buffet, even though it would have been a great deal more work. At least that way Julie could have been part of a small crowd instead of being the only guest. It all just felt so awkward. He wondered if he *had* jumped to conclusions in regard to her motives. He hoped so. Maybe she *was* just here for a vacation, and he was blowing it way out of proportion. He would just be glad when she left.

"Well, look at you," Julie said, and he looked up from the waffle iron to see her standing in the doorway between the guest dining room and the kitchen. She smirked as if seeing him in such a situation was terribly amusing.

"Yes, look at me," he said. "Chas isn't feeling well, so I've got breakfast duty. Fortunately," he put some effort into offering a kind smile, "she trained me well so it should be fairly tolerable."

"Oh, I'm not worried about that," she said.

Feeling awkward with her watching him cook, he said, "Why don't you help yourself to a cup of coffee; everything's on the sideboard. Have a seat and I'll have this ready in a minute."

He found her a couple of minutes later cradling a cup of coffee in her hands. He set her breakfast in front of her, and she made a noise to indicate she was impressed. "I can't take credit for the lovely arrangement of the fresh fruit," he said. "Chas did that last night."

"It looks delicious, thank you," she said.

"Enjoy your breakfast," he said as a good innkeeper would, and headed back to the kitchen.

"Why don't you join me?" she asked, and he turned around.

Jackson tried to keep it light. "I have a policy against fraternizing with the guests."

"Oh, stop being so stodgy and join me for breakfast. Clearly there's no one else to feed at the moment."

"I already ate," he said.

"Then have a cup of coffee."

"I don't drink coffee."

"Now, you're just being silly," she said. "I came all this way to see you. Sit down and talk to me."

Her coyness tempted him to feel angry, but he cautioned himself against jumping to conclusions and sat down after he peeked into the kitchen to be sure that Charles was playing contentedly. The kitchen was child-proofed and he knew that he could hear Charles if there was a problem. He suspected that Julie wasn't going to go away until he let her know very plainly where he stood. But perhaps he needed to hear her out first. Maybe she would surprise him. Maybe she would prove him wrong.

Jackson felt a little nervous when she scrutinized him closely, as if he had a smudge of dirt on his face, or something. She then reached across the table and *touched* his face. Jackson pushed her hand away abruptly.

"What *are* you doing?" he demanded.

"Scars?" she asked, and Jackson resisted the urge to flinch and look away. The *last* thing he wanted to talk about was how he got those scars. They weren't terribly visible except in certain lighting, but he was well aware of the little scar on his cheekbone, and another one next to his lip. They were daily reminders of the most horrid experience of his life—an experience he did *not* want to discuss with Julie.

"From a Marine brawl, I'd guess."

"You'd guess wrong," he said. "What is it you wanted to talk about?" he added, hoping to change the subject.

"I want to know how you got those scars."

Jackson felt tempted to lie, but it wasn't in him. He just had to get it over with quickly. "While I was on assignment with the FBI, I was taken hostage by drug lords in South America. They weren't very nice."

"Oh, my!" she said, but he sensed no concern or compassion. Rather, she seemed intrigued with the possibility of a heroic tale.

Jackson could have told her that they'd tortured him and starved him, and that he was rescued literally within an inch of his life. He could tell her he'd been in the hospital for weeks afterward because of the beatings and the parasites. He could tell her that he'd later been in the psych ward when the nightmares started overtaking his life. He could tell her that PTSD reduces a man to a level of humiliation and fear he'd never imagined. But he didn't tell her anything. He simply said, "Tell me what you've been doing the last thirty years."

"You go first," she said, pointing her fork at him, but she didn't ask for any details on the event he'd just brushed over. He was fine with that, but he also noted what that indicated about her character.

"You've talked to my sister. You already know."

"I want to hear it from you. She didn't say much."

"Oh, I bet she said a lot more than I usually would. You know I joined the Marines. I got a degree; joined the FBI. Retired a few years ago. I married Chas. We run this inn and we have two kids. It's the American dream."

"Is it?"

"It is for me," he said.

"You're right. She told me all that."

"Your turn."

Julie began to ramble about jobs, friends, and three husbands. She'd never lived more than an hour away from where they'd been raised, even though she'd avoided interacting with her dysfunctional family. Divorce number three had happened recently and she was hoping to find herself.

"You think you'll find yourself in Montana?" he asked.

"Maybe," she said, and Charles toddled out of the kitchen and climbed onto Jackson's lap, eyeing Julie suspiciously.

"Oh, he looks like you!" she said as if the notion was astonishing. She giggled. "He reminds me of you when you were a kid."

"Imagine that," Jackson said.

"You have another kid?"

"Yes, Isabelle was born last summer." In an effort to chalk up points toward all that he and Chas had between them, he added, "She was born with a genetic heart defect. She had open-heart surgery the day she was born. But she's doing great now."

"Wow. I think Melinda mentioned something about that."

"See," he said, "I have nothing to tell you." She smiled coyly again and he added, "Why are you here, Julie? I don't buy the vacation thing. People don't travel this far to stay in places like this alone without a good reason. Are you in trouble? Do you need something? Please tell me why you're here."

"I'm not in trouble and I don't need anything. The vacation thing is *partly* true. I decided to go on vacation where I could see *you.*"

"Okay . . . why? I'm a happily married man, Julie. Which, in my mind, makes your visit a little confusing."

"Come on, Jackson," she said, leaning over the table, "what we had was amazing!"

"What we had ended decades ago," Jackson said. "I thought it was amazing at the time, but now I know what real love is like." He resisted his temptation to tell her that he'd found a woman who had enough character to commit herself to a man even if his life wasn't convenient.

He leaned closer to her and spoke in a voice that was soft but imperative. "Listen to me, Julie, it's not my intention to hurt your feelings or make you angry. But your coming here just doesn't feel right to me. It doesn't make sense. And what you just said only adds to my suspicions. I'm not going to accuse you of anything, and I'm not going to ask for any further explanations. I just want you to go. Your stay here is on the house. Chalk it up to a gesture for old-time's sake. But you need to go. I'm sure you can find a room in Butte without too much trouble. I'm a married man with a business to run, and I don't have time to entertain you, or to deal with your games."

He took a moment to assess her response. Her expression was perfect astonishment, but her eyes reminded him of a criminal whose crimes had been exposed. "But . . . Jackson . . ." she said, sounding suitably baffled. "I was just hoping that you and I could . . ."

"Could what, Julie? There is no you and me; there never will be. Your implications are sounding very much like you came here with the hope that maybe my marriage isn't as happy as Melinda said it was." She opened her mouth to protest, then closed it again and swallowed hard, as if she had nothing to say in her defense. "Let me make this perfectly clear, Julie. I'm *happily* married, but even if it was not a good marriage, I wouldn't be complicating the problems by getting involved with another woman. It's just not in me to do something like that. I love Chas, and she loves me. Our commitment is one of the strongest things I've ever known in my life. I would never hurt her. *Never.*"

"So . . . you really have no interest in just . . . spending some time with me. . . ."

Jackson wanted to ask her if she was deaf or just stupid. But he mustered up the ability to be polite as he came to his feet. "I'm married to a woman I love. I'm not going to spend *any* time with you, for any reason. As soon as you finish your breakfast, you need to pack and go. Like I said, don't worry about the bill." He headed toward the kitchen and paused long enough to turn and say, "I wish you all the best, Julie. I hope you can find a way to be truly happy." He wished that he could tell her it had been good to see her, but it hadn't. He smiled and nodded and left the room.

He heard her leave the dining room less than a minute later, and a while later he was in the office with Charles when he saw her walk past and out the door with her luggage. He moved to the window and saw her drive away. For a few minutes he pondered what he'd shared with Julie enough to put it away for good. He was glad that Chas knew everything, and he was glad to have Julie gone. With any luck, the past would now remain where it belonged—in the past.

* * * * *

Jackson called Chas from the office to see if she needed anything.

"I'm okay," she said. "How'd it go with Julie?"

"I'll tell you later. I'll stay here in the office with Charles until Polly gets here, if you're all right. Call me if you need something."

"We're okay," she said. "Isabelle's being especially good."

"I can come and get her, too, if you need me to."

"No, she's fine, really. I'll get a nap when Polly gets here. How did it go with Julie?"

Jackson chuckled. "You can't stand it, can you?"

"No, and just because you're babysitting the inn doesn't mean you don't have time to tell me now."

"Okay, fine," he said and repeated the gist of the conversation.

"She really said that . . . that what the two of you had was amazing . . . right after she said she came to see you?"

"She really did."

"Okay, not that I think you would lie to me, but . . . she's pretty gutsy."

"And vain and arrogant," Jackson said. "I told her I was happily married and she needed to leave."

"Leave?"

"Yes."

"As in . . . leave the inn?"

"Yes. I told her she didn't need to worry about the bill, but she needed to go. So she did."

Chas considered this for a moment and couldn't deny that she felt some comfort to see that Jackson had not only declared his place in his marriage, but he'd made it unmistakably clear by drawing such a clear boundary. Julie had left knowing exactly what kind of man Jackson was and where she stood with him.

"I'm proud of you," she said. "And I'm glad to have a husband who honors me so well."

"Do I?" he asked. "I wasn't really looking at it that way. I just know she was out of line."

"I love you," Chas said.

"I love you too. How many days until we get that forever thing?"

"I don't know. I'm too sick to count, but it's getting closer."

"Yes, it is," he said. "Oh, I've got a call coming in. Talk to you later." He hung up and answered the other line to take a reservation for Valentine's Day. It was the only night of the year when the entire inn was full, and the reservations were made weeks in advance. Jackson had been concerned about leaving the inn for a vacation at such a busy time, but Chas had insisted that they needed to be sealed on the anniversary of his baptism, and she had worked it all out. Elliott would be getting a couple of days off to help at the inn. Michelle, who worked in the kitchen, would be putting in extra hours. She had worked here cleaning rooms for years before she'd been promoted to kitchen duty, and she'd helped fill in over the years in many ways. Tricia and Whitney, the girls who came in regularly to clean, would also be putting extra hours. Chas felt confident that everything would go smoothly while she and Jackson were off with their children having a glorious time in the nation's capital—a city that just happened to have a temple.

Polly came in a few minutes later. Jackson went over some business with her, then gave her the condensed version of the situation with Julie, if only so she'd know why they weren't billing Julie for the room, and why she was gone sooner than anticipated. Polly didn't say much, but she smiled enough for Jackson to know that she was as pleased as everyone else to have Julie gone.

Jackson left the inn under Polly's care and went to the house to look after his wife. She still wasn't up to even trying some clear broth or juice, but he took charge of Isabelle and left Chas to rest. More than once during the afternoon while he took care of his babies, did some laundry, and loaded the dishwasher, he smiled to think of the joy he found in the life he lived—and Julie's opinion of it. If nothing else, her visit had reminded him of how far he'd come and of how good life could be.

Chas felt much better by evening. She had some chicken broth from a can and some Jell-O that Jackson had made. She slept well that night apart from Isabelle waking up for the usual once-a-night feeding, but Jackson handled it and Chas went back to sleep. She woke up feeling immensely better, and she was glad to know that Michelle was coming in to serve breakfast to their guests. Polly would be putting in some extra hours so Jackson could look out for the kids, which meant that Chas could use the day to rest. As wiped out as she felt from that twenty-four-hour bug, she was grateful for such a day.

Chas was sitting up in bed reading when Jackson appeared in the doorway. "Jodi is here. She wants to talk to you. Should I send her up here so you can have some peace and quiet?"

"Oh, that would be fine," Chas said, glancing around to see how bad the room looked. Jackson apparently had the same thought as he grabbed some dirty clothes off the floor and tossed them in the hamper in the bathroom. Other than that it didn't look too bad. Chas was glad she'd showered and looked relatively presentable. She and Jodi were good friends, but she hadn't achieved the comfort level with her that she'd long ago found with Polly. Jodi had never actually been in Chas's bedroom, except right after the house had been finished when Chas had given her a quick tour.

Jodi entered the room less than a minute after Jackson left. "You don't look so bad," she said.

"Oh, I'm fine," Chas said. "Just tired. Jackson spoils me. It's nice that our work is often flexible and he can be around."

"That *is* nice," Jodi said. She sat down in an old-fashioned wing-back chair near the bed. "I hope it's okay that I came by."

"Of course," Chas said. "What's up? Did you need to talk about something, or . . ."

"Actually, yes . . . and I'm hoping that you might be able to help me with a project."

"Oh, tell me!" Chas said. Jodi had been so good to Chas that she would welcome an opportunity to help her in any way.

"I have this group of friends," Jodi said. "There are seven of us. We've been close since the sixth grade. We all lived in the same neighborhood south of Salt Lake City. We were all in the same ward—all members—and we all went to the same school. Looking back, it's pretty awesome that seven girls could all get along so well and have so much fun together. I mean . . . sometimes two or three of us would get together to do things, but there was never any of that 'best friend' stuff among us. Whoever was available to play was welcome. And most of our parents were pretty patient with this big group of giggling girls. Well . . . we mostly got together at my house or Mia's.

Our houses were bigger and our mothers more patient, I guess. But it all worked out.

"Anyway, we all stayed in the same neighborhood through junior high and high school. Even though our differences became more evident as we got older, we still managed to keep track of each other, and we always got together for a movie or a sleepover once a month or so. We all graduated together, and then little by little we went to college, got married, moved away. Three of them still live within an hour of their original homes and they see each other somewhat regularly. The rest of us live in different states, but we all keep in touch—some more than others. But it's always like . . . no matter how long it's been since you've talked to any one of them, you can pick up the phone and it feels so comfortable and easy to talk. But life is busy, you know.

"E-mail has helped us keep each other updated, but we've only been all together three times since high school. Even when there have been weddings and stuff, there was always at least one who couldn't make it. These three gatherings we've had in . . . what . . . about sixteen, seventeen years . . . something like that . . . have just included going out to lunch or visiting at someone's house. We've always talked about *really* having a vacation together someday. We've all speculated and joked about getting a week all together where we could really renew our friendships and make some great memories."

"That sounds wonderful," Chas said. "I can't even imagine what a great thing that must be! I've considered myself lucky to have *two* good friends."

"It *is* great," Jodi said. "But you know . . . sometimes it takes a crisis to make people do things they've been putting off."

"Has something happened?" Chas asked.

"No one is dead or dying," Jodi said, "but one of these women has really hit a crisis in her life. Tammy and I—she's one of them—have both been talking to her quite a bit. It's Rachelle. I have to use their names to keep track of them, even if you don't know who I'm talking about."

"Yes, go on," Chas said.

"So, Rachelle has been going through some really hard things and it's just . . . draining the life out of her. Tammy and I have been talking, and between us we decided that it was time we did get us all together. We can do it just because we've always talked about doing it, but if we can do it soon, we might be able to give Rachelle some support. And I'm sure she could use a vacation."

"It's a great idea," Chas said, wondering why Jodi was telling her all of this, and what her role might be in this *project.*

"The thing is . . ." Jodi sounded mildly nervous, "I'm wondering if we might be able to do it here . . . at the inn."

"Oh!" Chas said with excitement. "Oh, that would be wonderful!"

"Of course, we would pay a fair price for your services," Jodi said. "I'm just wondering if you could maybe give us a group rate for renting the entire inn for a week, so we could be the only ones here."

"That would be great!" Chas said, the very idea making her almost giddy.

"I was thinking that if the inn provided breakfast, we could all just pitch in on buying groceries, and we can work out the other meals if you're okay with letting us use the kitchen. And you wouldn't have to do much with the rooms every day. The sheets wouldn't have to be changed during the week, and we can clean up after ourselves to some degree. What do you think?"

"I think it's a fantastic idea. I would love to do that. We just have to see when we have a week without reservations."

Jodi bit her lip. "I figured that would be the case. I'm just praying that you might have something soon. As it turns out, everyone is either unemployed, or has vacation days coming, or has other circumstances where getting away in the next couple of months would be easier than later on. As far as Rachelle and her crisis are concerned, the sooner the better. Tammy and I have already talked to everyone about the possibility, and everyone could come. But I'm afraid it's just too much to hope that you could have a full week without other guests here."

"Well, let's see what we've got," Chas said, picking up the house phone, which she could use to call the office where Polly was working. "If we could begin in the middle of one week and go to the middle of the next, then we're only dealing with one weekend. It's usually the weekends that are busier. We often have times during the week without guests." Chas dialed the number while she kept talking.

"Except for Valentine's Day, most people don't book too far ahead, so maybe it's not as difficult as you might think."

"Oh, that would be so awesome!" Jodi said, crossing fingers on both hands.

"You miss me?" Polly asked in lieu of a greeting. Caller ID made it impossible to ever surprise her on the phone.

"I do, actually. But I have a scheduling question." She briefly recounted the gist of Jodi's request and asked if there was any stretch of six nights in the near future without any reservations.

"Um . . ." Polly said and was silent while she checked. "Bingo. From the last Wednesday in January until the following Thursday, we have nothing scheduled."

Chas laughed softly and repeated the news to Jodi, who squealed with excitement and jumped up and down. Chas laughed again and said to Polly, "Okay, book the whole inn for Jodi and her friends. We'll work out the details later."

"Done and done," Polly said. "Wow, she sounds really happy."

"Yeah, I think the stars are lining up," Chas said and ended the call.

"Oh, I can't believe it," Jodi said. "I mean . . . I guess I *do* believe it, because Tammy and I have been praying a lot, and we felt so right about it. It just seemed too good to be true that your place would be available, but I wanted so badly to have it work out here. I just . . . had a good feeling about it." She looked around. "You have such a sweet spirit in your home, Chas, and in your inn. I think this is the perfect place for my friends to find healing and peace."

"I'm honored," Chas said. "And yes, we will give you a really great deal. We can work that out later. I assume all of your friends are paying for their own travel and pitching in on the accommodations."

"Actually," Jodi said as she sat down again, "this is one of the awesome things. You see, some of them could pull the money together but it would be kind of a strain. There are a couple of them who can't afford even an extra dollar. But Tammy just got an inheritance. Her mom died last year, and they just sold her parents' home. They're already well off; not rich, but very comfortable. She said that one of the first things that came to her mind when she realized that the money would come through, was doing this for her friends. She got enough that this trip wouldn't take even a fourth of it, she said, and it's her own money. But she was worried about the others being too proud to accept it, one or two in particular. She was praying about it, wondering what to do, and she was reading in the Doctrine and Covenants and . . . well, she's always been active in the Church, always lived her life that way, praying and searching for answers. She's awesome! You're going to love her."

Jodi took a breath and continued talking quickly, as if she couldn't get it all out fast enough. "So, she reads about the law of consecration and the answer hits her. Since she *can* afford it, and others can't, it's her privilege to give what she has in abundance to bless the lives of these women she loves. She wrote this beautiful letter about her feelings and sent it to all of us. I was the only one she'd talked to about it before. Everyone agreed to come if we could make arrangements for a place . . . and now we have!" Jodi let out a delighted laugh. "It's so awesome!"

"Yes, it certainly is," Chas said and laughed with her.

"Now, there's one more thing I want to talk to you about," Jodi said. "We'll have to work out all the little details, I know, but there's one thing that I've thought about a lot, or . . . well, it's probably more true to say that the thought just won't leave my brain, so I think it's important."

"Okay," Chas said eagerly.

"I want you to be involved with what we're doing; not like every minute or anything. But I would like you to share meals with us, and if we're doing anything specific together, I'd like you to be there."

"Why?" Chas asked, not so eagerly. "If the seven of you have been close all these years, you're not going to want some outsider sitting in on your time together."

"Actually, I think we do. It's hard to explain, but . . . in spite of staying close, there have been some differences over the years, and there are some *big* differences in personalities, and in the way our lives have turned out. Tammy and I both were thinking it was too bad we couldn't have someone there to be kind of like a moderator. We just think that it might keep things on a more even keel with someone there who *doesn't* know all the history, who can take everything at face value. Seven days is a long time to be under the same roof after so many years. I just think that . . . Tammy does too . . . we think it would be good for you to be there. I know it's a lot to ask, but I was wondering if we could include in the fee some extra babysitting money for Polly or something so that you can kind of make it a little vacation for you as well. What do you think?"

Chas was taken off guard and could only say, "I'm going to have to think about that one."

"And pray about it," Jodi said with perfect confidence, as if she knew what the answer would be. "I don't want to put you on the spot or make you uncomfortable, but . . . that's how I feel."

"Okay," Chas said, "I'll give you my answer on that in a few days. But consider the rest taken care of. It will be a joy to have you and your friends fill the rooms of our inn."

"Yes." Jodi smiled. "I think it will."

CHAPTER THREE

Chas and Jodi talked in detail about the plans for the friends' reunion for more than an hour before Jodi finally left. Chas was thrilled about the entire thing—except for Jodi's request for her to be personally involved. It just felt awkward and uncomfortable. She did as she'd promised and took the time to ask her Heavenly Father about it, then she drifted off to sleep and woke up to see Jackson sitting where Jodi had been sitting earlier. He was reading a book and concentrating intensely. For a minute she just watched him, then she had to share her most prominent thought.

"I love you, Jackson Leeds."

"Well, hello," he said. "I love you too. Did you get some rest?" He rested the book against his thigh, keeping his finger between the pages to mark his place.

"I did, thank you. It's not only wonderful being married, but it's wonderful being married to an innkeeper whose job makes it possible for him to spoil me."

"I would strongly second that motion," he said.

"It's awfully quiet."

"Yeah, they're both taking a nap at the same time. It's a moment worth savoring."

"What are you reading?" she asked.

Jackson held up the book, and she could see that it was *Great Expectations*. "It's been a while since I've indulged in Mr. Dickens."

"You run the Dickensian Inn," she said with soft laughter.

"It's not quite the same thing, though, is it. Besides, I love this story. It's time I read it again. I actually read it while I was in the hospital—whenever that was—but I don't think I retained much."

"How *is* Pip doing?" Chas asked in reference to the main character.

"Pip is having some trouble."

"That's pretty much true for most of the story."

"But he comes through okay in the end."

"Yes, he certainly does."

"So, what did Jodi want? If you don't mind my asking."

"It's no big secret. She wants my help . . . *our* help . . . with a project. Her group of friends, seven women altogether, will be renting the entire inn for a week."

"Really?" Jackson said. "That is . . . great. I think it's great. Is it great for the inn to be overrun by seven women for a full week?" He chuckled at his own teasing.

"Yes, it's great. Of course, I told her we'd give them a good deal. They won't require much maid service while they're here, and they'll use the kitchen to cook most of their own meals; we'll just have to do breakfast. Since there are eight rooms and seven guests, we're going to have a local massage therapist set up in the extra room for a few days, and she'll be giving each of the ladies a turn at some pampering. The ladies will also be doing some projects . . . crafts, or scrapbooking, or something; maybe both. Polly checked the calendar and we have a clear week beginning the last Wednesday of January."

"That's . . . what? Three weeks from yesterday?"

"Yeah, but we don't really need to do anything. It's all good. And after they leave, we'll have just more than a week before our big vacation."

"Wow. It's really that close?"

"It really is," Chas said. They shared a loving smile, then Chas recalled, "Oh, there is something else Jodi asked me that I'm having a little trouble with."

"What?" he asked and she repeated Jodi's request for Chas to be involved with the activities.

"I think it would be good for you," Jackson said.

"I don't know. I just need to pray about it . . . give it some time. It sounds awkward to me."

"Well, it's for you to decide," he said. They heard the waking-up sounds of Isabelle through one of the two baby monitors sitting nearby.

Chas pondered the situation throughout the remainder of the day. That evening she and Jackson watched a video together in spite of numerous interruptions to care for the children. After the movie was over and the children were asleep, they shared their usual night-time prayer. Chas snuggled close to Jackson and shared more details of the things Jodi had told her about this group of friends, and how the timing of this gathering was important because one of them was in crisis.

"Wow," he said.

"Wow what?"

"Do you think this is part of the fulfillment of that promise?"

"What promise?" she asked, leaning up on her elbow.

"When the house was dedicated and that beautiful blessing was given on behalf of our home . . . and our inn. Don't you remember?"

Chas let out a little gasp. "I'd forgotten." She thought about it. "We were told that—"

Jackson finished the sentence. "That this would be a place of refuge for the troubled in spirit who seek healing and peace, that people would be drawn here to find new beginnings. Yes, I remember it well. It was one of those great moments in my life."

"I should have remembered it better myself," she said. "I'm sure you're right. It will be interesting to see if anything good comes out of this grand gathering."

"Yes, it will be interesting to see, but I think I'll watch from a distance and I'll just . . . watch the kids and buy groceries and stuff so you can be with the ladies."

"Polly can help."

"I'm sure we'll manage either way. Does that mean you're going to do it?"

"I don't know yet. I'm still . . . pondering. I'll let you know when I get permission to bow out."

"Or not." He chuckled and turned over to go to sleep.

Chas lay for a couple of hours thinking about all that Jodi had told her about this group of friends. She wondered more specifically about the crisis that Rachelle was facing, and if her friends would truly be able to help her get through it by bringing her here for a week. Chas felt warm inside to think that her inn could be used for such a wonderful event, then she got chills to think of what Jackson had mentioned about that blessing. She knew it was true, because she'd felt it so deeply at the time. People *would* come here to find healing and peace. But chances were that having a guest stay just one night wasn't likely to accomplish such things. Which made her think that this opportunity was something she should take seriously, and she should do everything in her power to make it work the way that her Heavenly Father would want it to work, in order to bless the lives of these women.

Still, trying to imagine herself being integrated into this group felt way too awkward for her. She believed that she could be a great hostess, hover on the sidelines to see that they all had what they needed and were comfortable, and perhaps still accomplish what Jodi wanted from her. Perhaps Jodi's request wouldn't be so well received by the others. Maybe it was just Jodi's way of trying to make Chas feel included; perhaps she was trying to mesh old friendships with new ones. But Chas felt certain that in this case, it probably wasn't a good idea.

Chas knew she'd spent too much time in bed during the day when she found it so difficult to sleep. She got up and checked on her babies, wandered a few minutes through the house, then went back to bed, breathing deeply to try to clear her head of all thoughts in order to relax. She was just starting to do so when Isabelle woke up, and Chas changed and fed her. The baby went back to sleep quickly, and Chas was grateful that she was only waking up once during the night. She went back to bed, glad that she now felt sleepy.

Her next awareness was of getting out of bed and walking down the stairs, almost as if she were sleepwalking. She glanced down at her flowing, white nightgown and realized she was dreaming. She'd gone to sleep in flannel pajamas covered with bright pink penguins. She felt like a character in a historical novel as she left her house through the kitchen door and went into the inn. She was immediately struck by a sense of the house being new and shining with its original beauty, as opposed to the carefully restored beauty it had now. She stood in the kitchen and noted the water pump there instead of the modern faucet and sprayer. She was amazed at the detail on the old cookstove that was there instead of a modern range with a double oven. She felt compelled to move on and walked through what she knew as the guest dining room, but it looked entirely different.

She didn't stop to absorb details. She was drawn ahead by a light shining through a crack in the door that led to the formal dining room. This was a room that remained closed most days, but it was used for special occasions—Thanksgiving and Christmas dinners, or nice meals with guests. Approaching the door, Chas could hear conversation and laughter as if a large gathering was taking place. She peered carefully through the crack in the door and could see that many people were seated around the table, chatting and enjoying themselves. There seemed to be more people there than what the table actually had the capacity to accommodate. Having a desire to be a part of the celebration, Chas pushed open the door, slowly and with care, not wanting to intrude. She gasped at her perfect view of the woman sitting at the head of the table. "Granny," she whispered, glad that no one had noticed her. She wanted to just stand there and watch her grandmother.

Granny looked about the age she'd been when Chas had lost Martin and her first baby, before she and Granny had decided to turn the old house into a bed-and-breakfast. She'd technically been elderly at the time, but she'd been healthy and full of vigor and energy. She could keep up with Chas in almost every way. Chas recalled the joy they'd shared when they were officially able to open the inn, and how they'd worked together with some minimal hired help to run the place. Then, within a few years, Granny's age had began to catch up with her. She'd never lost her vibrant spirit, but her body had become tired and slow. Her passing had been one of the most difficult things Chas had ever faced.

But there she was—just how Chas remembered her. Chas wanted to rush into her grandmother's arms. It occurred to her that she was dreaming, but it felt so real that she didn't care. She could only feel the absolute reality that she was in her grandmother's presence.

Chas took a moment to peruse the other occupants of the table. There were men and women of many ages, none of whom Chas recognized, but her grandmother was having a wonderful time visiting with them. From this angle, Chas couldn't see who was sitting at the foot of the table, directly opposite Granny, with people lining both sides of the lengthy table. There were too many to count with a quick glance. She became intently focused on this man she could see from behind. There was a strange familiarity about him, but she couldn't place it. His hair was longer and worn in a style that was not at all how men wore their hair in the present time. Perhaps that was in keeping with the new feeling of the house. Of course, that would have been years before Granny was even born, so she had to assume this dream had no sense of consistency in time.

Chas saw Granny's eyes come to rest on her, and she could hardly breathe. "You're here!" Granny said, coming to her feet. "Come here, child. Let me look at you."

Chas rushed into the room and down the length of the table, seeing no one or nothing but Granny. They shared a long, tight embrace that felt absolutely real to Chas. It filled her with strength, hope, and perfect peace. Most of all it filled her with the perfect love Granny had always given her, a love she had missed so desperately since Granny's death. Somewhere in the midst of the hug, Chas had to acknowledge reality. "I'm just dreaming," she said to Granny. "You're dead."

"Death is relative, my dear. We all live in harmony here together, but there are some things you can do that we cannot, and the other way around, of course. We can help each other, but you must do your part. There's a work we need you to do for us," Granny said imperatively. "We cannot do it for ourselves. We didn't know it needed to be done when we were on the other side of this veil that separates us. You must do it, Chas. You must." She motioned with her hand as if to show Chas something. She turned, and the wall of the dining room seemed not to exist. Instead it was as if she were looking into a temple sealing room, where Chas and Jackson were kneeling together, facing each other over an altar. "You must do it, Chas," Granny said. "No one else can."

"Of course, Granny," she said. "I will; I promise."

"I know you will," Granny said. "And Jackson; he's such a nice young man. This is a work you must do together."

Granny turned and motioned in the other direction with her hand, and Chas once again saw the people sitting at the table. She didn't recognize any faces, but now there was a familiarity about them. These were ancestors; relatives of one kind or another. She had the impression that both of her parents were among them, but she didn't see any faces clearly. She also had the impression that Jackson's parents were there, and that some of these people were *his* relatives. While everyone seemed to be enjoying each other's company, Chas became aware of the absence of any food on the table. It was set beautifully with fine china and crystal goblets, but there was no food. As this idea settled into her mind, she once again heard Granny say, "We are waiting for the bread of life, my sweet child. We are waiting." She then motioned toward the far end of the table where the gentleman who had drawn Chas's attention earlier was sitting. "Except for him, of course. He's all taken care of, but I think he wants to talk to you."

Chas realized this man was watching her intently, and she became so focused on him that everything and everyone else in the room seemed to fade away. She felt utterly attracted to him, but not at all in a romantic way. It was more as if she could have spent endless hours in mesmerizing conversation with this man; as if they could have been best friends. She walked toward him as he stood and moved to the side of his chair to face her directly.

"Hello, Chas," he said with a British clip. His eyes sparkled as if he knew many delightful secrets he might like to share with her. He took her hand and kissed it in a manner that was wholly flirtatious but not at all inappropriate, as if he knew she was a married woman, and he was likely attached as well. It was simply his manner to be so coy with women. "I love what you've done with the place," he said, putting her hand over his arm to guide her out of the dining room and into the main hall.

Now the inn looked as it did in the present, fully restored and filled with Chas's personal touches. "You keep up the good work now, my dear, and you'll always have help from us. Remember," he said, touching her nose with his finger as if she were a little girl, his eyes dancing with merriness, "angels will always be with you. *We* will always be with you."

He took hold of both her hands and leaned toward her ear, whispering with a dramatic lilt, "Never forget that . . . it was the best of times, it was the worst of times." He stepped back, then turned away, but he glanced over his shoulder and added with a wink, "You really should go to that party. You will do much good there. And you know how I feel about friendship."

Chas came awake with a gasp, as if someone had nudged her, but it only took a second to realize she was in her bed with no one else in the room except Jackson, who was breathing evenly in his sleep. For a long moment she tried to remember what she'd been dreaming, then it rushed back into her mind in perfect, vivid detail in what seemed a nanosecond. And with the memory came clear thoughts of understanding, and undeniable feelings of validity. It had been more a vision than a dream, full of symbolism that wasn't terribly difficult to decipher. But the enormity of it dazzled her and left her flattened against the bed in awe, staring into the darkness above her for more than an hour while she replayed it over and over in her mind.

She finally slipped out of bed and found her journal without disturbing Jackson. She hurried downstairs where she could turn on the light. She plopped down on the couch and began writing vigorously so that she could record the dream before its memory faded, although she doubted that what she felt would ever leave her memory. It was too powerful and intense to imagine ever forgetting.

Chas wrote frantically, not wanting to miss a single detail. Her hand ached and she had to stop and stretch it in every direction before she could go on. Huddled under a lamp, she didn't realize the sun was coming up until she stopped to stretch and found the room had lightened. On the home stretch of writing down her experience, she pressed forward until she could think of nothing more. She thought all of it through again to be certain she hadn't missed anything, feeling a warmth as she did so that verified its meaning and source to her once again.

"What are you doing?" Jackson asked, startling her.

"I had the most amazing dream," she said, reaching for his hand. He set down the baby monitors he was carrying and took her hand, sitting beside her. "I have never experienced anything like it—not even close—ever before." She held up her journal. "I had to write it down so that I won't forget the details, but I'll never forget the feeling."

"Wow," he said, looking at her intently. "It must have been something. You look so . . ."

"What?"

"I don't know . . . happy . . . glowing; not literally, though. You don't look radioactive or anything."

"Oh, ha ha," she said, then held the journal out toward him. "Would you like to read it?" She wanted to share it with him, but figured this would be easier than trying to repeat it all aloud.

"If you want to share," he said, "I'd *love* to read it." As she thumbed back through the pages to find the beginning, he asked, "How long have you been down here writing?"

"I don't know. I lost track. I didn't even look at the clock." She kissed him quickly and stood up. "I'll be back. Take your time."

Chas hurried to take a shower and get dressed for the day. She checked in on the babies, then made the bed, pausing to look at a picture of herself with her grandmother that was on the dresser. She smiled and felt a warm rush. She finished tidying up the bedroom and went downstairs to find Jackson still reading, but he held up a finger and said, "I'm almost done."

Chas sat down and waited for him to finish, anxious to hear his opinion. She wondered for a moment how she might feel if her husband credited the experience to some kind of simple nonsensical dream. It wouldn't make her question the clarity of what she'd seen and felt. But she would far prefer that he understand what this meant. He took in a deep breath as he finished reading. She saw his eyes lift from the book, but he said nothing for at least a minute, lost deep in thought. He turned to look at her but still said nothing.

"What do you think?" she asked when she couldn't bear the suspense.

"It's . . . I can't think of a word. It's . . . wow. The detail you remember, and the feelings. It's . . . wow."

"I guess the meaning is pretty self-explanatory."

"I think so," he said, "but tell me anyway."

"We'll be going to the temple soon, Jackson. And after we've done that, we can do the work for our families . . . our loved ones who have passed on. Remember when *you* had a dream about your grandfather? The message was in essence the same . . . in a roundabout way."

"It must be pretty important for us to *both* get the message, especially in such a remarkable way."

"Maybe we just need to be reminded so that we don't lose our focus on what's important. If opposition comes up—and it probably will—we need to remember that it's not just *us* we're going to the temple for. That's just the beginning."

Jackson was thoughtful again and muttered softly, "Incredible." He looked at Chas and asked, "So, who was the man . . . the one you spoke to in your dream?"

Chas laughed. "You don't know?"

He shrugged and gave her a comical glare. "Why would I know?"

"Come here," she said and took his hand. She unlocked the door that divided their home from the inn, led him up one flight of stairs and pointed to a small wall hanging. The inn was full of little excerpts from Dickens novels and quotes from the man himself, but Jackson hadn't necessarily paid that much attention to most of them. He leaned forward to read, *The pleasure of a generous friendship is the steadiest joy in the world. —Charles Dickens.* Chas commented, "He said that I knew how he felt about friendship."

Jackson looked at Chas, eyes wide. "That was Dickens . . . in your dream?"

"It was a dream, Jackson, not some kind of visitation from the other side."

"I don't know," he said with a little chuckle. "You felt like you were really with Granny, so maybe he *was* there. You're the one who taught me to believe in angels."

"Well, it doesn't really matter whether it was actually him or not; the message is clear."

Jackson looked at the quote again, then at his wife. "Does this mean you'll be getting involved in Jodi's project like she asked?"

"I guess it does." She led the way down the stairs and stopped in the main hall, recalling how it had felt in her dream. She felt a little chill to think of the great writer—her hero and the namesake of her inn—actually standing here. Understanding the principle of the ministering of angels, specifically what she'd learned from practically memorizing Moroni chapter seven, she knew it was possible. It just seemed so incredulous. But speculating over such things was irrelevant. She'd been given a beautiful reminder that life after death was real, and she'd felt a renewal of the love of her grandmother. She knew she needed to make the temple work for their family members a high priority, and she knew that she needed to do everything she could to help Jodi and her friends during their stay here.

Jackson nudged her out of her daydreaming. "You okay?" he asked.

She smiled. "He likes what I've done with the place." She looked around again. "Remember how Granny used to talk about Mr. Dickens as if they were great friends?"

"Oh, I remember."

"Maybe they are," Chas said, and they went back into the house, knowing their babies would soon be awake and the day would begin.

* * * * *

Chas almost floated through the morning, still feeling attached to her dream with a keen sense of peace and joy. In the middle of washing the dishes, the thought occurred to her that sometimes a great spiritual experience was meant to give a person strength to carry them through difficult times ahead. It had certainly applied to her own life in the past more than once. She was startled by the idea, and a cold dread dropped a rock into the glassy surface of her spiritual high, sending ripples of fear through her. It only took a minute to put her faith in check and utter a prayer for help in being able to replace any fear with faith. If challenges arose, they would deal with them. They'd survived much, and she and Jackson would survive whatever life might throw at them. The love she shared with Jackson was unshakable, as was their mutual testimony of the gospel. It was the rock in their life. With those things in place, surely anything else was manageable. She could think of a hundred things that might test that faith, but not one of them that could break it. Then she pushed such thoughts away and instead pondered her dream and the precious gift that it was.

Chas called Jodi at the bakery she managed, and asked if she could bring some lunch to the bakery for the two of them to share. Jodi was thrilled, and Chas left the children in Jackson's care to do a few errands before she picked up some Chinese food she'd called ahead to order. She knew Jodi's favorite, and she was looking forward to such a fun meal after her little bout of stomach flu. There was nothing like being ill to make one appreciate good health—or a good meal.

Chas went into the bakery and greeted one of the regular employees who was working behind the counter. "I'll get Jodi," she said and went into the back.

Jodi came out a moment later and hugged Chas in greeting. They sat together at one of the little tables where customers could sit to eat a roll or pastry with coffee or cocoa. They shared small talk for a good while as they ate their sweet-and-sour chicken and egg rolls before Chas said, "I prayed about it."

"About spending time with the group, you mean?"

"That's what I mean."

"And?" Jodi asked with eager excitement.

"Apparently it's the right thing to do. You must be inspired."

"Oh, that's great!" Jodi said with delighted laughter.

"I just hope I can handle whatever you think might come up."

"Who knows *what* will come up," Jodi said. "But whatever it is, your being there will make it go more smoothly; I'm certain of it."

"I'll be praying for that," Chas said. "Now, tell me more about these friends. It would probably be good if I got to know more about them before they come. Are they *all* coming?"

"They are!" Jodi said. "It's nothing short of a miracle . . . the way everyone is available, the way Tammy's money came through, the way the inn was available, the way *you* are available. It's going to be wonderful!"

"I'm sure it will," Chas said, then she encouraged Jodi to tell her about these women.

"Well, Tammy is the steady one. She's the one I've stayed closest to through the years. She lives in West Valley . . . that's in the Salt Lake area. She's always been strong in the gospel. She's very wise, great at giving advice . . . not in a presumptuous or bossy way, though. She just seems to have a sixth sense about what's appropriate and right. She grew up in a pretty good home; not perfect, but pretty good. She married a good man. The marriage has had its ups and downs, but nothing really big. Or maybe it's because they're both great people and they're both committed to working things out instead of letting them overtake you. You know what I mean?"

"I do," Chas said, thinking of her own marriage.

"Sometimes people have to go through a lot of hard times to gain wisdom, I think. But for Tammy, it's like her wisdom is just a gift. I mean, her life hasn't all been a bed of roses, but she's made wise choices and it's been good. It's been better than most of the rest of the group—let's put it that way."

"I can't wait to meet her," Chas said.

Jodi then told her about Mia, who now lived in San Diego. She'd never married, but she had a really good life in every respect otherwise. The problem was that she often couldn't see past feeling sorry for herself because marriage and children had never been a part of her life.

"But she's a hoot to be around when she's in a good mood," Jodi said. "She is *so* funny. Whenever we're together, she's the one that gets us laughing."

Jodi told Chas about Kristy, who was coming from Iowa, and Marianne, who now lived in Denver. "Then there's Luci," Jodi said. "That's short for Lucinda. She *hates* that name, so she's always gone by Luci. She lives in Salt Lake City. She actually lives about a mile from where she grew up, so she's the closest to our original neighborhood."

Jodi told Chas a little about the situation of each of these women, but Chas knew that right now she could never remember it all or keep it straight. She hoped that when she actually met them it would be easier.

"And then there's Rachelle," Jodi said. "She's the one facing the big crisis right now. She's always seemed to have a charmed life; everything's been great for her all along. Or so we thought. So *she* thought. Turns out her husband has been living a double life right from the start; even when they were dating. She discovered one problem a few months ago, then the whole façade just began to crumble, and now she's found out all kinds of things he's been doing. *Horrible* things. Needless to say, she's pretty shaken."

"That's terrible!" Chas said, so grateful to know that her husband had character and integrity.

"Yes, it is. But hopefully this little vacation will give her the strength to be able to face it more realistically and be able to get through it."

"I hope so," Chas said.

"And then there's me," Jodi said. "You know all about me."

"Not *all* about you. You haven't told me how you fit in exactly."

"Well, I'm the one who had kind of a wild streak in high school. That's when I met Patrick; he was kind of a bad boy back then. We got married young, but he's always been a good husband. I just wish he would go to church with me."

"He'll come around eventually," Chas said. "It's evident that your friends have had different challenges."

"I've stayed closest to Tammy. I told you that already. But I talk to all of them at least once every month or two."

"It's so wonderful that you've all stayed close this way," Chas said. "I'm really looking forward to it." She laughed to recall something. "Which reminds me . . . I had a great idea. I was talking to Polly this morning about what we could do to make this nice and relaxing for the ladies, and she said that the place where she gets her hair done does the greatest pedicures. She said that she overheard them talking once about doing pedicure parties, where two or three ladies will come to your home and bring little tubs for everyone to soak their feet, and they take turns getting a foot massage, and having their toenails done, while they all sit and visit. How does that sound?"

"Oh, it's divine!" Jodi said. "What a great idea! I've also arranged for some of our greatest delicacies that we make here at the bakery to be delivered. A new dessert each day. This is not a week for dieting. Of course, we'll have some great healthy stuff on the menu, but . . . hey, life is too short to not have dessert, especially when you're on vacation."

"Amen to that," Chas said.

* * * * *

Jackson listened politely to Chas as she told him all about the plans for the week-long ladies' gathering at the inn. Finally she said, "Doesn't it sound great?"

"It sounds great for ladies," he said. "I think it's going to be wonderful, and I'm glad you're going to be involved. I think it's a good thing."

"But?" she asked in response to his lack of enthusiasm.

Jackson chuckled. "I'm a guy, Chas. I'm sorry that I can't get overly enthused about pedicures and chick flicks. I'll be glad to tend the kids and stay out of the way. Maybe I'll bribe Elliott to hang out with me here and there to help balance out the overflow of estrogen that will be radiating from the inn."

Chas laughed. "You are so . . . *male.*"

"Guilty," he said and kissed her. "You wouldn't want me any other way."

"No, I wouldn't. And the other way around."

"Precisely. I'm more than happy to let you and the ladies have your little vacation. I think you've earned it, and I'm sure these other women have as well. I'm just going to keep my distance."

"Fair enough," Chas said. "With the way we're working it out, Polly can cover the office, Michelle will be doing breakfasts except for one day off, and Jodi insists we'll do toast and cereal that day so I won't have to work. Tricia and Whitney will come in to do minimal room cleaning, and that about covers it. Since the entire inn is being rented, the ladies are going to pitch in and take care of everything else. But with women everywhere, it's probably not a good week for you to be doing any maintenance or extras, anyway. Maybe you could take the week off as well—as much as you can while being in charge of the kids. But you don't have to do that *all* the time. I'm not going to be with the ladies every minute of the day."

"It'll be fine," he said. "I'm just glad we built this addition. I'm not sure renting the whole inn would have worked very well if we had actually still been *living* in it."

"Yes, that would have been challenging. But as it is, it's all going to come together perfectly."

Jackson smiled to see his wife's enthusiasm. She truly had an innkeeper's spirit. It was one of her gifts to be so skilled at taking care of people, making them comfortable, and helping them enjoy their time away from home. He'd once been the recipient of that gift, and it had left such an impression on him that he'd never wanted to leave. He was glad that Jodi and Chas had become friends, and that this project was involving Chas in a broader capacity than simply providing rooms and meals. He really did think it would be good for her. And he was going to enjoy a relatively easy week, just hanging out with his kids. He too was looking forward to it, but more than that, he was looking forward to having it behind them, which would put them within days of going to Washington, DC, for one of the greatest events of their lives. He was counting the days!

CHAPTER FOUR

A week prior to the scheduled grand reunion, Chas and Jodi sat down with Polly to go over the plans and make certain everything had been covered. Even though Polly wouldn't be directly involved, she was excited to be a part of the planning, and she would be getting a massage just like the other ladies while the massage therapist was set up to work at the inn for a few days.

At Jodi's suggestion, Chas had personally phoned each of the other six women to extend a personal invitation to stay at the Dickensian Inn, and to express her pleasure at the opportunity to meet each of them and get to know them better. Jodi had believed it would be a way for Chas to become a little better acquainted with them beforehand, and it might ease some awkwardness when they all arrived. To incorporate more purpose into the phone call, Chas asked each of the women if they had any special needs that the inn could help accommodate. She told each of them that they would all have their own rooms, but since the rooms varied in size and elegance, she wanted to assign rooms in a way that would make everyone comfortable and relaxed. She found it interesting that every one of them said they'd be thrilled with anything as long as it had a bed and a shower, and that she should give the elegant rooms to someone else. Chas told each of them in return that she would try to be inspired. Since they were all LDS women, she knew they would understand.

Chas also took a few minutes with each phone call to give each woman a little bit of history about the inn. In most cases the conversations ended up lasting more than an hour, and Chas *did* feel like she'd gotten to know each of them a little better. Having Jodi provide pictures for her to look at while she talked to them helped her feel more prepared to meet them and keep their names straight.

The Sunday before the ladies were to arrive, Jackson and Chas shared a monumental event that they'd both been looking forward to for a long time. Chas's joy was deep when Jackson was given the Melchizedek Priesthood and ordained an elder. Many times since his baptism, Jackson had expressed a desire to be able to have the privileges associated with this priesthood; she knew this step meant a great deal to him, but no more than it meant to Chas. In all the years since she'd joined the Church, she had never been blessed to have a priesthood holder in her home who could give her a blessing if she needed one. And now Jackson could. And he could do the same for their children. She'd simply never felt more happy, especially with the prospect of the temple on the near horizon. She told him so that evening after they'd shared their usual prayer. Hugging him tightly, she added, "Granny would be proud."

"Yes, I believe she would," he said, and Chas saw an added contentment in his countenance that warmed her.

* * * * *

The day before the scheduled arrival of Jodi's friends, all of the prayers for fair weather seemed to be working. The weather forecast was bright and clear for the next few days, then a big snowstorm was expected. But by then they would all be safely comfortable at the inn with everything they needed. Chas and Jodi both agreed that a storm with the right timing could add to the coziness of the experience.

Polly looked after the inn while Jackson watched the children so that Jodi and Chas could go buy all of the groceries and other amenities that would be needed for the week. Menus had been planned in such a way that all of the food could be purchased in advance and refrigerated or frozen if needed. They also bought some odds and ends to finish up some projects they'd been putting into place for the ladies, as well as a gift bag for everyone.

Chas was enjoying everything so much that she now wondered why she'd felt so hesitant when Jodi had initially suggested she be personally involved. Even though she didn't fully understand Jodi's reasons for wanting an outsider in the middle of everything, she now had to admit that if she *wasn't* going to be involved, she would be completely jealous and feel left out. Ironically, Polly felt the opposite. She was more than happy to stay on the outside and be able to help make everything go more smoothly—as long as she got that free massage.

When they returned, Jackson was there to help carry in all the groceries and put them away. Chas was more than eager to let him carry things downstairs that needed to go in the freezers or overflow pantry they had in the basement. Since the babies were both asleep, they were able to get everything arranged and put away without any interruptions.

Chas was finally able to look around and declare, "I think we're all set. Now we just have to pick the women up at the airport tomorrow and let the good times roll."

With everything ready for the following day, Jodi went home to pack for the week and make certain that her own home was prepared for her lengthy absence. Her husband, Patrick, was actually using some vacation time to help with the children so that she could have the same opportunity for a getaway as the others who were traveling many miles from their homes.

Chas felt confident that everything was under control, but she also felt tired and had no desire to cook supper. When she expressed her feelings to Polly, she said, "Oh, I bet we could make some decent sandwiches that would be sufficient." Polly often hung around into the evening when Elliott was working a swing shift so she wouldn't have to be alone so many hours, and it was typical for her to eat with Chas and Jackson when she did.

"Excellent plan," Chas said, and they started digging through the refrigerator in the kitchen of the inn. They were each making their own sandwiches when Elliott came in, wearing his uniform.

"What are you doing here?" Polly asked him before he greeted her with a kiss.

"They made a mistake in shift assignments and they had too many of us there," he said. "The good news is they sent me home. The bad news is that I have to make up for it sometime in the next few weeks."

"Well, it's a nice surprise today," Polly said, but Elliott was distracted by teasing Charles, who was sitting in his high chair, more playing with his own version of a sandwich than making much effort to eat it.

Jackson entered the kitchen carrying Isabelle, who wore a freshly changed diaper. He said to Elliott, "What are you doing here?"

"Am I not welcome?" Elliott asked, feigning hurt feelings.

"Not if you cry like a little girl when I ask you a question," Jackson said and put Isabelle into the little baby plaything where she could sit surrounded by the attached brightly colored toys. She'd inherited it from her brother, and Jackson fondly called it the spaceship. Once the baby was buckled safely into the little seat, she started bouncing up and down, squealing with delight. The adults all chuckled, then Chas announced, "I didn't feel like cooking, so we're having sandwiches for supper."

"Works for me," Jackson said and started making himself a sandwich. "Although, I'll probably be eating lots of sandwiches this week while you're partying with the girls."

"I'm sure you'll manage," Chas said.

"You still need me to come and hang out while you tend kids?" Elliott asked him.

"You're welcome as much as your wife will let you keep me company around your work schedule."

"Anything for a good cause," Polly said with a sideways smile. She pointed at the sandwich ingredients spread over the counter and asked her husband, "Want one?"

"Do we have to *feed* him?" Jackson asked facetiously, then he chuckled.

"Maybe I could earn it by cleaning some toilets or something," Elliott said while he was washing his hands.

"Oh, you've earned it," Jackson said. "A lifetime of sandwiches could never pay you back for taking care of my inn all those weeks we were out of state when Isabelle was born."

A moment of silence brought back a deluge of difficult memories. Isabelle had been born with a heart defect, and the family had stayed in Salt Lake City for weeks while she had recovered from open-heart surgery. Elliott had been staying at the inn during those weeks, since a young woman living here at the time had become tangled up between two notorious crime families. The culminating incident had nearly cost Polly and Elliott their lives. It was truly a miracle that it hadn't. Jackson felt that he could never repay Elliott for putting his life on the line on behalf of his home and loved ones. It had strengthened the bond that had already existed between them after working together for years in a dangerous profession. And Jackson was only too glad to have him around now. But he *did* like to tease him.

When they were all seated around the table in the kitchen eating, Elliott said casually, "Oh, Jackson . . . you remember Serena?"

Jackson felt immediately uncomfortable with the memories that rushed to his mind. He met Elliott's eyes with a firm gaze, silently cautioning him to take care in the conversation. He wasn't sure if Elliott understood or not when he said, "Of course you remember Serena."

"What about her?" Jackson asked.

"You knew, of course, that she had cancer."

Jackson set down the glass in his hand. His reaction to the news squelched his efforts to try to remain discreet. "No, I didn't know she had cancer," he said, only realizing how angry he sounded when his wife's expression showed alarm. "What do you mean by *of course?* Why would you assume that I knew?"

"Well . . ." Elliott looked confused and flustered. "Everyone knew. I just assumed you knew."

"Everyone?"

"Everyone . . . who knew her . . . who worked with her . . ."

"Well, no one told *me* she had cancer. Is she okay?" As soon as he asked, he realized Elliott had been speaking in past tense. That fact combined with the shadow that rose in Elliott's eyes made Jackson's heart pound. "What's happened?" Jackson asked more quietly.

"Jackson, she . . . she died yesterday. Ekert left me an e-mail, but I didn't check my messages until this afternoon. He told me to tell you. He sounded like you already knew she'd been sick. Maybe we all just assumed that someone else had told you, but . . ."

Jackson rose abruptly and rushed out of the room. He was so overtaken by anger and grief and regret that he feared making some kind of ugly outburst beyond his own control. He needed to be alone. But even then he had no idea how to take this in or what to make of how he was feeling.

Chas felt unsettled and deeply concerned when her husband left so abruptly. A taut silence hovered in the room for a full minute before Chas said, "Apparently Jackson was very fond of this . . . Serena."

She noted a definite caution in Elliott's eyes. "Apparently he never told you about her."

Chas knew what that meant. The unsettled feeling increased. A string of emotions faced her all at once. But it only took her a moment to determine the most important one to take hold of and act on. Her husband needed her, and he needed her to be compassionate.

"Will you watch the kids?" Chas said, rising from the table. "I think my husband needs me."

"Sure," Elliott said the same time as Polly said, "Of course."

Chas knew Jackson had left the house because she'd heard the door after he'd left the table. She grabbed her coat from near the door and went out, seeing that a light was on in the garage. She opened the door to see him sitting against the edge of a work table, his hands planted on his thighs, his head low. He looked up when he heard the door, and she was stunned by the anguish in his expression.

"I'm not drinking, if that's what you're wondering," he said and turned his back to her. Chas recalled well the day she *had* found him here drinking when she had believed he'd given it up. But he'd come so far since then. He'd been through extensive counseling to heal the pain inside of him, and he'd been healed even more completely by his conversion to the gospel. She wasn't worried about him drinking. She *was* worried about why he would bring it up.

"No, I wasn't wondering that. Why would you think it would even cross my mind?"

"It crossed *my* mind," he said.

"Meaning . . . what? That if you still had liquor hidden out here you'd be having a drink?"

"No," he admitted through a sigh. "I wouldn't. I hope you know that."

"I *do* know that. You're not the same man you were then."

"Sometimes I wonder," he said, still keeping his back to her.

"Why?"

"Because I *want* a drink," he admitted.

Chas took that in and tried to be compassionate. "I would think that any recovered alcoholic might feel that way when he's facing a difficult moment. The important thing is resisting the temptation."

"I know," he said. "I wouldn't do it. I would never do it, Chas."

"I know," she said in the same tone. She added with caution, "Even though you're facing a difficult moment."

He looked at her then, but it was just a glance over his shoulder before he looked away again. "I used to take pride in not allowing people to be able to read me."

"Well, you weren't in the FBI squad room just now. You were in the kitchen with your wife and your friends. The people you love *should* be able to read you—especially me."

He let out a bitter chuckle. "You've *always* been able to read me."

"To some degree, perhaps." She decided to get to the point. "But you've managed to remain very mysterious about your past." She laughed softly to try to ease the tension. "I didn't know you spoke Spanish until you did it in your sleep. I didn't know you spoke Russian until you spoke to a Russian guest." Jackson shook his head. Even from behind, Chas could see self-recrimination in his body language. But she had to make her point. They needed to deal with whatever was going on. "And when we met, you summed up your past with women by telling me you'd had brief and meaningless relationships."

Jackson squeezed his eyes closed, waiting for her to throw darts of accusation at him. And he was prepared to take them; he deserved them. But her voice was kind as she said, "Apparently they weren't all so brief . . . or meaningless." He heard her sigh and could tell she'd stepped closer. "Apparently you once loved this Serena."

Jackson was unprepared for how much it hurt to hear her say that, but probably not for the reasons that Chas might suspect. "What makes you think so?" he asked, trying to sound nonchalant. He didn't want to be dishonest with his wife. But he didn't want to talk about it, either. He felt relatively certain, however, that keeping it to himself was no longer an option.

"You wouldn't be this upset over simply learning about the death of a coworker, because I already know the coworkers you were close to. And if she had only been a friend to you, Elliott wouldn't have looked so guilty after you got up and left the room."

Jackson chuckled tensely. "Remind me to give him a fat lip or something."

"You never would."

"No, I never would."

"Maybe you should be thanking him. Maybe it's time we talked about all the things that you've tried to avoid telling me; maybe you should tell me what your life was like before you met me."

"There are things you just don't need to know."

Chas thought about that. In spite of mixed feelings, she had to admit, "Okay, you're probably right. But . . . I need to know why you're upset *now*. You should know I'm not going to judge you or anything you did. You were a different man; it was a different time." Chas uttered a silent prayer and struggled to find the right words to urge him to talk as opposed to encouraging him to remain distant about his feelings. "I've told you everything about Martin. I was married to him. What we shared was significant. It's never been avoided in our conversations." She paused and added gently, "Tell me about Serena."

Jackson finally turned to look fully at his wife. Her sincerity was evident, but so was the uneasiness that she was trying very hard to hide. He tried to form the words to begin to tell her about his relationship with Serena and all that he was feeling upon realizing that she was dead. He couldn't have spoken the words that came to his mind in that moment if his life had depended on it. Everything that had felt sure and steady in his life half an hour ago suddenly felt like quicksand. He'd believed his past was put away. He'd believed that his skirting the truth and omitting facts had been sufficient in his relationship with his wife. Even with his confessions in regard to Julie, he hadn't believed that the years between Chas and his teenage follies had really mattered. But they *did* matter. And his holding out on his wife suddenly felt like he'd sinned against her. Still, he could recognize that he was seeing and feeling all of this through a lens of grief. He had sense enough not to be rash, and to give himself some time. And that's what he gave himself; that's what he needed.

"I can't talk about it right now," he said. "I appreciate your concern . . . and your understanding. I do, Chas—more than I could ever tell you. But I need some time."

Chas wanted to protest, but he was being calm and reasonable and appropriate. She just nodded and said, "You know where to find me when you're ready to talk about it."

"Of course," he said, but he truthfully couldn't imagine any scenario beyond continuing to avoid it—for the rest of his life if he had to.

"You should go to the funeral," she said.

He immediately protested. He couldn't imagine having the courage to actually go back to Virginia and face up to all of these memories and feelings. He far preferred to stay here and try to make them go away. "I don't know if—"

"I may not know anything about your relationship with her, but I do know that when you don't get closure with someone you care about, it can eat away at you. Haven't we already had enough of that kind of thing?"

Jackson almost felt like she'd slugged him in the stomach. The recent incident with Julie was nothing in light of how Chas had stood by him through the nightmares and traumas of PTSD. If anyone knew about the past eating a man alive, it was his wife. She deserved to have him handle this maturely and rationally; she deserved to have him act like a man and use the principles he'd learned in order to face this and deal with it.

"You should go to the funeral," she repeated, sparing him from having to answer her question. "You need to go there, see her, and spend some time with people you know who knew her. You need closure. And when you're ready, we'll talk about it. Fair enough?"

He thought about it and couldn't argue. "Fair enough. I'm sure you're right. I don't want to, but I'm sure you're right. As long as you're there with me, then—"

"I can't go," Chas said, wondering what kind of ill fate had committed her to be here at the inn when such an event would occur in Jackson's life. She told herself that maybe it would be better for him to face this without her. But a part of her felt terrified to send him back to that world in this state of mind without her being able to stand beside him. She'd felt good about the decision to have this group of women stay here at this time, and she had known beyond any doubt that it was right for her to be personally involved in their activities. She had to put her husband into God's hands, and hope and pray that He knew what He was doing.

"Can't go?" Jackson echoed, determined to renege on his need for closure if she couldn't be with him.

"That group of ladies will be arriving tomorrow. I have to be here. It's not something Polly or Michelle can do without me. It's a lot more complicated than our usual guests. We've already talked about this."

"Sorry. I'd forgotten. But . . . I can't go without you."

"You'll have to. Maybe it's better that way. Whether or not it is, you need to be there, and I need to be here. But it's not the nineteenth century, Jackson. We do have cell phones. We can talk as much as you need. We can still get through it together."

"I was thinking more of having you hold my hand."

Trying to lighten the mood, she said, "You can hold your cell phone in your hand. As long as it's with you, I'm as close as a phone call. And you can imagine me next to you every minute, because that's where my heart will be."

Jackson could only nod, suddenly overcome with a surge of emotion that was difficult to hold back.

"I should get inside," Chas said, knowing there was nothing more to be said right now—and with the mood he was in, staying longer would never make him talk. "You know I'm available if you need me."

"Thank you," Jackson said, thinking how this could have been an argument if he'd had a wife who wanted to focus on his omission of details of his past. Or if she had allowed feelings of jealousy to override her concern for him. She was a good woman. He just wasn't sure he deserved her.

She smiled and said, "Maybe Elliott could go with you."

"Maybe," Jackson said, but he knew that Elliott hadn't really known Serena that well. He wasn't sure he would want—or be able—to take the time off work and be away from his wife just to be Jackson's traveling companion. Not only that, if Jackson was going to be gone, Chas would rely more on Polly to help with the children, and Polly would rely more on Elliott. It wasn't feasible for *both* of them to be gone. Looking at the complications, he wondered if it was good for him to go at all. Perhaps he'd just have to find another way to get closure.

Jackson watched Chas leave, and the door seemed to close in slow motion behind her. He tried to comprehend that Serena was really dead. He couldn't believe it, and he couldn't even remember how long it had been since he'd seen her or talked to her. He'd always intended to contact her, just to tell her that the way it had ended wasn't her fault, just to let her know that his problems were no reflection on the kind of woman that she was. Now he'd never get the chance.

CHAPTER FIVE

Chas came back into the kitchen where Elliott was playing with the baby and Polly was putting the food away.

"Is he okay?" Polly asked.

"It's hard to say," she answered, then made eye contact with Elliott. "I think he needs to go to the funeral. I know practically nothing about how Serena ties into his life, but I think he needs closure. I don't suppose there's any way you could go with him."

Elliott shook his head. "I just can't," he said. "I haven't had this job long enough to be able to take time off yet. I have to take the shifts they give me. If it was an immediate family member, I could get a couple of days, but . . . not for this."

"I understand," Chas said.

"Are *you* okay?" Polly asked.

"I'm just . . . worried about him. I think he's pretty upset, but he doesn't want to talk about it." Chas looked again at Elliott. "Promise me something; promise me that you'll make yourself available to talk to him as much as possible. You knew this woman. You knew him before he came here and made so many changes in his life. You connect his old life to the new one. Just . . . be there for him. Maybe he'll talk to you more than he would to me."

"I'll do what I can," Elliott said. "But he doesn't have a reputation for being a real talkative kind of guy."

"I know. Just . . . be aware . . . and open."

"Of course."

"If he's going to the funeral, then you're going to need more help with the kids," Polly said. "I don't have any plans other than throwing some food at my husband once in a while. I can do that just as easily at your house. I can watch them as much as you need."

"You already do so much for us," Chas said. "I'm sure that I can—"

"Listen to me," Polly said. "You've given me more than I could ever tell you. You gave me a life, a home away from home, a friend; things I'd never had before I met you. Please let me do this for you. Why don't you just let us stay at your house for the week? Maybe you should just take the leftover room at the inn and make a little vacation out of it. We'll be fine. Won't we, honey?" She smiled at Elliott.

"Of course we will," Elliott said. "That's easy for me to say, since Polly does most of the work with the kids, but I love helping with them. You'll be close by if you're needed. I think it's a great idea."

"You've told me about a hundred times that you felt really good about being involved with Jodi and her friends," Polly said, "that you thought you might be able to make a difference to them. And I know you've been excited about it. Just . . . let us do this."

Chas thought about it a minute. She'd be close by and could spend as much time with the kids as she wanted, depending on what was going on with the ladies. But if she didn't have to be in charge of them, she'd be able to relax more. "Okay, you talked me into it," she said. "I think it would be better for Jackson if he knew you were going to do this. He'll likely be more willing to go to the funeral, and he won't be so worried about what's going on at home. On behalf of both of us, I accept your offer. And I intend to make it up to you someday."

"No worries," Polly said.

"There's one problem, though," Chas said. "There *isn't* an extra room at the inn. We have seven guests plus me, and eight guest rooms. We were going to use the extra one for the massage parlor."

"No, we decided to do the massages in the room that you and Jackson slept in before you moved into the addition."

"No, we were going to use that room to set up the extra tables and do the craft projects."

"And that's why we were going to do the massages in the room that used to be the nursery before you moved into the addition."

Chas thought about it. "Okay, I guess there's an extra guest room. I'd forgotten."

"So, it's all set," Polly said. "And Jackson can . . ."

They heard a door in the distance and she stopped talking. Jackson entered the kitchen and said, "It's a sure bet that someone's been talking about you when you walk into a room and no one is saying *anything.*"

"This investigator thing in your blood is so annoying sometimes," Elliott said in a light tone that eased the tension.

"It's in your blood too," Jackson said. He looked directly at his wife. "So, what were you talking about that stopped when I came back inside?"

Chas had no problem saying, "I told them I thought you should go to the funeral. Elliott can't go because of work, but you should go anyway."

"I don't need to go, Chas. I was upset to hear about her death, but it's not as big of a deal as you might think."

Chas knew him well enough to know that he was trying to draw attention away from his dramatic reaction earlier, and he was also hoping to simply avoid ever talking about it again. If he could declare that it wasn't a big deal, then it might just go away.

"With everything going on here at the inn, you need me to help with the kids. It's better if I just stay and—"

"Oh, that's all been taken care of," Polly said. "Elliott and I are staying at *your* house for the week, which would make it really awkward for you to stay there. And you can't hang around the inn because it will be crawling with women, and they might wander around in their pajamas or something. So, you might as well just go to Virginia. Go to the funeral. Visit old friends. We'll take care of the kids until you get back."

Jackson looked hard at Polly. "Funny how you've never had a problem telling me exactly what you think."

"Nope, never have," she said. "What are friends for?"

"And what if I don't *want* to go to the funeral? Are you just going to kick me out of my own house?"

Chas put a hand on his arm. "Obviously, no one is going to force you to go. The decision is up to you. But if you decide to go, you should know that everything will be fine here, so you don't need to worry. And my opinion is that you *should* go. And when you get back we can talk about it . . . or while you're there. I'm as close as your cell phone." She hugged him and added, "We've been blessed with very good friends. You should be gracious enough to accept their offer to help with the kids while you go to the funeral. Maybe you *will* see some old friends. The last time we went to Virginia, we had a great time."

"That's because you were with me, and it was a vacation. This is hardly the same."

"But necessary," Chas said. "You let us know, but if you're going, you'd better book a flight."

Jackson sighed, feeling torn between his desire to run and hide from these feelings and an instinctive need to face them head-on. He knew Chas was right. He knew that going there and having closure was likely the best solution to what he was feeling, and that he would be more likely to handle this better in the long run. He asked Elliott, "Do you know *when* the funeral is?"

"The day after tomorrow is what Ekert said in his message. I can call and have him e-mail you the details."

"Thanks," Jackson said and turned to leave the room.

"Where are you going?" Chas asked.

"To book a flight."

"Aren't you going to eat the rest of your sandwich?"

"I'm not hungry," Jackson said and hurried to the office, wanting to be alone.

* * * * *

Jackson planted himself in the chair behind the desk, but instead of turning on the computer to find Serena's obituary or to make flight arrangements, he just turned his back to the desk and stared at the wall. He'd only been there a couple of minutes when he heard Elliott say, "I'm sorry about that. Maybe I should have brought it up privately. I just . . . assumed you knew she was sick. And I assumed that Chas knew about her. I thought Chas knew *everything* about you."

Jackson turned his chair and glared at Elliott, but he was unaffected. They'd come a long way since the days when he'd worked for Jackson and had been easily intimidated by him.

"Apparently she doesn't," Elliott said.

Jackson looked away. "I didn't think the past mattered."

"Do you really believe that? Or is that what you've convinced yourself to believe because you didn't want to talk about it?"

Jackson glared at him again. Elliott chuckled and sat down. "I know you better than that," he said. "You are a master at avoiding any unnecessary conversation, especially when it's personal or sensitive. When it's both, you get *really* testy."

"And I thought I was hard to read."

"On the job you were . . . at least with people who didn't know you. But you taught me to be a good investigator, and we worked together for years. We couldn't have worked together well if we hadn't been able to read each other."

"Okay, you got me there," Jackson said.

"Again, I'm sorry I didn't tell you before. I really thought you knew."

"It's not your fault; it's not anybody's fault," Jackson said, wishing there was someone to blame for the way he felt. "The thing is . . . in the work we did, when people died, there was always someone to blame. Someone pulled the trigger or made stupid choices. Victims got vindication when criminals were punished. It doesn't work that way with cancer, does it."

"No, it doesn't," Elliott said. "But it probably would have been easier for you to handle if you'd actually known she was dying."

"Yeah . . . well . . . it's too late to wish for that. If she'd been killed in a car accident, I wouldn't have had a chance to . . ." He allowed the sentence to fade, not really wanting to go there.

"A chance to what?" Elliott asked. Jackson weighed whether to answer the question honestly or skirt around it and change the subject. Elliott proved how well he *could* read Jackson when he said, "Just tell me what's going on and get it over with. Who else are you going to talk to about it? It's got to be hard to talk to Chas when she didn't know *anything* about Serena. I knew her, and I know how close the two of you were. When I started working for you, the two of you were like Romeo and Juliet."

"Since that story was a tragedy, I'm not sure I like the reference. Or maybe it's accurate in that regard."

"I never understood what happened, why it ended."

"I'm not sure anyone did, least of all me."

"You mean she ended it?"

"No, *I* ended it, but to this day I'm not sure why. And I guess that's the answer to your question. I think something in the back of my mind always wanted to just call her up and apologize. I wanted to tell her that my reasons for not being able to commit to a long-term relationship had nothing to do with her. I don't think it was until I met Chas that I began to see how really messed up I was. When I first came here, I was in the middle of the tragedy with Dave getting killed."

Elliott nodded; his expression showed perfect empathy. They'd both been present when everything had gone wrong and one of their team members had been shot and killed. It was evident from the incident that there had been a mole in the FBI leaking information to drug dealers. Dave's death had been only one spoke in a wheel of nightmares and horrors, more for Jackson than anyone else. But they'd been a team, and it had been hard for all of them.

"I think I was more open, more raw, more . . . something," Jackson continued. "And Chas was just . . . there. She helped me get through that, and she's helped me through a lot of things since. But I've always been cryptic about my life before I met her. She's such a good woman; she's given me so much. I always felt like mixing that old me with the new one would only taint what we share. And I didn't want that."

"Well, I think it just got mixed," Elliott said.

"Yeah," Jackson said with self-recrimination. "But she's still kind and compassionate. It's far from the first time I've felt unworthy of her. Sometimes I think if she knew the *whole* truth, she'd send me packing."

"You don't *really* believe that. I mean . . . you've changed a lot the last few years; found religion and all. But Chas knows you weren't a saint before you met her. Right?"

"Yes, I'm sure she knows that. But when I was getting to know her, I summed up my past with women in one sentence that was barely true. I hardly knew her. I didn't figure it mattered. And then . . . as things progressed, I just . . . well, who wants to bring up stuff like that? It just didn't come up, or if it did, I just avoided details."

"So, if Chas had never even heard of Serena, then she obviously doesn't know that you lived together."

Jackson *really* glared at him. "We did *not* live together."

"Oh, is that one of those *barely true* statements you're so good at? I know how it worked. You both kept your own apartments, but you were usually together at either one or the other. Her place on weekends and yours during the week because it was closer to the office. Isn't that how it went? So, that's technically *not* living together, I assume?"

"Technically," Jackson said, feeling guilt consume him. Guilt for living that kind of life, and guilt for not being more honest with his wife.

"Well, for what it's worth, I agree with Chas. I think you need to go to the funeral. I think you need to deal with whatever it is that's got you so upset. And when you come back, I think you need to come clean with your wife in all things. You keep telling me the two of you are doing this temple thing, like getting married again, only forever. You really want to take a step like that with all this baggage you haven't told her about? That's my two cents anyway. Take it or leave it. You're my best friend and I care about you. I'm no shrink, but I know how to listen, and Polly tells me I've got a fair amount of common sense. While you're out there, or . . . anytime, ever . . . you know my number."

"Yes, I do," Jackson said. "Thank you. But I think I've got to figure this out on my own."

"Maybe you do, but don't go blowing it out of proportion. Chas has proven to be pretty understanding and forgiving, and while it's obvious that you have some regrets about Serena, that was a long time ago. There's no good in dredging it up any more than necessary."

Jackson nodded, appreciating the common sense in Elliott's advice. But at the moment, he wondered if it could get to his brain when there were so many emotional barriers it would have to break through.

Elliott stood to leave and added, "If you can't talk to Chas, you need to talk to somebody. I mean it when I say I'm available. Don't get all bottled up. It won't do anybody any good."

"Thank you," Jackson said. He meant it, but he also wanted to be alone. He had way too much to think about, and an inner churning of grief and regret that made it difficult to think at all.

Elliott gave a mildly awkward wave and left the room. Jackson once again turned his chair to stare at the wall until he finally got up the courage to go online and find the obituary. He lost his nerve before he could even type her name, so he went instead to the airline website he always used when he traveled. He debated what time of day to fly out, and ended up taking a very early flight the next morning. It didn't have any layovers, but it also held appeal in getting him out of here as quickly as possible, which would help him avoid any deep conversations with his wife until he'd had a chance to sort all of this out. He then debated when to return. He didn't actually know the date of the funeral yet. Chas would be entertaining an inn full of women. The occasional wish he had to be able to just drop by FBI headquarters in Norfolk and say hi to people he knew there gave him an excuse to stay a little longer. In the end, he just booked the flight to Virginia and left the return trip open.

With that done, he stared at the wall for several more minutes before he pulled up the obituary. Now he had evidence. It wasn't just a rumor or hearsay. Serena really was dead. But he wondered how Chas would feel if he admitted to her that a little part of him felt as if it had died with her.

* * * * *

Long after Polly and Elliott had gone home, Chas tried to give Jackson some time and space. When it was nearly time to get the children ready for bed, she took them with her to the office where Jackson was sitting behind the desk, reading something on the computer. But Chas couldn't see what it was.

"You okay?" she asked, glad for the way little Charles broke the ice by running to his father, excited to see him.

Jackson picked up Charles and hugged him, laughing and talking to him as if nothing at all was wrong.

"It's almost bedtime," Chas said.

Jackson glanced at his watch. "So it is." He turned off the computer, knowing he'd reread Serena's obituary too many times. Doing it again wasn't going to convince him that she was really gone.

"I'll catch up with you," Jackson said as he turned off the light and locked the office door. "I'll make sure everything is locked up."

"Okay," she said and headed slowly toward the house with Isabelle while Jackson took Charles with him to lock the doors and see that all of the lights were dimmed for nighttime. He came through the kitchen door just a few steps behind Chas and turned to lock it behind him. She smiled at him and he returned it, determined to behave as normally as possible. He didn't like where his thoughts and memories were taking him, but he didn't necessarily believe he needed to share all of it with Chas in order to deal with it and move on.

A few minutes later they were each putting a child into pajamas. They said prayer with Charles, even though he was barely old enough to understand that he needed to fold his arms. They wanted to start him out young with good habits. After both of the children were put down for the night, Jackson said to his wife, "You're awfully quiet."

"I'm just wondering how *you* are," she said. "I'm not sure what to say."

"You could say something like, 'I'm sorry your friend died. I'm sure you'll be fine. It's been years since you've even talked to her so it's probably not that big of a deal.'"

"How could I say that when I know it *is* a big deal?"

"What makes you think so?" he asked.

"Oh, come on, Jackson. I know you better than that, and I'm not a fool. I saw the way you reacted, and trying to pretend now that you were *over*reacting isn't going to fly. Why don't you just admit that you're upset? Why don't you talk to me about it?"

Jackson was amazed at how well she could read him, even though he shouldn't have been. But he didn't want to talk about it, and he was willing to keep up the façade for as long as he could. "I'm fine, Chas," he said with a lighthearted chuckle that he hoped would convince her. "I'm flying out in the morning. My flight is early; it was the only one without a layover that didn't get me there too late tomorrow to get a decent night's sleep. I'll call you when I get there."

"When are you flying back?"

"I didn't book that yet. Since you're going to be partying with the girls, I thought I'd just see what's going on while I'm there. I'd like to see Ekert and his family."

"Of course," Chas said. She'd met Agent Ekert and his wife on their visit to Virginia. They were good people, and Jackson had worked with Shawn Ekert for a long time.

"So, we'll just see what happens."

"Okay," Chas said, and Jackson gave her a very normal kiss, followed by a very normal smile. "I'm going to miss you."

"I'll miss you too. But it won't be that long. Let's get some sleep. I've got to get up at four-thirty."

"*That* early?"

"That early," he said. "I'll wake you before I leave." He kissed her and settled into the bed.

Chas doubted she could sleep at all as thoughts of Jackson's pending trip to Virginia—and his reasons for going—mingled with her anticipation of the grand gathering of friends at her inn. The excitement she'd been feeling over the latter had been overshadowed by the death of Jackson's friend, or rather his reaction to it. The point being that they'd obviously been much more than friends. Chas couldn't help wondering about Serena. But she had to draw a line in her thoughts between simple jealousy and a desire to help Jackson deal with the grief of this turn of events.

Chas knew she'd slept when the baby woke her. She got up and took care of Isabelle, and when she came back to bed, Jackson eased close to her, wrapping her in his arms.

"I love you," he whispered.

"I love you too," she replied and kissed him, feeling inexplicably better from hearing his assurance as well as from being able to hold him close.

Chas woke up again when the alarm went off. Jackson told her to go back to sleep, but she was surprised that she did. Her next awareness was Jackson sitting on the edge of the bed, bending over to kiss her face. "I've got to go," he whispered. "I'll call you when I get there."

"You'll be in my prayers . . . as always."

"Then everything will be all right," he said. They shared a lengthy kiss and he added, "You enjoy yourself and don't worry about me."

"I'll do my best," she said, and a minute later he was gone.

Chas didn't go back to sleep. She took time for a long prayer while she was still snuggled in her bed. It was something she enjoyed doing sometimes, where she could just feel completely relaxed and tell her Heavenly Father all of her hopes and fears, her concerns and joys, her gratitude and love. When she finished her prayer, her mind strayed to her husband and the continuing prayer she would hold in her heart throughout the length of their separation. She looked forward to his return when they could have a long talk and take another step toward putting the past to rest.

In the meantime, today was a big day with all of the ladies flying to Butte and getting settled into the inn. She knew everything was under control except for one thing that had just occurred to her. Polly and Elliott would be staying in the house, and Chas needed to pack enough personal items to go live in a room at the inn without having to come back into the house every time she needed something, especially since someone else would be using her bedroom and bathroom. Chas showered and got dressed. She changed the sheets on the bed and made it up nicely. Then she packed a bag without feeling too much concern, knowing she *could* come and get something if she really needed it.

By the time the first child woke up, she really *was* under control for the day. If not for the unrest she felt for her husband, she would have been in a great mood. Knowing there was nothing she could do to help him at the moment, she said another prayer for him and pressed forward with her day.

* * * * *

The plane might as well have been a time machine for Jackson. In his mind, he could almost see his life moving backward. Back before he'd become the father of two. Back before he'd made the gospel a part of his life. Back before Chas. Back before he'd even considered that his own personal code of ethics might not be the best formula for long-term happiness. Back to a time when he'd been holding on to the anger of a troubled youth. Back to when he'd had no one or nothing to consider but himself, and he'd managed to push away the temptation to dwell too long on the collateral damage he might have left behind by his selfish motives. It might have mostly been driven by a distorted version of self-preservation. But it was still selfish.

When the past felt like nothing but a vacuum of regret, Jackson tried to bring his mind back to the present. But the clash between these two worlds was so intense that he was struck with physical pain. He opted to dwell in the past for now, hoping he might find some answers there that could help him fully make peace with the present so that he could move into his future with tranquility and understanding. He'd believed that he *had* made peace with his life before Chas. But the emotions that had slapped him in the face since he'd heard of Serena's death had proved him wrong—*deeply* wrong.

Realizing how tense he felt, he stretched his neck and shoulders and tried to focus on relaxing so he wouldn't end up with a migraine or something. Just what he needed—to fly to Virginia so he could endure a headache in a hotel room and miss the funeral. He leaned his head back and closed his eyes, trying to think of anything but Serena. Maybe he could even get a little nap.

Jackson gripped the stair rail with unnatural tightness, leaning on it with each step he took up the flight of stairs. He moved slowly but with a purpose that he didn't understand. At the landing he lumbered down the hall but leaned against the wall and tried to catch his breath before he could even consider knocking on the door. He'd been to Serena's place more than a dozen times over the last year or so, but never like this.

Ever since she'd come to work for the Bureau, pushing papers and answering phones, she'd made herself the center of social life for anyone like her, anyone who had no family anywhere near. There were several agents and employees who fell into that category, and Serena came up with all kinds of excuses for parties and gatherings at her place. Her apartment wasn't that large, but she liked to crowd in ten or twelve people and just eat and talk and drink, sometimes watching a game or a movie. She had a way of making everyone who came into her home feel welcome and accepted. She had contributed to better camaraderie in the office, and she had helped more than one person that Jackson knew of to get through difficult times. It was just her way.

Jackson had come to admire and respect Serena, and he couldn't deny that being at one of Serena's parties was surely the highlight of his pathetic life. But he'd never imagined coming to her place like this, never wanted to be one of those that would turn to her for help and comfort at a difficult moment. Now, here he was. Practically shaking, drained of strength, barely holding it together. He told himself to just knock on the door, tell her what had happened, and get it over with. He knew she'd offer comfort and simple advice, and maybe it would even work and he'd feel better. But he was instinctively a private person. The thought of telling her what had happened felt ludicrous. He went back toward the stairs with amazing vigor considering how weak and shaky he felt. Then he stopped, turned around, and knocked on the door before he could talk himself out of it.

It took half a minute for the door to open. She was tying a fluffy bathrobe over flannel pajamas. She was wearing her glasses. She'd been reading.

"Jackson," she said and looked at him hard, as if she were a fortune teller who could tell him what had happened. "Who died?" she asked with no hint of humor. She did know.

"I don't know his name," Jackson said. "But it was me who killed him."

She spoke volumes of understanding in her expression and gave him a hug before she motioned him in and he sank onto the couch.

"Tell me what happened," she said, sitting on the same couch. She turned toward him and tucked one foot beneath her.

"I'm sorry to bother you like this," he said. "I could say it's your own fault, the way you take in strays. You should expect them to show up at your door when something goes wrong."

"I'm glad you came," she said. "I'm glad you feel like you can. Where else are you going to go? Those idiots you work with aren't going to let you cry."

"What makes you think I'm going to cry?" he asked.

She gave him a sidelong glare and said, "Tell me."

Jackson looked away. "We went to arrest a suspect."

"We?"

"Ekert and I. When we got there the suspect had a gun. Of course, we took the usual precautions."

"Which would be?"

"We both had our weapons drawn. Then the guy points the gun at his own head. I tried to talk him out of it. I was saying all the right things. He lowered the gun. Next thing I know he's pointing it at me."

"So it was you or him?"

"I hesitated too long. He shot me first."

"What?" she screeched.

He looked at her. "I was wearing a vest."

"You would be dead if you weren't wearing a vest?"

"Yeah," he said. "Sick irony."

"Are you okay?"

"Pretty sore, but I'm okay. I'm shaky, but I don't know if that's from the impact of the bullet knocking me flat, or the fact that I pulled the trigger before I went down."

"What about Ekert? Apparently he hesitated too."

"Yeah. It was a weird situation. He got reprimanded; Henry said if the gun was pointed at me, Ekert should have been the one to take him down. I don't want Ekert to have any grief over this. Sometimes we all just . . . miss the best choice by a split second." Again he looked away. "I killed him."

"It's not the first time you've had to kill someone for duty's sake."

"No, and I'm sure it won't be the last. But this was different. He wanted me to kill him. I think he knew I was wearing a vest. Henry said it was suicide by FBI agent." Jackson shook his head. "I know this kind of thing isn't supposed to be easy, but . . . I wish it didn't have to be this hard."

Serena took his hand. "That's why you're so good at what you do, Jackson. A man who finds it easy to kill should not be in law enforcement."

Jackson closed his eyes, but it only brought the memory of that moment closer. He remembered his back hitting the floor as the kick from his own gun combined with the jolt of the bullet that hit him, halted by the protective vest.

Jackson jerked unwillingly and found himself on a plane, dozing in a mental state where dreams felt real. He glanced around, glad to realize no fellow passengers had noticed him jolting out of his sleep. Or if they had, they were gracious enough not to show it. He leaned his head back again and took in the memories. That was the first time he'd spent time alone with Serena. But one visit became two, and two became ten. He was still stunned to think of how badly that particular incident had shaken him. But Serena had helped him through it. She became a friend in a way he'd never known, not even in his youth.

He didn't recall at what point exactly his need for her friendship became attraction. It had all just evolved so easily, with no apparent thought or effort. She became the center of his life. She made him believe that there was more to life than fighting crime and hanging out with friends occasionally. He'd never really paid any attention to the beauty of the city before. He'd never bothered to stop and consider the good things in life. Serena guided him to a place where he could see his world through different eyes. Looking back, he knew that she had been there for him at a time when he could have easily gone off the deep end. It was a time when his ugly childhood could have overtaken him, when he could have lost control of his drinking. He'd been teetering on the dangerous edge of an emotional cliff, and she'd saved him.

But somewhere along the way it started falling apart. That too had been a slow and effortless evolution, and something he'd regretted even though he'd felt helpless at the time to stop their relationship's dissolution—or even to explain it to himself. Chas had filled the holes and healed the wounds left from his relationship with Serena, even if he'd been doing very well at keeping them in the category of himself marked *Top Secret—Do Not Disturb*. But now it had been disturbed, and it was no longer a secret. He just wished that Serena was still alive so that he could tell her how he felt.

CHAPTER SIX

Satisfied that the inn was in perfect condition, Chas locked it up and put out the No Vacancy sign. She got into her SUV at the same time that Jodi got into her own SUV. They gave each other a thumbs-up and headed in their separate vehicles toward the freeway. They'd agreed that there was no need for anyone to waste money on renting a vehicle when the ladies would not likely even be leaving the inn, and if they did, Chas and Jodi both had vehicles available.

While she drove, Chas went over a mental checklist of plans for the day, knowing that her babies were safe and well in Polly's care. Elliott would be working a swing shift, but he was there with Polly now. They truly seemed to enjoy the children so much that Chas almost felt like she was doing them a favor to let them become temporary parents. Elliott commented more than once that he was glad for the practice since they had a baby on the way and he'd never been around children at all.

At the airport, Chas and Jodi parked side by side, then walked inside to meet their guests near baggage claim. Tammy, Luci, and Rachelle were flying in together from Salt Lake City. Mia, Kristy, and Marianne were all coming in on different flights from their respective homes, but all of the flights were supposed to arrive in Butte within an hour of each other. Chas and Jodi found some seats where they could easily see all of the passengers coming from the gates.

"You must be excited," Chas said to Jodi.

"I am, yes. And a little nervous."

"Nervous, why?"

"I don't know. It's just been a long time since we were all together, and I'm hoping we can give Rachelle the support she needs."

"I'm sure you will," Chas said.

"How about you? Are you excited?"

"I am, actually," Chas said. "But I'm probably more nervous than you are. I've never even met these women."

"Once you spend five minutes with them, you'll forget you were ever nervous."

"I could say the same to you," Chas said, and they both laughed.

"Oh, my gosh!" Jodi said. "There's Marianne." Jodi stood up in order to make herself more visible and Chas did the same.

"Remind me," Chas said.

"Most gorgeous, worst marriage. Well, it was until Rachelle found out what *her* husband was really like."

Chas recalled Jodi telling her that Marianne was well aware of her husband's many problems, but she assumed a constant stance of patience and long-suffering, keeping everything perfectly under control while her husband behaved like a child—tantrums, irresponsibility, treating his wife and children unkindly, and never apologizing. Jodi had told her that Marianne was so good at managing the home and children and making a decent living that it was easier for her to avoid confronting her husband. But Jodi and others in the group had been concerned for years about the impact that such denial would have on the children. Now that they were becoming teenagers, that effect was starting to manifest itself, and their worry was increasing. Chas wondered, not for the first time, if it was good for her to know these women's problems before she even met them. But Jodi had said more than once that the biggest purpose of this gathering—beyond relaxation, fun, and pampering—was to hopefully help those who were struggling come to terms with their problems a little better. Jodi believed that Chas might be able to help facilitate that. Chas couldn't imagine how, but Jodi was convinced that she'd had an undeniable spiritual experience in which it was made evident she needed to include Chas and keep her in the middle of the activities. Who was Chas to argue with the Spirit?

Chas stood at a discreet distance while Jodi got Marianne's attention and they shared a tight hug and lots of laughter and excitement at seeing each other. They talked for a couple of minutes before Jodi turned toward Chas and introduced them.

"We talked on the phone," Marianne said, and Chas had to agree that she was certainly gorgeous. Her hair was auburn and swept perfectly into a clip. She was taller than Jodi and wore a classy pantsuit. She carried an expensive purse, and Chas could see that her nails were professionally done. She was vibrant and radiated the energy that Jodi had spoken of. Chas could easily imagine this being the kind of woman who could do it all and do it well, but she wondered what might happen to Marianne's life if something unexpected happened and she could no longer do it all.

"It's so nice to finally meet you," Chas said, surprised by Marianne giving her a hug. "I've heard so much about you."

"If it wasn't good, don't believe her," Marianne said, and they all laughed.

Chas saved some seats while Jodi went with Marianne to get her luggage. They returned with three rather large suitcases. Chas wondered what Marianne might be needing for a week away. Fortunately the bags all hooked together and had wheels so that Marianne could manage all of them on her own. They sat down and continued chatting while Chas just listened and pretended to be people-watching. She felt sure that she'd be more of an observer than a conversationalist throughout the course of the week. But that was okay. She was intrigued by the nature of these women's friendships, and was looking forward to an opportunity to observe them together with their different personalities and challenges.

A few minutes later Kristy arrived from Iowa, and the greetings were repeated. Chas noticed that Kristy looked tired and unnaturally thin. She wondered if she had some kind of illness that Jodi had forgotten to mention, until Marianne said to Kristy, "You have lost a *lot* of weight."

"Oh, thank you," Kristy said. "You noticed."

Chas saw a cautious look of concern pass between Jodi and Marianne while Kristy looked down at herself. Apparently Kristy was oblivious to how unhealthy her thinness looked, and Chas knew her friends were suspicious. But it was quickly glossed over as the conversation moved on. They collected Kristy's luggage, and Chas noticed that it was only one conservative bag.

Kristy had brown hair that was starting to show some traces of gray. She wondered then if the others colored their hair, or if Kristy had just gone prematurely gray. Chas was near the same age as these women and as of yet she'd seen no hint of gray in her own hair, but she knew it was different for every woman. Where Marianne wore a lot of makeup, Kristy wore none. They seemed far too different to be close friends, and yet they were thrilled to see each other, and were having a marvelous time chatting.

Mia arrived next from San Diego. She had blond hair and was shorter than any of the others. Like Marianne, she was well put together and her persona spoke of a successful career. Chas recalled that Mia had never married, but she had succeeded in every other aspect of life. She was currently serving as the stake Young Women president. She too seemed pleased to meet Chas, and gave her a hug as the others had. And she too commented on how thin Kristy looked. And again Kristy seemed oblivious to her friends' perception that she was *too* thin.

With all the luggage gathered, the four friends chattered and giggled like little girls. Chas could immediately see why Mia had the reputation for being the clown of the group. She just had a way of saying things that made the others laugh, but Mia laughed the loudest. It was an infectious laugh that Chas enjoyed listening to. She couldn't help laughing herself, even though she didn't understand a lot of the humor connected to their discussion of past events.

They all waited for about forty minutes before the flight from Salt Lake City arrived, but they were so busy talking and catching up that they didn't seem to notice. Since Chas was more of a bystander in the conversation, her mind kept wandering to Jackson. She wondered if he was okay, and she prayed that all would be well for him during this journey into his past. And as always, every time she considered the possibilities regarding his relationship with Serena, she felt uneasy and mildly jealous. But she knew Jackson loved her, and whatever he had to face, it would be faced with a ghost. Serena was gone and Jackson had a right to grieve. She just wished she could be with him.

Chas was pulled from her thoughts when Tammy, Rachelle, and Luci arrived and the flurry of greetings among all seven of the women was overwhelming. Chas just stood back and watched in amazement. They were all so excited that the collective group was practically radio-active. They finally got around to introducing Chas, and she received a hug and genuine kindness from each of them. These three women seemed more alike. Chas knew they saw each other more because they lived in the same area, especially Tammy and Rachelle. They all had similar coloring, which was the average side of dark, and they were all just a little overweight; not heavy, just the kind of weight that came with having children and being too busy to exercise much. Even though their features were all different enough that they could never be mistaken for sisters, they were all the same type. Chas wondered if at least part of the reason was due to continuing to live in the same area. However, she felt sure there were many other contributing factors.

While the rest of the luggage was being collected, Chas's cell phone rang. Her heart quickened. It was either Polly calling with a problem, or Jackson calling to say he'd arrived safely. The chances of it being anyone else were extremely slim. She glanced at the caller ID to see Jackson's number, and her heart quickened further. This response was a combination of her love for him as well as her concern for his present situation.

"You made it?" she said in lieu of a greeting.

"I did," he said.

"Did you get any rest on the plane?" she asked.

"A little," he said. "How are things there?"

"We're still at the airport, but everyone has arrived. As soon as we get the rest of the luggage, we'll be on our way."

"How is it so far?" he asked with a normalcy that implied there was no death or grief or past loves on his mind. "The ladies club?"

"It's not really a *club,* but it's fine," Chas said. "They've all been very kind. The differences and similarities in them are fascinating. If nothing else, it could be a very entertaining week."

"I hope you have a wonderful time," he said.

"Thank you. I'm sure it will be fine, but . . . I wish I could be with you. I'm worried about you."

"I wish you could be here too," he said, almost feeling as if he were lying. A part of him wanted her here, but a bigger part of him didn't want her to get too clear a picture of the life he used to live. She'd come to Virginia before, but the circumstances had been entirely different. Most of all, he just wanted to be alone. In spite of feeling down and confused and dreading the funeral, he said, "There's no reason to worry about me. I'll be just fine."

"You'll call me every day?"

"Just once?" he asked, sounding deceptively lighthearted.

"At least once; the more the better."

"I know. As long as I have my cell phone, it'll be like you're holding my hand."

"Something like that," she said, noting that the ladies were ready to go. She started walking with the group while she continued her call. "Next time you fly out of state, I'm going with you. I'm counting the days until we'll be in DC."

"It'll be great," he said but felt like he didn't mean it. Right now he couldn't imagine feeling right with Chas, especially not right enough to be going to the temple together. But he'd cross that bridge after he got through this funeral and returned home. "I should go," he added. "I've got to get my car, and I'm hoping to get a nap once I get checked in."

"Okay, well . . . thanks for calling."

"Have a good time," he said.

"I wish I could say the same, but it doesn't really fit for a funeral. I hope you'll be able to see Shawn . . . and maybe some other people. I hope you can have a *little* fun."

"Maybe," he said blandly.

"I love you, Jackson. Don't you ever forget it."

"I love you too, Chas," he said, wishing he didn't feel so unworthy of such unconditional love and acceptance. He couldn't believe how one incident could turn his life upside down in an instant.

With the call ended, Chas put the phone in her purse and kept walking.

"Was that Jackson?" Jodi asked.

"Yeah, he got there safely."

"That's good," Jodi said. Chas had told Jodi that Jackson had to go to Virginia for the funeral of someone he'd known there, but she hadn't said anything else. If she *did* end up talking to Jodi about the situation, it wouldn't be when they had so many other people around.

It didn't take long for the luggage to be loaded into the SUVs, and for the ladies to choose a seat in one vehicle or the other. They didn't seem to mind who they rode with. Any combination was good for enjoyable conversation. Chas ended up with Mia, Kristy, and Luci in her vehicle. While she drove, she enjoyed listening to them chatter about memories from their youth mingled with a little bit of asking how things were in the present. They all seemed to be doing well, although Chas sensed a little bit of what Jodi had told her about Mia: she carried a subtle attitude that implied her own unhappiness with her life due to the fact that she'd never married or had children, even though her life was gratifying in so many ways. Luci was genuine and seemed to have a great deal of gratitude for her life. Chas recalled that she was the one who had been through a very ugly divorce and she'd even lost custody of her children for a while due to lies her husband had told in court. Chas found it ironic that Mia and Luci had ended up in similar situations for different reasons, yet their attitudes were such a contrast. Kristy was more quiet than the other two, and Chas almost wished she felt like she could be involved enough in the conversation to draw Kristy out a little with some questions about herself, but the other two were chattering way too much. Perhaps before the week was out, Chas could get to know Kristy a little better.

"So, Chas," Mia said about half an hour into the drive, "tell us a little more about you."

"Oh, there's not much to tell," she said. "I have two kids and I run an inn. My husband is in Virginia at the moment. He used to live there and had to go back for a funeral."

"Anyone close?" Luci asked.

"An old friend," Chas said. "Thankfully I've got good friends who are watching my kids so I can hang out with you guys." As an after-thought, she wondered if any of them disagreed with Jodi's desire to have her hanging out with them. "I hope that's okay."

"Oh, I think it's great!" Mia said, and the others heartily agreed.

Chas didn't sense any false diplomacy and was relieved. She hoped the women in the other car weren't chastising Jodi for bringing a stranger into their midst. Kristy said eagerly, "I think it's great to bring in some fresh blood. New friends keep the old ones from getting stale."

The others laughed, then Luci said, "How true. How true."

"You said on the phone," Mia said to Chas, "that your inn has a Dickens theme."

"That's right. My grandmother inherited the house, and she also inherited a passion for Dickens and his work. It's like a legacy in my family. If you don't read Dickens, you're a black sheep. Except that I'm an only child of an only child, so there aren't any other sheep to compare me to."

Apparently the comment was funny, because they all laughed heartily. When the laughter settled, Mia said, "I remember studying Dickens in school, but I don't think I've ever read anything by him just because I wanted to. But then, work keeps me busy."

"It's not easy to take on a Dickens novel," Chas said. "But it's usually worth it. The movies are good as well. There are some really great miniseries that let us enjoy his stories without relearning the English language."

"Oh, I've seen a couple of those!" Luci said. "There was one on TV a while back and I really got into it. I'd never even heard of it before then, but it was very good!"

"Little Dorrit?" Chas asked.

"Yes, I think that was it," Luci said. "I didn't realize Dickens was such a romantic."

"Oliver Twist sure wasn't romantic," Mia said.

"No, that's for certain," Chas agreed. "But *Little Dorrit* is, and so is *Our Mutual Friend.* Even though these stories aren't as well-known, they really are very good—some of my favorites."

"I really did enjoy that," Luci said. "I'd kind of forgotten about it."

"Well, I have the DVD at the inn," Chas said. "It's about eight hours long, though. I don't know if anyone would want to get into it, but it's an option."

"I think it sounds great," Kristy said. "The others don't have to watch it if they don't want to. We've got all week. I'm in."

"I'd love to see it again," Luci said.

"I'm game," Mia said. "I could use a little culture, some broadening of my boring life." She said it in a mildly martyred tone, but Luci skillfully changed the subject, asking Chas more questions about the inn.

When they drove into Anaconda, the ladies became more interested in what they were seeing out the windows. They commented on the quaintness of the town, then they oohed and aahed when the inn came into view. A new excitement came over all of them as they expressed pleasure at being able to spend an entire week in such a beautiful place with friends that were dear. Jodi's vehicle pulled in less than a minute later. As the ladies got out of both cars, they were all in the same mode of excitement and couldn't wait to get inside. But Jodi insisted they all stop on the front porch of the inn for a photo. Chas was prepared with her camera and took several shots to be sure they could get a really good one, which they needed for one of their surprises for the group later in the week.

Chas opened the front door with a key and invited everyone to leave their luggage in the hall while they had a brief tour, after which they could settle into their rooms.

"Before we get started," Chas said, taking on the role of innkeeper and activities coordinator, "I want to remind you of some of the things we discussed in our phone conversations. The rooms are different sizes with different amenities. Jodi left it up to me to make room assignments, and our hope is simply that you'll all be comfortable. Of course, most of the time we'll be gathered as a group, but we want you to also get some nice rest. What I finally decided, since you're staying six nights, is that after the third night we will do a room change, which doesn't require much work. This way, each of you will be able to have a few nights in a more luxurious room with a jetted tub."

She received a chorus of agreement and approval and a couple of comments on how anything would be fine. Chas then started the tour, telling them as they went through the house about how there was TV and Internet available in the parlor, a snack fridge, and a kitchen in which they were welcome to make themselves at home.

"Normally," Chas said while they all peeked through the kitchen door to see it, "I don't invite my guests into the kitchen, but it's all equipped for your stay with menus that Jodi and Tammy have coordinated. Since you will all be pitching in on the cooking, you are welcome to the kitchen. The only rule is to clean up after yourselves." They all chuckled as Chas moved back through the guest dining room and up the stairs. The women were all impressed with the decor and atmosphere and thrilled with the opportunity to be there. Chas realized

Jodi had been right. She didn't feel nervous at all. In fact, she was enjoying the positive energy of the bonds of friendship these women made readily evident. Their excitement at being together with a full week ahead of them was a joy for Chas. She loved making people happy here at her precious inn.

After they'd completed their tour all the way to the top of the third floor and back again, they all went back to the office, near where they'd left their luggage. Chas graciously accepted compliments on the beauty of the inn, then she passed around a plate of cookies that had come from Jodi's bakery.

"Now," Chas said, also passing out a paper to each of them, "we've come up with a tentative schedule, although it's flexible and some activities can be rearranged. I suggested to Jodi that each morning at breakfast we can discuss the day as a group and do whatever we agree on. But we need to stick to somewhat of a schedule so that the together time really has everyone together. You'll notice that meal preparation and cleanup has been divided up and assigned. It's kind of like girls camp, but it spreads the work out evenly. While we're doing morning activities, maids will do a quick cleanup of your rooms and provide fresh towels. They'll only change sheets on the day we're changing rooms."

"What's this on the schedule?" Rachelle asked, and Chas noticed that she looked tired. "Each of our names have a time with an *M*."

"That's one of the surprises," Chas said. "You'll notice that you each have an appointment over the course of three days. *M* stands for massage." They all made exaggerated noises of pleasure. Chas laughed softly and continued, "We have a local massage therapist who will be setting up here at the inn so that we can each be pampered a little."

"What's a 'ped party'?" Marianne asked.

"Some ladies from a local salon will be coming over one evening and bringing everything for each of us to have a pedicure, complete with a foot soak, massage, and painted toenails."

They all made swooning noises, and Marianne let out a wolf whistle that made everyone laugh.

"We can all make sandwiches for lunch in about forty-five minutes," Chas said. "While we're having lunch we'll talk about our plans for the afternoon. I think the rest is self-explanatory. I will keep a cordless handset with me all the time. If you have any questions, or problems, or you need something, just pick up the phone in your room and dial me. I'm looking forward to getting to know all of you better, and I hope you have a wonderful time."

They actually applauded, and Marianne whistled again. Chas passed out cards with room assignments and keys, then she and Jodi helped the others find their way to the right rooms. So far, everything was going exactly as planned. Chas hoped it continued that way.

* * * * *

Jackson drove his rental car aimlessly through the city, going past where he'd lived, where Serena had lived—places they'd spent time together, places he'd haunted on his own. He went to his once-favorite deli and got a sandwich when his hunger began to make him feel queasy. After eating, he wandered on foot a little, then drove to the hotel where he'd be staying. While he was checking in, his early morning caught up with him and he felt tired. Once alone in his room, he locked the door, took off his shoes, and crawled into the bed.

When he woke up it was dark. He laid there for a while orienting himself to being in Virginia for a funeral. He still couldn't believe Serena was dead. Trying to distract himself, he considered calling Ekert to let him know he was in town. But he couldn't find the motivation to call his old friend, and there was no one else that he cared to see or talk to. Of course, there were people that he would enjoy saying hello to, but no one he'd go out of his way to find.

He unpacked and cleaned up, thinking he should at least go down to the hotel's restaurant to get something to eat. But he ended up ordering room service and spending the rest of the evening in front of the TV. Chas called, but they didn't talk long. She told him everything was going well. He missed her and he told her so, but he wasn't sure how he would have handled being in the same room with her while his head was so lost in another time and his emotions were all tangled and twisted. He loved Chas with all of his heart, and his love for her was in no way diminished by his present confusion. What he felt for Serena had stopped being romantic a long time ago. But it was difficult to explain that to Chas at the moment. He just needed a chance to think it all through. It was better this way, he thought, and kept flipping through channels until he found a guy movie that he could escape into, at least for a little while.

* * * * *

Chas checked in with Polly and spent some time with her kids while the ladies were settling into their rooms. The children were pleased to see her, but as always they were doing fine in Polly's care.

Elliott said to Chas, "You look worried."

"Is it that obvious?"

"At the moment, yeah."

"Only when I think about Jackson," she said.

"He's going to be just fine. You and I both know that sometimes he just needs to go into that . . . imaginary . . . man cave he has, and . . ."

"You made that up just now, didn't you."

"Yeah," he said and laughed. "You know what I mean."

"I know exactly what you mean."

"He'll be fine," Elliott said. "Enjoy your little stay-cation."

"I'm sure I will," she said, and turned her attention to Charles, who was showing her the little car he was playing with.

Chas left the children having their lunch and found Jodi in the kitchen of the inn, setting out a sandwich bar. While Chas was helping her, the ladies began arriving. They all ate in the guest dining room where there were several small tables that each seated two people, their purpose being perfect for a bed-and-breakfast where single occupants or couples would eat. Chas hadn't shown them the formal dining room yet, because they had a project set up in there that was kind of a surprise. Because of the project, however, they would all be eating in this room throughout the course of the week, and they impulsively rearranged the little tables and pushed them together so the eight of them could eat together.

Chas felt more involved in the conversation already. She was asked questions about the inn and herself, and she was able to ask them others things about themselves. She was already finding that she could match up the faces with the names and personalities.

Everyone pitched in to clean up lunch, and it took about three minutes. Chas then said, "Okay, I want to take you into the formal dining room, which we're not going to use for dining." Chas opened the door from the hall and guided them in while she was saying, "In the letter you received as an official invitation, one of the things you were asked to bring was any photos or mementos. Jodi's made me aware of the scrapbooking jokes among the group." Everyone chuckled. "I know that some of you enjoy that kind of thing, and some of you don't. But what we have set up in here will accommodate your taste, whatever it is." She motioned to some computer equipment that had been set up on an extra banquet-sized table that had been brought into the room. "We have a computer, photo scanner, and CDs for backup so that you can share photos with each other that can be taken home and kept. Or you can just print out copies of the photos here; there's plenty of ink and paper. Or both."

This brought on some soft noises of excitement, and Marianne said, "That is such a great idea, I wish I would have thought of it myself."

"It was Tammy's idea," Chas said. "I just had my husband move the equipment from our office into this room." She then motioned toward the large dining table, which had a protective tablecloth over its fine wood surface. In the center were piles of colored paper, scissors, adhesives, and enough page protectors for everyone. "If you want to make any scrapbook pages while you visit, everything is here to do that. If you want to just visit, you can do that, too. I'm sure you'll all have a great time reminiscing over the things you've brought. So, right now why don't you all get your things and we'll spend the afternoon here until supper. We have other time slots during the week to keep working on these things, or you can come here anytime day or night unless something else is going on for the group."

"It's wonderful, Chas," Kristy said.

"I just helped Jodi get the stuff together," Chas said. "Make yourselves at home and have a wonderful time."

They all scattered and returned within minutes with aging photo albums, tacky scrapbooks, or in some cases old shoe boxes full of memories. Chas stayed on hand to help run the scanner and printer if she was needed, but she enjoyed hearing the laughter and stories that came bubbling out as pictures and other memorabilia were passed around.

Chas slipped out later in the afternoon when she knew her children would be up from their naps and Elliott would be off to work. She sat and visited with Polly for more than an hour while she interacted with the children intermittently. She wasn't surprised to have Polly bring up Serena.

"How are you doing with that?"

"I'm mostly just worried about Jackson. He's taking it hard."

"But aren't you just a little miffed that he had some kind of important relationship with this woman and you didn't know about it?"

Chas had to ponder that for a minute. "He told me early on that he'd had relationships. When he told me that it had never occurred to him to save sex for marriage, it wasn't hard to put two and two together. He lived a worldly life. I grew up sheltered by a grandmother who taught moral standards. It's unfair to compare the two."

"Okay, but . . . why don't you tell me how the real, deep-down you is really feeling about this. It's *me* you're talking to."

"I feel blindsided and utterly jealous," Chas said so quickly that she realized the feeling hadn't been too far beneath the surface. "In a way I'm glad I didn't find out about it until I knew she was dead. But in some ways, a ghost from the past could be harder to compete with. Memories can become distorted and revered."

"You think he still has feelings for this woman?"

"Truthfully I don't know what to think, and I don't know what he's feeling. He's avoided it very skillfully. I just need to give him time, and I need to remember exactly what he's told me a number of times."

"What's that?"

"I know everything about him from the day I met him. And I know that he's a good man with integrity and a lot of inner strength."

"You don't sound convinced," Polly observed.

Chas sighed. "If I'm being completely honest with myself, I also have to acknowledge that he's a man with a very damaged life. I didn't meet him until he was in his mid-forties. His childhood was unimaginably horrible. He's been through a lot of terrible things, and he's survived them. But sometimes I see hints of this . . . hurt, scared little boy somewhere in there that I think will always be a part of him. It's not hard to imagine that part of his personality taking over in the face of trauma. And whatever he shared with this Serena, I can say for certain that hearing of her death *did* traumatize him. So . . . yes, I'm worried. I just hope he can make peace with whatever he needs to and that he doesn't get depressed. Given his history with PTSD, I don't believe it would take much to bring back some of the feelings he struggled with then."

"Maybe you should forget the party and fly out there to be with him."

"I've thought about it," Chas admitted. "But I know I'm supposed to be here. In spite of my concerns, maybe it's best if he faces this on his own."

"Maybe so," Polly said.

They were distracted by the children, then Chas needed to get back to the inn. On her way to the door that divided one kitchen from the other, Polly hugged her and said, "You know where I am if you need to talk."

"Yes, thank you," Chas said and hurried back to the dining room to find the ladies having a marvelous time.

She was thinking they hadn't even noticed her absence until Tammy said to her, "Oh, good. You're back. You've got to see this."

Chas was ushered to a chair in the middle of the group and shown some photos taken at a sleepover when the girls had all been ten and eleven, and they were all wearing pajamas, making silly faces. Chas had fun trying to figure out which child matched up with each woman. She got it wrong a couple of times and they all laughed. Then Kristy said, "Hey, where are *your* photo albums, Chas? Just because you weren't with us when we were kids doesn't mean we don't get to see pictures of you when *you* were a kid."

Chas was quickly talked into sharing and she hurried back to the house to grab some photo albums, giving Polly a quick explanation on her way in and out. Charles was so mesmerized by a Disney DVD that he didn't even notice her. Isabelle was distracted by toys on the living room floor.

Supper ended up being late since the ladies all had a wonderful time seeing pictures of Chas and her Granny and some glimpses of what the inn had looked like before she and Granny had completely restored and remodeled it as a bed-and-breakfast inn. Her history with Granny brought up some questions about her childhood.

"We all know everything about everybody but you," Mia said. "Tell us why you were raised by your grandmother."

"Putting pieces together, it seems there's a genetic heart defect that has shown up repeatedly in my family. My grandmother is the only one of her siblings who survived, and my mother was the same. But my mother's heart was weak, and she died giving birth to me. I never knew my father. So . . . Granny raised me. And since Granny was obsessed with Charles Dickens, she had been hoping for a boy. She wanted to name me Charles, but since I was a girl, she used the abbreviation for Charles instead."

"Oh, that's so cute!" Tammy said.

"If you don't mind my asking," Luci said, "what was the deal with your father?"

"That is kind of a sensitive topic," Jodi said, giving Chas the option to gracefully bow out of an explanation. But Chas felt no qualms about telling these women the truth. She wondered if that meant she'd dealt with it, or if she just felt comfortable with them. Probably both.

"Actually, my conception was a crime," Chas said, and she was answered with expressions of concern and a few gasps. "I didn't know about that until I was a teenager, and I had some trouble dealing with it at first. But eventually Granny helped me understand. She always loved me enough that it just didn't matter."

"Tell them what happened more recently," Jodi prodded. "It's such a great story."

"Well," Chas said, "it turns out that my father was a real black sheep in his family. After his mother passed away, his father decided to find me. He'd known enough about the situation that it wasn't too difficult. So, after all these years of just having Granny—before she passed away—I now have a new family. My grandfather lives in Butte, and we've become very close. Last year I met all of his children and other grandchildren when the family got together at his home. It was quite amazing."

"That *is* a great story!" Rachelle said.

"What about your father?" Marianne asked. "Where is he now?"

"He died in prison while he was serving time for what he did to my mother. I know very little about him, actually. The family doesn't talk about him much, other than saying that he was difficult and that he hurt a lot of people."

"But you're living proof that good things can come out of hard situations," Luci said.

"How true!" Tammy said. "And I hear you've been a really great friend to Jodi."

Chas looked at Jodi, certain she hadn't done that much. "I thought it was the other way around," she said. "Jodi takes very good care of me. And hey . . . her baked goods give the finishing touch on a great stay at the inn."

"I thought the inn did a great job of showing off my baked goods," Jodi said.

"That's how friendship works," Tammy said, and the others agreed.

By the time supper had been cleaned up, the ladies unanimously agreed that they were tired from all the effort it had taken just to get their lives in order and get to Montana. They shared hugs in the hall and all went to their separate rooms to call it a night. A glance at the clock told Chas that her children were already asleep. She tried to enjoy the luxury of a beautiful room and the promise of a full night's sleep before her, but her heart was in Virginia.

CHAPTER SEVEN

Jackson's efforts to sleep were definitely inhibited by the long nap he'd taken, as well as tenuous thoughts of Serena and the reality that she was dead. No matter how he tried to think of other things, count his blessings, or indulge in any possible distraction, memories of a former life kept trickling almost passively into his every train of thought. He finally took half of an over-the-counter sleeping pill that he kept a package of in preparation for such moments. It was always harder for him to sleep when traveling anyway. At this point, he knew the mild sleepy hangover he'd have in the morning would be worth it.

Jackson woke up disoriented when the darkness of heavy drapes contradicted the clock. When he realized he would have to hurry in order to get to the funeral in time, he flew into a panic. Chas had said he needed closure. And he certainly did. But he knew enough about basic psychology to know that actually seeing the body made it immensely easier for a person to find that kind of closure and move on. As much as he dreaded seeing Serena in a casket, if he missed his chance to do so, he knew this would be even harder. He didn't want his mind playing tricks on him in the future, making him believe that she was still just out there somewhere and he could actually call her up and apologize the way he should have a long time ago.

Jackson arrived to find a line still waiting to see her. While he stood there waiting, he felt eerily alone. The people in front of him and behind him were in small groups and they had a lot to talk about. He didn't overhear any conversation directly related to Serena, and he figured these people had already privately shared their shock and grief, or else they didn't know her all that well and their attendance was simply an obligation.

Seeing her took him off guard, as much as he'd tried to be prepared. She looked beautiful, and she looked at peace. She didn't look sick, but she looked much older than she should have for the number of years that had passed since he'd seen her. He managed to avoid any conversation with her family members except for her mother, who shook Jackson's hand and said, "You look very familiar. I'm sure we must have met some years ago. You're one of Serena's friends?"

"Used to be," he said.

"Tell me your name, dear," she said as if he were twelve.

"Jackson," he said, hoping to avoid anything further. He'd only met Serena's mother a few times when she'd come to visit, but she certainly had good cause to remember him. He knew she was going to figure it out, and then he wondered if she would slap him or tell him how he'd broken her little girl's heart.

"Of course!" she said, but she said it with a smile. Then a wink. "You're the one that got away. I remember you well."

"I remember you too," he said. "Your daughter was an amazing woman." In an impulsive attempt to unburden himself, he added, "I wish I would have told her that." Jackson was only answered with silent compassion, so he added, "I didn't . . . know she was sick. I've moved to Montana, and . . . uh . . ."

"So, you're not with the Bureau anymore?" she asked.

Jackson looked over his shoulder, worried that they were holding up the line. But people were moving around them and talking with other family members. No one seemed to be noticing their conversation at all. "Um . . . no. I retired a few years ago."

"And tell me what you're doing now, Jackson," she said with the kind of genuine concern that reminded him of Chas's grandmother.

"I got married," he said, "and we have a couple of kids. We run a bed-and-breakfast."

"Oh," she said with a warm smile, "I'm so glad to know you found someone. Serena would be pleased."

Jackson could only nod and swallow hard. It occurred to him then that if he *had* done the right thing by Serena and married her, he might well have been grieving over a dead wife right now. The thought made his insides churn, but he couldn't shake it.

Responding to the way Serena's mother wouldn't let go of his hand, or stop looking at him as if *she* might give *him* comfort, he couldn't keep himself from saying, "She was very good to me. I don't think I deserved her. Maybe it was my believing that that made me leave. I've never been quite sure. But I know it wasn't her fault. I've always wanted to apologize to her, and now . . . I'll never have the chance."

She smiled and said, "I think you just did. I'm sure she understands."

Jackson took that in, wanting it to penetrate his foggy brain and strained emotions and give him the comfort he was seeking. But he still felt more shock than anything else. He then took notice of what seemed obvious. Serena's mother was apparently doing well.

"This must be very hard for you," Jackson said. He glanced around at other family members who were falling apart.

"I've known for a long time that we would lose her," she said. "I didn't handle it at all well when she first got the word *terminal* attached to her diagnosis. But we dealt with it together. In the end, she was ready to go, and I was tired of seeing her suffer. I have my moments, but right now, it's nice to see how many people loved her."

"She loved a lot of people," Jackson said. "That's just the way she was."

"Yes, that's true," she said and surprised him with a hug. "Thank you for coming, Jackson."

"Thank *you*," he said. "You were always so kind to me."

"And the other way around," she said. Then someone else approached her and Jackson moved discreetly away after taking one more long glance at Serena in the casket.

Jackson's relief at having survived the viewing was overshadowed by his dread of sitting through the funeral. The chapel was crowded and he couldn't see many options for a place to sit, and none of them was anywhere near the few people that he knew. He wished then that he'd spoken to Ekert or one of his other old coworkers ahead of time so that he wouldn't have to be here alone. During his years of living in Virginia, he'd become accustomed to being alone most of the time unless he was on the job. Since he'd left here and started a new life, he was rarely alone. Taking a seat on a hard bench, he felt that sense of being torn between two worlds, and he wished in that moment that Chas could have been there with him.

"Is this seat taken?" he heard a woman say. He looked up.

Since there was just enough room on the bench for one more person and she appeared to be alone, Jackson said, "No, have a seat."

He slid closer to the gentleman sitting on the other side of him, even though he didn't want to. He was even more dismayed when this woman tried to strike up a conversation. "So, you're here alone?"

"It's obvious," he said, trying to discourage her from talking to him. The conversation he'd had with Serena's mother was enough for him. He just wanted to think about what had been said.

"Yes," she laughed softly as if he'd made a joke, "it *is* obvious."

Jackson folded his hands on his thigh in a way that made his wedding ring obvious, but that didn't keep her from talking. "So, how did *you* know Serena?"

Jackson felt taken off guard by the question. In his mind he could admit, *I loved her once.* But aloud he said, "We worked together many years ago . . . and we were friends as well." Then he heard himself adding, "I didn't know she was sick. I only heard after it was over." He wondered when he'd taken to saying such things to strangers. He had justified saying it to Serena's mother. But did he really need to talk about it so much that he would blurt it out while at the very same time attempting to avoid any conversation at all? It was as if that very fact bothered him so deeply that he couldn't keep from instinctively trying to get some kind of validation or sympathy for it—even with a stranger. He looked the other way and hoped for silence, but he'd just added his own fuel to the fire of the conversation. Now it would be even harder to avoid it.

"Oh, I *knew* she was sick," the woman said, and Jackson wondered if he was supposed to ask how *she* knew Serena. He didn't, and she went on. "Serena and I have been friends since college. We've stayed close all these years, even though we lived in different states. I was one of the first people she called when the pathology report came back. But I wasn't a very good friend after that."

Jackson realized this had turned into some kind of confessional for unburdening guilt over a mutual friend. He turned more toward her as she went on, "I mean . . . I kept in touch with her as much as I always had, but I should have done *more*. I should have made some extra effort, you know. I should have come to see her, and . . ." Her words faded while she dabbed at her eyes with a tissue, taking care not to smear her eye makeup. Jackson looked straight ahead and said nothing. He feared that if he actually started consoling her, the conversation would never end. She'd end up wanting to talk to him *after* the funeral, and he was planning a quick getaway.

"I think I must have been in more denial than I thought I was. Or maybe I just didn't want to see her like that. I really didn't believe she would die, even though she'd told me she would. I kept telling her to be positive. I kept talking about getting together the way we used to, but . . ." she sniffled, "I never came to see her. And now it's too late. It's over."

Jackson wished the funeral would begin so he could be spared any more of this woman's grief. But it didn't. The silence made him feel like he needed to say *something*. "At least she's not suffering anymore," he said. "And I'm sure she understands."

The woman turned to look at him, astonished, and perhaps even more upset. "Serena is *dead,*" she said as if he might not know. "It's *over.*"

Jackson was struck with the reminder that he wasn't at a Mormon funeral; people here didn't necessarily believe in life after death. He wondered what he could say to her now, but he wanted to be able to say something to give her some kind of hope in that regard. He couldn't even imagine believing that a person's spirit was as dead as his body, and that there was nothing after this life was over. Then he realized that until he'd met Chas he *had* believed that. He'd never thought about it too deeply. Looking back, he knew that something inside of him had believed in some kind of supreme being. But when it came to death, he'd never stopped at all to consider the possibility that spirits might live on. Now he wondered if his blocking out any effort to even think it through had been some form of denial. Seeing the complete lack of hope in this woman's countenance, he could understand *why* he would have preferred not to think about it. Without the knowledge that he had now, death could be a pretty hopeless prospect. He couldn't possibly end this conversation without making some effort to share a little bit of that hope. But he wondered how to say it briefly and get the point across. Some divine guidance would be nice.

"I don't believe it's over," he said gently. "It's difficult to explain *how* I know, but . . . well . . ." He felt himself stammering, and her expectant expression made him nervous. She really *wanted* some reason to believe that it wasn't over. An idea came and he added, "Since I lost my mother, there have just been times when I've felt something that I couldn't explain, and I just knew that her spirit was with me, that she understood all the things I wanted her to know. I've felt the same way about my wife's grandmother."

Jackson recalled in that moment the experience he'd had before he married Chas, when he'd been held hostage for weeks by sadistic drug lords. He'd been wanting only to die and end his misery, but he'd known beyond any doubt that Granny was with him in those darkest moments, helping him hold on until the rescue team arrived. He considered it a sacred experience, but he was surprised at how right it felt to share it with this woman. If it could give her some hope and understanding of the present situation, that wasn't a bad thing.

"You really believe that?" she asked, and he couldn't tell if that was cynicism in her eyes, or just grief.

"I really do," he said, but before he could think of how he might share his experience with her, the funeral began.

During the service, Jackson felt mostly numb. He became distracted from his own regrets in regard to Serena when he realized that the temperament of the funeral was dark and depressing. Was everyone else in the room in a similar frame of mind as the woman sitting next to him? Did they *all* believe that it was over? That death was the end? He wondered if Serena's mother making peace with her daughter's death was a belief that her spirit lived on, or an acceptance that it was truly over. He wanted to march up to the front and announce that there *was* life after death. It wasn't that anyone actually said there *wasn't,* but nothing was said to the contrary, either. The implication was obvious. Jackson wanted to tell them that God existed and He had provided a Savior. For the first time since his conversion to the gospel, he truly felt sorrow to think of the ignorant state of the majority of mankind. He could understand the zeal of the missionary force, going out into the world with a strong desire to share the ultimate message of hope. Jackson's sorrow surfaced as he thought about how he had once been blindly moving among the ignorant and hopeless. The life he'd lived before felt so eerily close that he believed it could snatch him back if he thought about it too deeply.

He quickly forced his thoughts to the moment and tried to focus on the speaker at the podium, but the speaker's droning delivery encouraged Jackson's thoughts to focus on the part of his life he'd shared with Serena. The memories became so clear and close that he felt like a stranger to the life he'd left behind in Montana. A nagging voice in the back of his mind tempted him to believe that he wasn't worthy of that life, that he'd been fooling himself to believe that he *was* worthy of it during these years he'd spent with Chas. Maybe he was simply more suited to the life he'd stepped back into by coming here. The thought caused pain, but he shoved it down deep and indulged in his memories. For the moment they felt more comfortable and right than anything else.

Once the service ended, Jackson gracefully got away with no fuss or attention. He was glad that he'd managed to avoid any further conversation with the woman sitting next to him. He had the fleeting thought that he'd like to share his knowledge of the gospel with her, but in his present frame of mind he doubted he'd make a very good missionary. At the moment he wasn't feeling good at anything—especially all things spiritual.

At the cemetery Jackson found a place to stand unobtrusively among a small crowd of nondescript mourners. Wearing dark glasses and a dark suit, he blended in perfectly. He scanned the faces that he could see and recognized a few that were vaguely familiar, but none that he knew well enough to strike up a conversation. But that was just as well. He didn't feel like talking. He just wanted to be here alone for these final moments when he would be in any proximity to what was left of Serena's life in this world.

He didn't listen very closely to the words being spoken over the grave by the same boring man who had monopolized the funeral service. His mind was scanning through the relationship he'd shared with Serena. He remembered how it had started and how it had ended. He remembered how good she had been to him, and how unfair he had been to her. And it made his heart hurt. He felt almost lost in a trance until he realized the service had ended, except for some kind of musical number. When he noticed the two bagpipers standing a short distance away, he was chilled. He'd forgotten that Serena had some Scottish heritage, and she loved all things related. She'd been to Scotland prior to their meeting, and she'd had several mementos in her apartment. As the first lengthy note of music broke the air, Jackson's emotional turmoil increased, but it was difficult for him to determine which emotion was most prominent. While a magnificent rendition of *Amazing Grace* was played, the well-known lyrics to the first verse filled his mind. The concept certainly fit his own life, but he felt too weighed down by grief to fully consider its implication.

When the song ended, the contrasting silence was deafening. Jackson stood where he was, vaguely aware of people slowly dispersing. He heard lots of crying mingled with distant pieces of conversation. But he just stood there and stared at the ground, trying to make some peace with the situation. He wished that he could talk to Serena. He believed that her spirit lived on. But what made him think that if he *did* have a conversation with her, that she'd be anywhere near enough to hear what he wanted to say? Of all the people her spirit might want to connect with, he knew he had to be very low on the list. He felt like such a heel, such a jerk. And he felt sure if Chas knew how he'd behaved—in many regards—she would entirely agree with him, and possibly even reconsider her notion of choosing him as the man she wanted to be with forever.

"Leeds? Is that you?" he heard and looked up to see Shawn Ekert. They'd worked together for years. Beyond Elliott Veese, who now lived in Montana, Ekert had been the closest thing Jackson had had to a friend when he'd lived in Virginia. "I wondered if you would come," Ekert added, giving Jackson a handshake and quick hug. "You should have called and told me."

"It was kind of last minute," Jackson said, then his eye went to the woman standing nearby. "Karla," he said and received a tight hug from Ekert's wife. "The trip was worth it to see you."

"You always say the sweetest things," she said, and an associated memory with Serena caught him off guard.

"How are the kids?" he asked, knowing they had two but not even recalling their names at the moment.

"Oh, they're great," Karla said. "Speaking of which . . . I've got to leave and go help one of them with a project at school." She hugged Jackson again. "It's so good to see you."

"You too," he said. "I'm still holding a great room for you two at the inn when you decide to actually take a vacation."

"You talk him into it and you'll be my biggest hero," she said with a little laugh and a comically scolding look toward her husband. Again her words triggered an uncomfortable memory.

"I've tried," Jackson said, showing an easy nonchalance that contradicted his inner turmoil.

"Well, keep trying," she said. "And keep in touch." She then turned to her husband, "I'll see you later, then."

"Yeah," he said and gave Karla a kiss. Jackson had been expecting them to leave together, and he was surprised to see them parting. Ekert turned to him and said, "You coming?"

"Where?" he asked.

Ekert shook his head and chuckled. "You haven't been gone *that* many years. Have you forgotten our tradition? We need to share a toast for the fallen."

"Of course," Jackson said, realizing now what he meant. There was a bar near the FBI office where Jackson had once worked. It was a place where many gatherings had taken place for friends and fellow workers. If there was any cause for celebration or grief, anyone who could get there would meet to share a drink. There was a wall commemorating *the fallen,* with pictures of those who had died in the line of duty, since it had been the most popular hangout for FBI employees for many years. Serena was never an agent, and her death didn't qualify as dying in the line of duty, but it did require a toast from those who had worked with her and cared about her.

Jackson felt momentarily torn. Drinking had been an issue for him in the past. Going into a bar didn't seem terribly wise. But he didn't want to be alone, and he had known Serena better than the majority of people who had worked with her. It seemed appropriate that he go along, and he knew there was plenty to drink that wasn't alcoholic. He could participate in the toast without compromising his standards.

"Sure," Jackson said. "I'll meet you there."

"Great," Ekert said and patted him on the shoulder before they walked to their separate vehicles.

While Jackson drove across the city, memories continued to dominate his thoughts. When he stepped into the noisy bar, its familiarity made his life with Chas seem like nothing more than a distant dream. The sounds, the smells, the people all shoved him back to a time when he had been a different man, living a completely different life. He noticed the group gathered that was obviously here to honor Serena. He saw many familiar faces among these people, and some he didn't know. But he knew well the purpose of the gathering. His anxiety and discomfort relented as he eased himself into the group and was greeted by many people who were glad to see him. When he realized that drinks were being ordered and served, leading up to the toast, he went to the bar and ordered a tonic water with lime. It was something he'd had occasionally even during his drinking days when he'd been on duty or when he'd needed to drive.

A man called the noisy group to attention and said that he would start the toast. Jackson recognized him as Serena's supervisor at the Bureau; he probably had been her supervisor until she'd no longer been able to work. He said many nice things about Serena, offered a toast, and everyone lifted their glasses and took a sip of their drinks. Many people took a turn saying something, and the pattern continued. Jackson remained quiet and withdrawn, just listening and remembering. He didn't particularly want to draw anyone's attention to recalling that he had once shared a romantic relationship with the woman being honored. When the casual ceremony was finally completed, the noise level elevated again as conversations between friends and coworkers began to buzz. Jackson talked for a few minutes with people he'd known way back. He enjoyed telling people that he was married with two children. He loved their reactions to hearing that he was now an innkeeper. He hated it when someone mentioned recalling that he'd once been involved with Serena. He would only comment casually, "Yeah, she was a great person."

The crowd began to break up. Jackson wondered what to do now. He noticed Ekert across the room, but he was deep in conversation with someone Jackson didn't know. He didn't want to go back to a hotel room and flip through TV channels, but he wasn't entirely thrilled about hovering in a bar, either. Since Ekert was the only person in Virginia he really *cared* to have a conversation with, he decided to give him a few minutes and see if he became available. He found an empty booth and sat there to finish his drink, even though it didn't taste that great. The thought crossed his mind that adding some gin would improve it significantly, but he pushed that thought away abruptly. A server asked if he would like another one.

"Gin and tonic?" she asked, taking his empty glass. It was as if the devil had prompted her to say it.

"Just the tonic," Jackson said, refusing to think about how he'd once relied on alcohol to calm his nerves and soothe his emotions. And he was certainly struggling with both at the moment.

A minute later she returned with the drink and Jackson paid her. He smelled it to make certain there had been no mistakes before he took a sip. Then he looked up to see the woman he'd been talking to at the funeral standing next to his table.

"Is this seat taken?" she asked with a little smirk, since it was exactly what she'd said at the funeral.

Jackson didn't want there to be any mistake about where he stood, so he just said, "That depends on why you want to sit down. I'm happily married. *Very* happily married."

"Oh, I already knew that," she said and sat down. "You're wearing a ring, but you also put off those vibes that scream in neon that you're taken. Don't worry. I'm not here to flirt or pick up a date. I've got my own relationship back home. I got here late. I guess I missed the big toast, but . . . when I saw you here . . ."

"What?" he asked and took a sip of his drink.

"Our conversation got interrupted earlier. I have to admit that it's stuck with me. You said something about your mother, and your grandmother, I believe."

"My wife's grandmother, actually," he said, recalling now that he'd felt good earlier about sharing his experience with this woman. If it could give her some hope and perspective, that wasn't a bad thing. Even if she thought he was crazy, he had nothing to lose.

"Would you mind . . . expounding a little? You said that you really believe that spirits live on. That you'd . . . felt something."

"Yeah, I think that's what I said."

This woman looked at him as if to size up such beliefs. She made a contemplative noise and said, "Funny. I've heard other people say that and I've always thought they were delusional. Maybe there's something about the way you said it, or . . . maybe it's just that you don't *seem* delusional."

Jackson chuckled. "Maybe I am."

"Maybe. I'd still like to hear about these . . . feelings you've had."

Jackson shrugged. "I could tell you the most dramatic experience I've had, but I do consider it . . . sacred; personal. That doesn't mean I'm not willing to share it. I'd just ask that you take it that way and not make light of it. And it's not something I want repeated."

"Of course. I understand."

"A few years ago I was in a hostage situation."

"You work for the Bureau?"

"I did," he said.

"That's how you knew Serena."

"That's how we met, yes."

"What do you mean by a hostage sit—"

"I was the hostage," he said. "I was kidnapped by drug lords in South America and held for more than three weeks."

This woman's face showed dramatic enlightenment before she said, "You're Jackson." Before he could cover his surprise and wonder how she could have possibly made that connection, she added, "Serena told me all about it. She knew you were missing. She was so worried about you. She cried on the phone to me more than once over it. And I remember how thrilled she was when she heard that you'd been rescued. And she'd also heard that a woman from out of state came to see you at the hospital, and she was glad you had someone to take care of you. Is that the woman you're married to now?"

"It is," Jackson said, trying to mesh Serena's concern and awareness of him with everything else that he was contending with. He pushed the emotional issues to a place where he could look at them later, and he focused on the moment. He'd been trying to tell her about a spiritual experience, but he was afraid the topic might not be recovered.

"I'm Lisa," she said. "I know you were close to Serena at one time. And I know she told you about me because we talked all the time, although I don't think you and I ever met."

"No, I don't think we did," he said. But he had to admit, "I do remember her talking about Lisa."

"How ironic is this!" she said, sounding thrilled. Jackson's reaction was the opposite. She then pointed a scolding finger at him, but she was smiling when she said, "You broke her heart, you know."

Jackson's first impulse was to come back with a flippant, *Did I?* But he realized he'd sound like even more of a jerk to seem so oblivious and indifferent. Instead he humbly said, "I know I did, and I'm still not quite certain why." It occurred to him that perhaps if he *could* figure out why, he might be able to let it go. He took another step toward his own reconciliation with Serena when he added, "It wasn't her fault. I wish I would have told her that."

"If you believe her spirit lives on, then you still can, right?"

Jackson felt strangely comforted by her statement, and relieved that the conversation had come back to where it had started. "I guess you're right," he said.

"You were telling me about being held hostage. It must have been horrible."

"It was," he said. "Unspeakably horrible."

"But you're talking about it."

Jackson chuckled tensely. "That took a lot of counseling . . . and the love of a good woman."

"Serena would be glad to know you found someone."

"That's what Serena's mother said."

"I think it's true."

"But if you don't believe in life after death, then why would she care?"

"I was more referring to before her death, but . . . I'm trying to keep an open mind. I wonder if you're trying to avoid telling me what you were going to tell me. You don't have to if you don't want to, but I promise to respect it."

"I'm happy to share it if it will help someone."

"And you think it could help me?"

"I don't know. I guess that depends on whether you think I was losing my mind when it happened, or if it was real."

"What do you think?"

"I know it was real. I know it as much as I know I'm sitting here."

"Wow," she said. "You sound pretty sure."

"Absolutely."

"So, what happened?"

"I was praying that I would die. I was ready to give up in every possible way. And I felt Chas's grandmother's presence with me. I heard her speak to me. I can't tell you for sure if I actually heard her voice or if it was inside my mind. But I know that she was there. She said, 'Hold on a little longer, young man. You have much to live for. You're just getting started.' I was rescued soon after that. But the remarkable thing about that experience is that the memory is brilliantly clear. It hasn't faded with time. I *know* she was there."

Lisa looked more mesmerized than skeptical. She said in a reverent voice, "And this was your wife's grandmother?"

"Yes. I only knew her a matter of weeks before she died. But we bonded quickly; we were close. And she had raised Chas . . . who is now my wife. She was the only family Chas had known. She called me 'young man' all the time. She made me feel younger than my years." He shrugged. "Anyway, that's my story."

"And you've felt similar things with your mother?"

"I have. Not so dramatic, but I've certainly had moments when I knew she was with me." He paused to consider her thoughtful expression, and how he might tip the scale toward believing in something bigger than herself. "Listen," he said, "it can be difficult to take something you've believed your entire life and decide that maybe it's not true. I used to be where you are. I never bothered to consider whether or not God existed, or if life continued after death. When I met Chas, she asked me if I believed in angels. Well, I do. She taught me a lot of amazing things, but the spiritual things I've learned since I met her have changed my life in ways I never thought possible." He heard the conviction in his own voice and felt some reassurance to realize that he *had* changed. He wasn't the same man who had broken Serena's heart.

"Is Chas like Serena?" Lisa asked.

Jackson thought about that. "They're from completely different worlds. Technically, they would have very little in common."

"Then you must have changed a great deal."

"I have," he said. "I can tell you there is one way that they are very much alike. Serena had a big heart. She was kind and compassionate, and she was never judgmental or critical. In that way, she and Chas are a lot the same."

He realized that Lisa was dabbing at tears. She'd just lost a friend. He'd only lost a piece of his past.

"Lisa," he said, certain he'd never see her again, "I don't want to sound pushy or presumptuous, but I wish someone had shared with me years ago what I know now . . . about spiritual matters; how they *really* work, what they *really* mean. Would you be all right with my referring you to some missionaries who could come to your home, give you some things to read, and answer your questions? Or I could just send you to a website that might help."

Lisa thought about that for a minute, and Jackson's heart quickened with the hope that she wouldn't back off. "Okay, I can live with that. I assume I can kick these missionaries out if they get pushy."

"You sure can." Jackson pulled a pen from his inside jacket pocket and wrote down the website. He knew it well from his own initial study of the Church. He also wrote down his e-mail address and phone number. Lisa wrote hers on a separate napkin.

They traded napkins and put their pens away, then Lisa put her hand over his on the table. "Thank you, Jackson. You've helped me get through a tough day. I should go. I have a policy against hanging out with married men." She laughed softly. "I also have a policy against spending too much time in a bar when I'm depressed."

"Yeah, I used to have that policy."

"Used to?" she said.

"Well . . . until today, I haven't been in a bar in a long time." He held up his drink. "Just tonic. I stopped drinking. It's high on the list of the smart things I did in my life."

"Good luck with that," she said and stood up. "Thank you again."

"Take care," he said and watched her walk away.

Jackson glanced around and couldn't see Ekert. He figured he must have left. But Jackson could call him later or tomorrow. He took another big swallow of his drink, left a tip, and decided to go. This really wasn't a good place for him to be wasting time. By the time he got to the door, Lisa had just gotten her coat on. He opened the door for her and said, "If anything those missionaries have to say makes a difference, I'd like to hear about it."

"I'll let you know," she said and stepped to the curb to hail a cab. Jackson felt like he should stay with her until one had picked her up. As a result of his work in the FBI, he was painfully aware of the awful things that could happen to a woman alone. He'd just feel better, even this once, to see that she was safe.

When every cab that passed was occupied, they ended up standing there longer than he'd expected. "You really don't have to wait with me," she said. "I do this all the time."

"It's okay," he said.

"Tell me about your wife," she said as if she sensed his awkwardness in standing there with her, knowing he was a married man.

For a moment he felt pulled away from the darkness he'd been feeling. He laughed softly. "When I met Chas it was like . . ."

"Like what?"

"Well, that's just it. It wasn't *like* anything I'd ever experienced or felt before. I had no point of reference to work from. I'd simply never imagined feeling that way about a woman, or just wanting— almost instantly—to give up everything to have her. She threw me completely off kilter from the very first moment. How could I not do whatever it took? I didn't sacrifice anything to make myself a part of her life. I was ready to let it all go, but even if I hadn't been . . . even if it had been hard to leave the Bureau for her sake, I would have done it and I never would have regretted it."

"That all sounds a little too good to be true, Jackson."

"Yeah," he sighed, "it does, doesn't it." He wondered how that must have sounded to the friend of someone he'd once been involved with.

"So what are you doing here?" Lisa asked.

"That's a good question," Jackson said as a cab pulled up to the curb.

"Take care," he said, opening the door for her.

"Thank you," she said and got in.

Jackson walked to his car and drove back to the hotel, stopping at a drive-through to get some fast food on his way. By the time he got to the hotel, all the sorrow and regret had taken over again, squelching the temporary high he'd felt from sharing his convictions with Lisa.

He hoped that Lisa might follow his suggestions—then he didn't give her another thought.

CHAPTER EIGHT

Chas enjoyed her day with the ladies, even though she kept wondering about the funeral and what Jackson might be doing afterward. She slipped away from the group while they were cleaning up supper. They were all very insistent that she not be doing work on their behalf. Since it had been a late supper and they'd visited a great deal while they were eating, it was now bedtime for the kids. Chas tucked Charles into bed herself, then she rocked Isabelle with a bottle until she fell asleep while she visited quietly with Polly.

Assured that her children were sleeping safely, Chas went to the room she was using at the inn and used her cell phone to call Jackson. He answered, sounding tired.

"You okay?" she asked.

"Yeah, I'm fine," he said.

"How was the funeral?"

"Boring; depressing."

"Did you see anyone you know?" she asked, feeling like he didn't want to talk and she was only going to get minimal information from him.

"I saw Ekert."

"His name is Shawn. He doesn't work for you anymore."

"Okay, I saw Shawn . . . and Karla."

"Oh, that's nice. Anyone else?"

"Oh, a few people I know; no one special."

"Are you glad you went?"

"Yes," he said but he didn't expound. "How are things there?"

"Good. Everything is good." She expected him to ask about the kids but he didn't. After a long pause she added, "I feel like we're in junior high and we don't know how to talk to someone of the opposite sex."

"Sorry," he said. "I'm just tired. We can talk about it more when I get home."

"When will that be, exactly?"

"Not sure yet. I'll let you know. I didn't really get to talk to Ekert . . . Shawn. I'm going to call him in the morning and see if we can get together."

"That would be nice."

"Thank you for calling," he said. "It's nice to hear your voice."

"It's nice to hear yours too," she said. "I love you, Jackson."

"I love you too, Chas. I'll talk to you tomorrow."

"Okay," she said and added with hesitance, "bye."

"Bye," he replied and hung up.

Chas flipped her phone closed and cried, her worry amplified by his emotional distance from her. Nothing in the world felt right when things weren't right with Jackson. She wondered how long it was going to take him to deal with this and become himself again.

A knock at the door drew her away from her worry and self-pity. "Yes?" Chas hollered.

Jodi called back, "We're all getting into our pajamas and we're going to gab in the parlor."

"Okay, I'll be there soon."

Chas thought that it was good to have a distraction, but then if she hadn't had this particular distraction, she would have gone with Jackson. "Fifty-two weeks in the year," she mumbled to herself on her way into the bathroom, "and his old girlfriend has to get buried on *this* one."

* * * * *

As the ladies met up in the parlor, there was lots of laughter over comparing their silly pajamas. At first Chas thought that they had purposely brought silly ones to enhance the party, but it quickly became evident that this was one thing they all had in common. Ever since their sixth-grade sleepovers, they'd all enjoyed wearing silly pajamas. They all found it funny that Chas was wearing flannels with pink penguins when she hadn't even known about the unspoken rules of the group. There was flannel and fleece and silk and tricot, but they all had crazy colors and goofy pictures and patterns on them.

"Okay," Jodi said after the pajama parade was over, "now that we're finally all together for the first time in years, I want to know how everyone is doing. I mean how you're *really* doing. We've all had different struggles—some more than others—but I think the most important thing about what we share is how we've been able to help each other through the hard times. But a lot of us just don't get the long conversations we'd like to when life is so busy. I think we need to take advantage of this time and talk. None of us has anything we have to get up for in the morning."

"I second the idea," Tammy said. "And if it gets late, the wonderful thing is that we can sort of push *pause* on the conversation and pick it up tomorrow. Even if it takes all week, we're going to have the best long talk we've ever had."

Chas noticed that Kristy seemed uncomfortable. She was being discreet, but Chas felt certain something was going on in her life that the others didn't know about. She wondered if anyone else had noticed, but since they had all week to talk, whatever it was would surely come up. She wondered if the problems weighing on Kristy had anything to do with her excessive weight loss.

"Well, I might as well start," Rachelle said. "I'm well aware that you all know what's happened at my house, and I also know that it's probably part of the reason that this wish of ours for a real vacation together has finally happened. I admit that at first I was a little squeamish about having my problems being talked about, and I was thinking I didn't want to have them dampen the fun we're having. But Jodi and Tammy have both talked some sense into me. I realize that if friends can't help you through the hard times, what good are they?"

There were comments of agreement, and also some joking about the need for laughing, eating, and scrapbooking. And especially giggling together in their pajamas. Then Luci said, "I *never* would have gotten through my divorce without you guys. I talked to some of you more than others. But you were all concerned; you all kept in touch with me. Every time I talked to any one of you," she got teary, "you would tell me you were praying for me. I felt those prayers. I felt your love and acceptance. I was judged and criticized and ostracized in my ward, my neighborhood, even with some members of my own family. But you guys were nothing but supportive. Sometimes you told me things I didn't want to hear, things I didn't want to face, but I knew it was said out of love, and you kept me from making some stupid choices. The years after the divorce were every bit as hard as the years that preceded it. But you were all there, all the way through."

Chas noticed that they were all a little teary. Tammy commented, "And how are you doing now? You seem great!"

"You know what? I *am* great! Money's tight, and I feel like it's always a balancing act to make ends meet, but I have so much to be grateful for."

"Do you see your kids?"

"Not as much as I'd like," she said. "Even though the custody ruling has changed and I've legally got them more than every other weekend, they're more comfortable at their father's. He's so good at letting them see what he wants them to see, and he's even better at making them believe I'm evil. The kids have varying degrees of anger toward me. Some of them don't even want to see me at all."

"How can you live with that?" Mia asked, horrified. Chas thought again how they were very much in the same position but for different reasons. Mia had never married or had children. Luci had lost her husband and only had limited access to her children, which was surely heartbreaking. But Luci's attitude was so different from Mia's.

"Well, first of all, there's nothing I can do about it," Luci said. "I learned a long time ago that the jerk is going to tell people what he wants them to hear. He's smooth and slick. That's why I fell in love with him. It's hard to fault people for falling into the trap of believing he's a nice guy, when I did the same thing. I've also learned that trying to manipulate the kids—the way their father does—is not going to endear them to me in the long run. I believe that when years pass they will see the truth. And if some of them don't see it in this life, they'll see it in the next one. I know that as long as I do what *I* am supposed to do, I can only make the most of what I have. I know I'm right with the Lord. The rest is just . . . day to day, trying to be grateful for what I've got. I didn't end up with the happily-ever-after I'd hoped for, but that doesn't mean life isn't good. It's a lot better than being in a marriage that was destroying me spiritually and emotionally. But that's ancient history now."

Chas noticed Mia looking thoughtful. She wondered if Luci's perspective could help her with her own. But surely she'd heard Luci's story before. Perhaps some people would simply never see the most obvious path to their own happiness.

"Sorry for running on," Luci said. "I just want Rachelle to know that there's no better place to be than right here with these women to find all the love and support she will need in order to get through tough times. What we have with this group is a rare blessing we shouldn't take for granted. It's really quite amazing that we've been able to stay this close all these years. None of us is perfect and we have our differences, but we really care about each other, and we all have the same value system—even though some of us have struggled to remember that sometimes. I'm just . . . grateful for you guys; that's all." She motioned toward Rachelle. "I pretty much interrupted you. We really need to know what's going on and where you're at."

Rachelle took a deep breath. "Well . . . I'm actually doing a lot better than I thought I would, or maybe I should say I'm doing better than I was a month ago. I think looking forward to this has kept me from going over the edge."

"Does that mean you'll go over the edge when this is over?" Mia asked.

Rachelle shook her head. "I sure hope not. To tell the truth . . . a part of me still can't believe it's real. How is it possible that I could be that . . . gullible, that . . . stupid?"

"He was *trying* to deceive you," Jodi said. "And he obviously worked very hard to convince you that things were as they appeared."

"He was choosing the side of him that he let you see," Tammy said.

"I'm more out of the loop," Kristy said. "I know the basics, but . . . can I ask how you found out?"

Rachelle then told the story that Chas had heard in brief summary from Jodi. She cried some as she talked about how searching for some insurance papers in her husband's home office had led her to the discovery of a bank account she'd not known existed. And that had led her to discover charges he'd made at restaurants, florists, jewelers, *and hotels.* Once she had some proof that she had reason to be suspicious, she could look back and see that she had purposely ignored a hundred little things through the years, certain her husband was trustworthy, not wanting to be a possessive wife. As the truth had begun to unfold, Rachelle had discovered that he'd been unfaithful to her while they'd been dating, and even after they were engaged. He'd been promiscuous his entire life, and she'd believed that he'd been completely loyal to her right from the start.

Now that the ugly reality had been exposed, Rachelle's husband had become cruel to her in defending his actions, threatening her with all kinds of horrible things if she tried to divorce him or keep him from seeing their children. Rachelle had gotten an attorney anyway, but she feared what the future would bring. Through no fault of her own, her life was being turned upside down. The world as she knew it had come to a screeching halt. She cried hardest as she said, "The only thing I'm guilty of is being too trusting, too naïve. I thought I had a good self-esteem when I married him. Why did I attract someone like him? Where did I go wrong?"

"You *did* have a good self-esteem," Tammy said. "Better than the rest of us, in my opinion." Many agreed with her. "Who knows why any of us got dealt what we were dealt? I mean . . . look at us." She motioned with her hand to include the group. "We all had the same goals, the same values."

"Well," Jodi said, "I went off the deep end in that regard for a while there."

"But you came out of it with a pretty decent husband."

"Yes, I did," Jodi said. "He's stubborn, and we don't always agree. I don't know if I'll ever get him to church, but he treats me and the kids very well."

"So, what makes one marriage turn out well, and another fall apart?" Luci asked.

"Or no marriage at all," Mia said with chagrin.

"Exactly," Tammy said. "None of us is perfect, but we weren't smoking or drinking or doing drugs. We weren't promiscuous or careless. We just wanted to get married and live happily ever after." She put an arm around Rachelle and handed her another tissue. "I'm sure there are a lot of things we're never going to figure out in this life, but we are going to stick together, and we're going to get Rachelle through this."

"I'm so grateful for you guys," Rachelle said tearfully, then she chuckled and added, "but I think we'll need to wait until tomorrow for all the good advice I know you're all going to give me. I am utterly exhausted." She yawned, and many of the others did too, then they all laughed.

Chas glanced at her watch. "Good heavens! It's past midnight. No wonder we're all tired."

They were all shocked at how late it was and agreed that being together made time fly. After sharing hugs all around, including Chas, they all went to their separate rooms. Chas made certain everything was settled for the night and went to her own little guest room. "The Dorrit," she said aloud as she sat on the edge of the beautiful bedspread. This room had been named after sweet Amy Dorrit in Dickens' *Little Dorrit*. She smiled to recall the conversation they'd had about this story on the drive home from the airport. She'd have to find the DVD for the miniseries tomorrow in case anyone was really interested in watching it.

It felt strange to Chas to fall asleep in one of the guest rooms of her inn. But it was a good kind of strange. She *felt* like a guest, and it was a feeling she'd only experienced once before. That was when she and Jackson had used one of the rooms for their wedding night. Memories of all they had shared lured her away from her worries. She drifted to sleep with clear images in her head of Jackson lying close beside her, touching her face, kissing her, whispering to her of his love and devotion. But in her dreams she saw herself become another woman. And then she was facing Jackson, pulling blond hairs from his jacket, wiping lipstick that wasn't hers off his face, smelling liquor on his breath. She started shouting at him, asking how he could do something so stupid, so hurtful, so horrid.

Chas came awake with a gasp, reminded of when she'd had to urge Jackson out of his nightmares when he was suffering the worst of his PTSD. Of course, her dream was nothing like that. But it was still horrifying. She felt sick to her stomach, and it took several minutes for her heart rate to return to normal. She reminded herself that the woman who had induced mild jealousy in Chas was dead, and Jackson's involvement with her had occurred long before she and Jackson had even met. She also reminded herself that just because Rachelle's husband had led a double life and cheated on his wife, it didn't mean that Jackson was *anything* like him, *at all.* The evening's conversation had obviously mingled into her present concerns, coming together in a jumble that made no sense at all.

She felt a little disoriented trying to recall where she was. Normally when she woke up in the night for any reason, she would tiptoe down the hall and peek at her babies to make sure all was well. But Polly and Elliott were sleeping in her bedroom, and she knew the babies were safe. She had to admit it was nice to know she didn't have to get up with Isabelle when she woke up for the bottle she wanted in the middle of the night. She was glad Polly had talked her into arranging it this way. Having two babies so close together had made for years of exhaustion. As much as she loved her family, a break was really nice. With *that* thought in mind, she knew she was really going to have to do something great to make this up to Polly.

* * * * *

Jackson woke up to his phone ringing and felt like he had a hangover. He knew he hadn't had anything to drink, but he *had* taken another half a sleeping pill when his thoughts had kept him wide awake way into the night. He reached for the phone on the bedside table but knocked it on the floor where it kept ringing. He glanced at the clock. It was past ten. He threw back the covers and got out of bed to get the phone, just in time for it to stop ringing. He'd been expecting the call to be from Chas, but glancing at the caller ID he saw Shawn Ekert's name and number there. A beep told him he'd received a message. He listened to Ekert telling him he wanted to see him and catch up before he left town, and to call him as soon as possible.

Jackson pushed the button to dial the missed call and said into the phone, "Sorry, I was asleep."

"Wow. How much did you drink last night?"

"I didn't drink anything," Jackson said. "I stopped drinking a long time ago."

"Oh, yeah. I forgot."

"I took a sleeping pill. Are you working?"

"Actually, no; not today. How about if I meet you for lunch? Well, lunch for me, breakfast for you."

"Sounds good," Jackson said, and they set up a time and place. While they were talking, another call beeped through but he knew it was Chas and he could call her back in a few minutes. After he ended his call with Ekert, he noticed that Chas had left a message. He listened to her genuine concern for him and knew he should call her back, but he set the phone aside and took a shower. He picked up the phone to call her after he was dressed, but when he tried to imagine what he might say to her, he set it down again.

Leaving the hotel, he knew he needed to call his wife, but right now it just felt awkward. He pushed the speed dial for her cell phone and was relieved when it went to voice mail. He left a quick message, saying that he was fine and he was on his way to spend some time with Ekert. He didn't say that he would call her later; he felt sure she would call him back.

Jackson enjoyed his time with Ekert. Over their meal they caught up on trivial news concerning their wives and kids. Afterward they walked around an outdoor shopping district and talked about the good old days in the FBI. Eventually they ended up on a bench and Ekert said, "So how are you doing with this Serena thing?"

"Maybe we should go back to the good old days."

"That good," he said with sarcasm.

"I didn't know she was sick."

"What?" Ekert was shocked. "I was sure someone had told you. Everyone else probably thought the same thing."

"That's exactly what Elliott said."

Ekert chuckled. "You guys really must have become best buds or something. You're calling him by his first name."

"My wife insisted," Jackson said facetiously.

"You do everything your wife tells you to do?" Ekert asked lightly.

"My wife is a very wise woman," Jackson said. "Doing what she tells me is always the best option."

"Yeah, me too," Ekert said.

"So . . . Shawn . . ." Jackson said, enjoying his surprise. "Since you don't work for me anymore, I think we can do the first-name thing now."

"I'm good with that. And since we're on a first-name basis, you can tell me how you're doing with Serena's death."

"Not very well, I'm afraid. I'm not sure why exactly, but it's really getting to me."

"You're not sure why? But I bet you have an idea. I know how that investigator brain of yours works."

Jackson leaned his forearms on his thighs. "Yeah, I have an idea. You know as well as anyone that things didn't end well between me and Serena. I hurt her; I know I did. It took me a while to realize what jerk I had been, and somewhere in the back of my head I'd always intended to look her up and tell her that it had been my fault . . . that it fell apart. I guess I just . . . have a lot of regret, even though I know that regret doesn't really do anybody any good."

"It does if it makes you behave better the next time."

"Well, it *did* do that," Jackson said. "When you put it that way, I wonder if I ever would have made it with Chas if I hadn't learned what I did from my regrets over Serena."

"It's possible. I mean . . . we're a product of what we learn, right? And usually we learn it the hard way . . . especially guys like you and me."

"I don't know. You always seemed to have your life more together than the rest of us."

"I owe it all to Karla; seriously—she keeps me in line, keeps my head on straight."

"I know what you mean."

"So, how's *Elliott* doing? I actually talked to him this morning, but I'd like to hear it from you."

"He seems great."

"It still blows my mind . . . both of you finding wives in the same small town in Montana, of all places."

"And at the same inn," Jackson said.

"And I thought the two of you would be *eternal* bachelors."

"I thought that myself," Jackson said. "There are moments when I wonder if it would have been better."

"What is this? Problems with the wife?"

"No, no. Not at all." Jackson sighed. "But sometimes I think she could have done a lot better."

"She probably could have. All of our wives could have. But that kind of thinking isn't going to fly. When you start thinking like that, you start *acting* like that, and before you know it, you're proving she *could* do better, and if you're not careful she'll decide to find something better."

"Are you speaking from experience?"

"Not really. Sort of."

"Which is it?"

"I kind of went through this phase . . . work was tough, I was gone all the time. And I started thinking Karla would be better off without me. She set me straight in a hurry. What a woman needs is a man who cares enough to do the best he can, whatever the situation may be. Chas loves you."

"Yes, I know."

"So . . . does all this waxing philosophical have something to do with Serena?"

Jackson sighed again. "I'm not proud of the life I lived before I met Chas."

"But it was *before,* right?"

"Yes, but . . . I wasn't completely honest with Chas. I didn't lie to her, but I didn't tell her everything; practically nothing, actually."

"She didn't know about Serena?" His astonishment drove Jackson's guilt deeper.

"Nope."

"That's a pretty big thing not to tell your wife about, isn't it? I mean you and Serena were practically married." Jackson didn't comment and he added, "So, what went wrong? Serena wanted commitment and you couldn't give it? I've always wondered."

"It was something like that. At the time it felt a lot more complicated than that, but looking back, I think that's pretty much it. But I was such a jerk about it." He shook his head. "I still think of things I said to her and wonder what possessed me."

"Well . . . I can understand why this has thrown you for a loop, but I think you need to just sit down and have a good, long talk with your wife. She'll get it. And then you can move on. When are you flying home?"

"I don't have a ticket yet. The inn is being rented for the week by a group of women, and Chas is heavily involved. I was thinking some distance might be good until that's over."

"Ooh, good plan," Ekert said. "So, come to dinner at my house tonight. Karla told me to ask you to come over if you were still gonna be here. And tomorrow we can go into the office and you can check up on everybody."

"I think I'd like that, actually," Jackson said.

* * * * *

Chas felt her cell phone vibrate in her pocket, but she was on the inn phone line taking care of a reservation. When she tried to dial Jackson back, his phone was off. She listened to the message he'd left and hardly felt gratified. She'd been hoping that once the funeral was over he would snap out of this trance he'd been in since he'd heard of Serena's death. She called back and left him a message that expressed her love and concern. Then she said a prayer for him and went to join the others.

The massage therapist had come this morning and set up her things in the designated room. While the ladies took turns getting massages over the course of the next three days, they would continue to work on photographs and scrapbooks, as well as some other simple craft projects that a couple of them had brought materials for. Even though some of the ladies weren't into doing crafts, they seemed to enjoy working together on projects that didn't take a lot of thought or talent. And the projects were things that could be taken home and used for decor, offering a continual reminder of this week spent together as friends.

In the afternoon a few of the ladies bundled up to go out and get some fresh air, while others declared they were glad to be able to remain inside. The Montana cold was harsh in contrast to what most of them were accustomed to. Those that did go out came back quickly, invigorated but joking about the alluring ambience of the fireplace in the formal dining room.

It wasn't until after supper that they were all together again in a relaxed manner, all decked out in their pajamas. Once they were gathered in the parlor, the conversation picked up where it had left off. Rachelle had ended the previous evening with the details of her current circumstances, and a request for advice from her friends.

This evening she said that before they went on with her community counseling session, as she called it, she wanted to hear what was going on in everyone else's lives. Jodi started off, and nothing she said was a surprise to Chas, since they'd become good friends over the last several months. Life had its little challenges and frustrations, but overall she felt it was quite satisfactory. Her biggest frustration was going to church without her husband, but since she'd been inactive when she'd married him, it was difficult for her to expect him to change. *She* had changed, and the Church had come to mean a great deal to her. She just had to keep praying that eventually he would come around.

"Sometimes waiting patiently is all you can do," Marianne said. "You might have to be patient into the next life."

Tammy added in a voice of firm caution to Jodi, "Patience with a spouse being inactive in the Church is one thing. Patience with bad behavior that is destructive to the marriage and family is an entirely different matter."

"Oh, Patrick is a good husband and father," Jodi said. Chas knew that he was. She also knew that Tammy knew it. She realized then that the statement had been made for the benefit of someone else in the room.

"That's so great," Tammy said, and Chas figured the other comment would get dropped.

But Marianne took the bait. "What are you implying, Tammy?"

Tammy remained calm and unruffled. "I'm not implying anything, Marianne. I simply made a statement. I firmly believe that God wants us to be charitable and patient in our relationships, but I don't think he means that to include being mistreated and abused. Sometimes there's a fine line between being long-suffering and enabling bad behavior."

Marianne didn't sound angry, but it was evident she also intended to speak her mind. "You have a great marriage, Tammy; you always have. I don't know if you're in a position to make judgments on other people's marriage problems."

"I'm not making any judgments on anything. I simply made a statement that I believe to be true in regard to all marriages; not just marriages, but other relationships as well."

"I agree," Luci said. "And I *didn't* have a good marriage."

Now Marianne sounded defensive. "Just because you bailed out and got a divorce doesn't mean that I should. Sorry, Luci, I didn't mean that quite the way it must have sounded."

"Whoa!" Tammy said. "No one has *ever* said or implied that you should get a divorce. But as long as we're talking about it, I think we have *all* felt concern over the situation with your marriage, Marianne. You're a strong woman, capable of doing everything and surviving anything. And we admire you for that. But you cannot deny that your children are having some pretty serious struggles that are clearly a result of your husband's bad behavior. I think we're all concerned that if something doesn't change, these problems are just going to escalate."

Chas noticed that Marianne was trying to be patient with Tammy, as if she were a mischievous child and Marianne simply had to endure this lecture. Chas wondered if this was one of those moments that Jodi had predicted, when having a newcomer in the room would keep things from getting too out of hand. Tammy's voice was kind as she continued. "No one is going to dispute that it's hard to make such changes, but what kind of message about life and marriage are you giving your children when you simply put up with it, day after day, year after year?"

"He doesn't beat me," Marianne said. "And he doesn't cheat on me."

Chas saw Rachelle wince and look away.

"No," Tammy said, "but he's the king of emotional abuse. He's constantly full of contradictions and anger, and *you* are constantly walking on eggshells, worried that if you don't handle every little thing just so, he'll fly off the handle and take it out on you or one of the kids."

"She's right," Jodi said. "We're not saying these things to be critical, Marianne. We all love you, and we're worried. It's not like you haven't complained about him to every one of us. And we all know what's going on with the kids."

Chas wanted to ask exactly *what* was going on with the kids, but she didn't want to pry. In truth, she felt like an eavesdropper even being in the room. But no one seemed to notice. She just hoped that her being privy to all of these things might bring about something positive as the week progressed.

A mild disagreement continued for more than half an hour while Chas expected Marianne to get up and leave. It finally settled when Marianne tearfully admitted that she didn't know how to change her situation. She spilled details of the challenges with her husband and children that escalated Chas's concern. The conversation shifted as the others began offering gentle advice, much of it based on their own experiences. Tammy had not been through major difficulties in her marriage, but she had been close to people who had. She had also served as a Relief Society president and had seen a great many challenges in women's lives. Chas recalled hearing Jodi say that Tammy was instinctively wise. Chas could certainly see evidence of that.

Luci also offered sound advice based on her own bad marriage. She made it clear that their situations were entirely different and they required different solutions. But the principles of overcoming codependency were the same. When Marianne said she should write some things down, Chas got her a notebook and pen. For another hour, Marianne's friends rallied around her with support, love, and advice. Marianne came away with goals to get some counseling that might help her know how to appropriately overcome her own codependent behavior, and she also admitted that she needed guidance in helping her children understand that while she loved their father, she didn't agree with his bad behavior. Three of the women would be mailing books to her that had helped them in the past.

They all agreed that it would be a challenging journey, but Marianne had taken a huge step. She said it herself. She'd never been able to really admit that there was a problem. Jodi concluded the conversation by reminding them all that a *true* friend was someone who could tell you that you were making a mistake, and then stand beside you while you were able to correct it. Tammy pointed out that this was not the same as being bullied by a *supposed* friend who believed she had all the answers for you and became indignant when you didn't take her advice—because you knew it was wrong. She illustrated the point with a quick story about a woman in her neighborhood who had been very pushy about wanting her friends to run their homes and manage their lives according to *her* preferences, and then she would become offended when they didn't.

The conversation lightened with some reminiscing and laughter, and they all finally dispersed for bed after Chas left Michelle a message to let her know that they wanted breakfast at ten instead of nine. They all wanted to sleep in and enjoy the luxurious beds.

When Chas was alone in her own room she realized that her phone had not vibrated at all during the evening. She checked it and found no missed calls. She couldn't believe her husband hadn't even tried to call her back. What could he be doing that would keep him so busy? What was he thinking? She thought of the times he'd gone to Arkansas to see his sister without her, or when he'd gone to Virginia with Elliott to move his things here. He had always called her multiple times a day, telling her details of what he was doing, continually reminding her that he loved her and missed her. Chas's worry intensified. But she didn't know what to do about it.

CHAPTER NINE

Jackson felt guilty for not calling Chas. He'd had a nice day with Shawn, and he'd especially enjoyed his evening at Shawn's home. Karla had always been kind to Jackson, and she was a great cook. Being in their home was comfortable and familiar for Jackson. But when he returned to his hotel room, knowing it was too late to call Chas, clouds descended over him that were even darker than they'd been the day before.

He was awakened early by his phone ringing and managed to grab it without knocking it on the floor. "Hello," he said and wasn't surprised to hear Chas.

"Are you okay?"

"Just . . . tired," he said.

Chas decided to avoid the lack of phone calls the last two days and concentrate on the fact that she was at least hearing his voice. "What did you do yesterday? Anything fun?"

"I spent the day with Shawn. And Karla invited me to dinner. I was there late."

"You used his first name," Chas said with a lightness that normally would have made him chuckle.

"Yeah," he said tonelessly.

The silence became awkward. "Are you okay?" Chas asked.

"I'm fine," he said. More silence. "How are you?"

"Everything's fine here," she said, wondering why he didn't even think to ask about the kids, especially since she was in the same room with them and he could surely hear the noise they were making. "I'm worried about you."

"There's no need for that," he said.

"Convince me," she countered, but he only answered with silence. Chas had had enough! "What's going on, Jackson?" she demanded, trying to sound more assertive than angry.

"Nothing's going on," he said, and she wondered if his defensiveness was in response to her own tone of voice, or an effort to conceal his true feelings from her.

"You don't answer your phone, and when you do you won't talk to me. You're suddenly like a stranger . . . a different person. Should I not be concerned? If it was the other way around, *you* would be concerned."

He was silent way too long. When he did speak, he sounded like it was taking effort to be patient and polite, but it was subtle enough that she couldn't call him on being terse or unkind. "There's nothing going on, Chas. I just . . . need some time."

"Okay, I can live with that, just . . . give me a reason. Tell me something that makes sense."

He was silent even longer. "I'm just . . . trying to come to terms with some things, Chas. It has nothing to do with you."

"I'm your wife, Jackson; *everything* should have something to do with me. I completely understand that this could be difficult for you, but when you won't talk to me about what you're feeling, I think you're making it *more* difficult. Let me help you through this. Let me—"

"I need to go, Chas," he said, not in a tone that indicated he'd been interrupted or he had somewhere to be, but rather that he was refusing to hear what she had to say.

"Jackson, please listen to me and—"

"I appreciate your concern, Chas; I really do. But . . . I need to work this one out on my own."

When Chas heard evidence on the other end that he'd hung up, she stared at the phone in disbelief, as if doing so might help her understand what kind of brain damage had devoured her husband's ability to reasonably solve a problem. She lost track of how long she sat there, mentally putting all the pieces together in her head while she fought to keep her emotions out of it. The problem came when she *had* assessed the situation and realized that this was serious. Her deepest instincts combined with the logic of his behavior, and she knew she had solid reason to fear that she could be losing him. Was it really possible that his old life could have sucked him back into its vortex? Considering the frame of mind he'd been in when he left home, the answer was yes. *Yes,* it was possible.

Polly found her still sitting there, right after the tears had started to flow. "What on earth is wrong?" she asked.

"I'm afraid I'm . . . losing him."

"*Losing* him?" Polly echoed and let out an astonished chuckle. "We're talking about Jackson here. He's not going to go off the proverbial deep end just because he's having a hard time with this woman's death."

"I think he's *already* gone off that deep end," Chas cried. "He won't talk to me. He won't tell me what's going on, or how he feels, or anything. It's like his spirit isn't even there."

"Okay, well . . . just because he's not talking about what's going on, doesn't mean that what's going on is bad. We both know that Jackson is far too committed to you and the kids to do anything stupid. He's a good man, Chas. Don't let your imagination run wild. You can't fill in the gaps by thinking the worst."

Chas took a deep breath. "Okay." She took another and wiped her tears. "You're right. He'll come around. And just because he doesn't want to talk doesn't mean he's doing something he shouldn't."

"Exactly!"

"I think I've spent too much time with women whose husbands have been deplorable. Surely Jackson is not like that."

"No, he is not!" Polly said. "You need to stay busy and not worry so much. And Jackson just needs some time. A lot has changed in his life. Just give him a chance to let it catch up with him."

"That's a good point," Chas said. "I guess I should get back. They'll be gathering for breakfast soon."

"How's it going?"

"Good. I'm enjoying it, really. And I think I'm learning some things, too."

"Like what?" Polly asked.

Chas stood up. "That will have to wait."

She was about to kiss her babies good-bye for the day when Elliott came down the stairs.

"Hey there, Mrs. Leeds," he said. "How's the big deal going over there?"

"Fine. How are you coping with my children?"

"We're doing great," he said and seemed to mean it. "Overall, I think I'd prefer getting my own one at a time, but they're a lot of fun."

"Even in the middle of the night?" Chas asked.

"He's either working, or sleeping because he *was* working," Polly said. "He is not in a position to give that a fair answer."

"That's true," Elliott said. He gave Polly a quick kiss, then noticed Chas's expression. "You okay? You must be missing the hubby."

"I am, yes," she said. "But . . . I'm also worried about him. Has he called you?"

"No, I called him a couple of times and left messages, but he hasn't called me back."

Chas realized then that he seemed uncomfortable, perhaps nervous, with the topic of Jackson. She was wondering how to ask when Polly said, "Tell Chas that Jackson would never cheat on her or go off the deep end."

Elliott looked suddenly like a kid who'd been caught stealing.

"What?" Polly demanded. Elliott glanced with concern toward Chas, and her heart began to thud.

"I'm sure it's nothing," Elliott said. "I mean . . . you know Jackson well enough to know what he would or wouldn't do, right? So, it's nothing."

"*What* is nothing?" Chas demanded.

"Out with it!" Polly insisted when Elliott hesitated, looking terrified. "Just tell us what you know."

Elliott sat down, so the women did the same. Chas watched him across the kitchen table and felt like screaming. A part of her knew he would say something to confirm her suspicions, while a bigger part of her prayed that she would be wrong.

"Ekert called me the day after the funeral. He just called to shoot the breeze. He said that even though the funeral was very sad, it was nice to see some people he hadn't seen for a long time—one of them being Jackson. He said it was almost like old times when Jackson went to the bar with everyone after the funeral."

Chas gasped softly, but Elliott hurried to add, "It's a tradition. When someone died in the line of duty, we would all go to this particular bar that keeps pictures of the fallen heroes on one wall. And we'd all just share a toast. We'd also go there for a toast to celebrate good things or pay tribute for all kinds of reasons. His going to the bar with old friends isn't necessarily a bad thing."

"Okay," Chas said, "but I can tell you haven't told me everything yet. And you'd better tell me *everything*. I don't care if Jackson accuses you of being a gossip. I'm worried about him and I need to know."

"Fair enough," Elliott said. "So, here's the thing . . . Ekert said it real casually . . . so it wasn't like he was concerned at all, or that he thought anything was out of the ordinary, but then . . . Ekert wouldn't be as aware of the changes Jackson's made in his life, and . . . he would have been used to seeing Jackson at the bar, and—"

"Get on with it," Chas said. Realizing how impatient she'd sounded, she added, "Sorry. I'm just . . . stressed."

"It's okay," he said, "but what he told me is going to stress you more, and . . ."

Chas took a deep breath. "Just say it."

"Ekert said, 'It was great to see Jackson there, sharing a drink with the guys like old times.'" Chas gasped again, then Elliott added with even more trepidation, "And he said, 'I don't know who the woman was, but I assume they know each other. They were sitting together at the funeral, and they were holding hands over a drink. Must have been an old friend of his. I think they left together.' There. That's exactly how he said it." Chas could hardly breathe, let alone speak. "You can't jump to conclusions, Chas. It might be entirely different than it appeared to an innocent bystander."

"Or it might not," Chas said and hurried out of the kitchen, mumbling, "I need to be alone."

Chas went out the front door of her home and into the front door of the inn so that she could avoid passing by Michelle, who was in the kitchen, and the ladies, who would be gathering in the dining room for breakfast. She was glad to not pass anyone in the hall or on the stairs, and she managed to hold back her anguished sobs until she was in her room with the door closed. The energy it had taken to secure her solitude vanished and she sank to the floor, muttering over and over that it had to be a mistake, it couldn't be possible, he wouldn't have betrayed her like this. The drinking was bad enough, but it was more understandable. As horrified as she felt to think of him drinking after all the changes he'd made in his life, it was still not impossible to understand. If he was depressed, away from home, confused, it could happen. But a woman? It didn't even make sense. Holding to that thought, she worked it through in her mind. It *didn't* make sense. Depressed or not, it just wasn't in Jackson to stoop so low. Surely this *was* a case of false impressions. She needed to talk to her husband, and she needed straight answers. She wasn't going to waste a minute of unnecessary grief over something that hadn't even happened. But, of course, Jackson's phone was off. She remembered telling him that she was always a phone call away, that as long as he had his phone it would like having her there to hold his hand. She didn't like the implication of Jackson's silent phone in light of his present behavior, but she tried to remain calm.

A knock at the door startled her. "Yes?" she called.

"We're eating breakfast," Jodi called. "Are you coming?"

"Um . . . go ahead. I need to talk to Jackson."

"Is everything all right?" Jodi asked through the closed door.

"Um . . . I think so. We'll talk later. Just . . . have a good time. I'll be there later."

"Okay," Jodi said. "Let me know if you need anything."

"Thanks," Chas said and waited until she heard Jodi's footsteps descending the nearby stairs.

Chas did what she should have done the minute she'd been alone. She knelt next to the bed and prayed with all the fervor of her soul that this situation was not what it seemed to be, that her husband would come to his senses and come home to her, that she would know what to do. Following the amen Chas knew she needed to call Shawn Ekert. But his number was in the office of the inn.

Now that she had composed herself, she checked in the mirror to make certain she didn't look suspiciously emotional, then she hurried down the stairs, avoiding any attention from the ladies in the dining room. She slipped into the office, where she closed the door and locked it. It only took her a minute to find Shawn's cell phone number, and she was glad to see his home number listed as well.

Perhaps a conversation with Karla couldn't hurt. Jackson had eaten dinner there last night. Maybe she would have some insight. First she would see how it went with Shawn.

Chas dialed Shawn's number, trying to ignore her nerves. She was expecting to leave a message but he answered after the second ring.

"Hi," she said, "it's Chas Leeds."

"Oh, hi!" he said. "I'm just on my way to pick up your husband. We're going into the office today to hang out."

"I'm sure he'll enjoy that," she said. "Maybe you could tell him to call me."

"Has he *not* been calling you?"

"Apparently he's not in a very talkative mood." She wanted to get to the point of what Shawn had told Elliott, but she also needed to ask, "How has he seemed to you?"

"Oh, he's definitely down; not really himself. I guess he's taking this pretty hard."

"So it seems," Chas said. "Listen . . . I need to ask you something, and I want you to be absolutely straight with me."

"Okay," he said, not sounding concerned.

"You told Elliott you'd seen Jackson at the bar . . . after the funeral."

"That's right."

She wanted to ask about the drinking, but since Shawn was a drinking man she didn't want to make that the issue of the conversation. She would cross one bridge at a time. Right now she had a more prominent concern.

"And you told him that Jackson was with a woman . . . that they left together."

"Whoa!" Shawn said. "I had no idea that was going to get back to you like that. No . . . I didn't mean it like that. I'm not keeping any secrets from you; nobody is. It never even crossed my mind that Jackson would be seeing another woman, Chas. I just assumed they were friends."

"But you didn't know her?"

"No, but we had very few mutual acquaintances. You can't really be worried that he would be . . ."

"You and I both know it's not in his character to do something like that. The problem is that he's avoiding any conversation with me

at all. Given the fact that he's depressed and he's dealing with stuff
from his past that I don't know anything about, you can understand
why I would be concerned."

"Yes, I *do* understand."

"I'm sorry for putting you in the middle of this. I just needed to
know the truth."

"All I can tell you is that I saw him sitting next to her at the
funeral, and then they were talking in the bar."

Chas wanted to ask about the holding hands, and their leaving
together. But she already felt like the proverbial nagging, paranoid
wife. She just needed to talk to her husband. If nothing else, perhaps
Shawn's concern over the misconceptions would prompt him to talk
some sense into his friend.

"Just . . . tell him to call me," Chas said. "Tell him I need to know
what *really* happened."

"I'll tell him," Shawn said. "And . . . I'm sorry, Chas, if I gave
Elliott the wrong impression."

She wanted to say that there never would have been a problem if
Jackson would engage in some reasonable conversation, but she only
said, "It's okay, Shawn. I hope the two of you have a good day. And . . .
see if *you* can get him to talk."

"We talked a little yesterday, but I'll see what I can do."

"Thank you. Tell Karla hello for me."

"I will."

"And we really want the two of you to come and stay at the inn. I
think you're long overdue for a vacation."

"I know we are."

Chas hung up the phone and wanted to go back to bed. Right
now she didn't feel like making scrapbook pages or crafts or indulging
in pleasant conversation. She just wanted to be alone, and she felt
utterly exhausted. And the day was just getting started.

While Chas sat there and thought about the situation, she was
surprised to realize how angry she felt. She wasn't terribly worried
about this other woman thing, but she wouldn't be at all surprised to
learn that he'd been drinking. And if that was the case, it was going to
significantly set back their goal of going to the temple together. But
Chas felt most angry over his cutting her off like this. The very fact

that she heard such a thing without first hearing from him what *really* happened was what truly ticked her off. She looked at the dormant cell phone in her hand and wondered if he'd actually have the nerve to call her once Shawn gave him the bad news that he'd been busted. She wondered for a moment if it was really possible that this was the beginning of some ridiculous disintegration of their relationship. The idea was so painful that she pushed it away and focused on her anger.

* * * * *

Jackson had just walked out of his hotel room when his phone rang; the caller ID told him it was Ekert. He wondered if he'd been delayed in picking him up. But he answered it to hear, "Boy, are you in the doghouse! You'd better call your wife, and you'd better do it now. If you don't want me to listen to that conversation, then you'd better do it before we leave."

"She *called* you?" Jackson asked, feeling angry that Chas would bring Shawn into this problem.

"I'd say she had good reason to call me. When I talked to Elliott I happened to mention that I saw you at the bar with a woman, but I didn't know who she was." Jackson groaned and leaned against the wall in the hallway, glad he was alone. "I'm sure it was completely innocent. It never would have crossed my mind that you'd cheat on your wife. I don't think it would cross Elliott's mind either, but somehow wires are shorting out here, buddy. She says she hasn't talked to you. Maybe if she *had* she wouldn't need to call me to get the story straight. Call her. I like you too much to let you blow your marriage just because you're having a bad week."

Jackson sighed. "I'll call her. But . . . apparently this could take a while."

"Oh, I always have a book on hand," Shawn said with a chuckle. "Call me when you're done and I'll pick you up."

Jackson returned to his room, wanting to be angry with Shawn, with Elliott, with Chas. But he knew the truth. He could only *really* be angry with himself. His lack of communication with Chas *was* the source of the problem, and going into this conversation with anger and frustration would accomplish nothing. He sat on the edge of the bed, took a deep breath, and saw evidence on his phone that enhanced his guilt. Chas had tried to call three times this morning. He dialed her cell phone, thinking that if she'd just finished talking to Ekert, maybe she'd be available and answer it.

Without any kind of greeting, she answered and said, "So, I take it you answer the phone when Shawn calls you. I can't think of any other reason for the timing of this call, unless it's just a happy coincidence that you've finally decided to talk to me. Or maybe I shouldn't assume that just because you called, you'll actually *talk.*"

"I don't know what to say," he muttered truthfully.

"That seems to be a big problem lately. But I'll make it simple for you. I need some straight answers to some simple questions, and if you're lucky, I'll believe you're telling me the truth."

"I would never lie to you, Chas."

"I've always believed that. And I think I was doing a pretty good job of completely giving you the benefit of the doubt on all of the things about your past I didn't know about. At the moment, however, I'm wondering how far your keen ability to *omit* the truth might actually take you."

Her silence implied that she expected a comment but he didn't have one. When she realized that, she said, "I'm assuming you've heard about the gossip that got to my ears. You can't blame Shawn *or* Elliott. They were being straightforward and forthright. You could take a lesson from them. The thing is, I was thinking about the time you came straight to me that time when Cortney was staying with us and she was behaving badly, and you didn't want me getting the wrong impression or jumping to conclusions. Given that experience, I have to wonder why you would do exactly the opposite in a situation that is full of all kinds of reasons for me to get the wrong impression and jump to conclusions. Please tell me I've gotten the wrong impression, Jackson."

"Maybe you should tell me your impression and I'll tell you if you're wrong."

"You were at the bar," she said. It wasn't a question.

"Yes, it's a tradition. I wanted to be included."

"Okay," Chas said. That rang true with what Elliott had said. "You were drinking."

"What?" He'd been expecting to hear questions in regard to the woman he'd been seen with, and he was prepared to answer them. This one threw him off.

"Shawn told Elliott it was good to see you there, having a drink . . ."

"Why do I feel like I'm being interrogated?" he asked.

"Because you are. How am I doing so far? I learned from the best." He didn't comment, and she said, "You're avoiding the question. It makes you sound guilty. So, you *were* drinking."

By the time Jackson realized it was a statement and not a question, she had gone on. "You told me you would never do it again; you promised! And if you were drinking, I can only imagine what might have happened. Who was she?" Chas demanded. "Tell me!"

"I was *not* drinking," he said. "And I—"

"So Ekert was lying to me?" She didn't wait for an answer. "He didn't say it to snitch on you. He just said it casually. He told Elliott that it was good to see you, that it looked like you were having a good time. He said you were drinking with the guys like the good old days, but he didn't know who the woman was, the one whose hand you were holding."

"Wow!" Jackson said. "Now do you want to stop talking long enough for me to actually tell you what happened?"

"Sorry," she said with sarcasm. "I've become so accustomed to having to fill in the silence and make assumptions that I didn't realize you actually had something to say."

"I don't think I have ever heard you this angry."

"I don't know if I've ever been this angry; I've never felt this betrayed."

"Betrayed? I did nothing to betray you, Chas. Nothing!"

"Listen," she said, wanting no room for doubt, "whatever happened we'll deal with it. Just don't lie to me. Whatever you do, don't lie to me, Jackson. The honesty thing is hanging by a thread here. Don't make it snap."

"I'm telling you the truth. Nothing happened . . . at least not the things you're accusing me of. I've been . . . depressed . . . confused . . . upset. But I did nothing to betray you."

Chas still wasn't convinced. She decided to take it on one issue at a time. "You were at the bar."

"Yes, I was at the bar."

"You were drinking."

"If you mean I was consuming a liquid beverage from a glass, yes I was drinking. If you mean that I was drinking alcohol, *no,* I was not drinking. Now, do you want to ask me about the woman?"

Chas had to think about that for a moment. A new thought occurred to her. She'd dismissed the possibility of his being unfaithful, but she'd believed it was possible for him to be drinking. And if he *had* been drinking, it might have turned out differently. If she believed that he really hadn't been drinking, she could never convince herself that he would cheat on her. As if he'd read her mind, he said, "Did you *really* think I would betray you in any way with any woman . . . ever?"

"Not if you were sober," she admitted. "But I thought you were drinking."

"I wasn't."

"Okay," she said, feeling much better to hear it from him. But she wasn't done with him yet. "Were you really holding a woman's hand?"

"She was a friend of Serena's, but I'd never met her before. She sat next to me at the funeral and got chatty. At the bar I was sitting at a table waiting for Ekert to get done talking. She saw me and sat down. I made it clear I was married. She made it clear she wasn't flirting. At the funeral she told me she believed Serena was gone for good, that this was the end. I told her I knew for myself that spirits lived on. At the bar she asked me to expound on that. We talked about angels. I told her to call the missionaries. She put her hand over mine on the table when she thanked me. We were talking in a room full of people, far from alone."

Chas's relief was growing, but she had to know *everything.* "Shawn said he thought the two of you left together."

"We *happened* to reach the door at the same time even though we hadn't left the table at the same time. I looked around for Ekert and couldn't see him. I thought he'd left. When I realized she was trying to hail a cab, I stood at the curb with her to make sure she got into one safely. I thought it was the gentlemanly thing to do. Then I got into my car and went back to the hotel. Is there anything else you want to know, Mrs. Leeds?"

He sounded angry, and Chas wondered how bad this was going to get before it got better. They'd had disagreements and tension in the past, but never anything like this.

"Just one more thing," she said. "It's not hard for me to believe that everything you just said was true, mostly because it makes sense and it's very much in character for you. I know you, Jackson. I wouldn't have been surprised if you'd given in to the temptation to drink. I would have been disappointed, even upset, but we would have started over and worked it through and moved on. In my heart it only took me a few minutes to realize that I knew you wouldn't have cheated on me. But I need to tell you why I'm *really* angry. I'm angry because I heard it first through gossip. I'm angry because I actually had to spend more than a split second wondering if it might be true. If you and I had been talking like we normally do, you would have told me what had happened. And when Elliott said what he did, I would have already known the story and we would have laughed over it. For all of your omission of telling me things about your past, I really do believe you wouldn't lie to me. But I did nothing to deserve having you cut me off like that. I've given you no reason to believe that you couldn't talk to me about *anything* without judgment or anger. I'll admit that this whole Serena thing blindsided me, but not nearly as much as the way you stopped talking to me. I deserve better than that from you. There. That's all I have to say." There was silence and she added, "You can talk now."

"I . . . don't know what to say. You're right; you're right about everything. You *do* deserve better than me."

"That's not what I said. Don't twist my words. I said that I deserve better than that *from* you."

"But I am who I am, Chas."

"You are everything I could ever ask for in a husband and father."

"But the life I lived before is—"

"Irrelevant," she said. "The only thing that matters about those years is that *you* make peace with them. They make no difference to you and me. *No difference!* Do you hear me?"

Chas sensed he was thinking and let him do so. He finally said, "I'm sorry, Chas. I really am. But you're right. I *do* need to make peace with it. And that's proving to be a lot harder than I expected.

I can't explain what's going on, but . . . this has really thrown me. I should have told you how I felt. I'm telling you now. I feel guilt, and regret; confusion, anger, contempt. Those last two are mostly toward myself."

"We need to talk it through."

"Maybe we do, but it's hard to talk to you about this. I'm not proud of the way I lived."

"You didn't know any better."

"I still hate it; I hate to look at it, think about it. But I can't seem to think of anything else. I feel like I sinned against you, Chas, even though I hadn't even met you. That may not sound reasonable, but that's how I feel. I just . . . need some time. I promise if there's anything important to say, I'll say it. I just . . . feel like I need to stay here a few more days. And we can talk it through when I get home and I've had a chance to sort it out."

"Promise?" she said.

"I promise."

"I love you, Jackson; I love you more than life."

"I love you too," he said. "I don't deserve you."

"That is simply not true," she said, but Jackson had trouble believing her.

"Is there anything else . . . that we need to talk about right now?"

"You haven't once asked about the kids since you left. That's not like you."

"I'm sorry. I know it's not like me. I've been self-absorbed and . . . a real jerk." He paused. "How are the kids?"

"They're fine."

That despicable awkward silence settled in again. Chas struggled to find something to talk about. "Shawn tells me you're going into the office today."

"Yeah, that was the plan."

"Was?"

"I'm not sure what he's doing . . . right now."

"What you mean is . . . this conversation is holding up your plans."

"It doesn't matter. This is much more important, and I'm sorry for that . . . again."

"I should let you go," she said, not wanting the impact of the conversation to get lost in this patronizing silence. "I should go too," she added to make it easier. "You'll call me this evening?"

"I will. I promise. Kiss my babies for me."

"I will," she said. "Jackson . . . please call me if you need to talk. Please don't just . . . try to hold it all inside." As an afterthought she added, "If you can't talk to me about this, then . . . talk to someone."

"I'll be fine," he said, but he didn't agree to talk.

Their good-byes were surprisingly brief, as if it suddenly became easy for him to get off the phone. Chas wiped away a couple of tears. She hung her head and prayed fervently on his behalf, then she tried to get a grip so she could go get some breakfast and be a good hostess. With any luck, she could distract herself enough from the drama of her own life to actually have a good time.

CHAPTER TEN

For a moment after he hung up the phone, Jackson felt the urge to get on the next flight out and get home to his wife. But his next thought was how utterly foolish he felt. He'd messed up his past, but now he was messing up the present.

Needing a distraction he phoned Shawn to tell him he was ready. By the time he walked downstairs and through the lobby, Shawn's car was waiting. When Jackson got in, Shawn said, "Did you get everything cleared up?"

"I guess you could say that," Jackson said.

"You want to talk about it?"

"Nope," he said. "Just . . . tell me what's been going on at work; tell me what I'm missing."

"You think it'll make you wanna come back?"

"Not in ten million years," Jackson said, and Shawn laughed.

* * * * *

Chas was startled by a knock at the office door, then she remembered that she'd actually locked it.

"Are you in there?" she heard Jodi call.

"Yes," Chas said and pulled open the door, hoping she didn't look as pathetic as she felt. Jodi's expression immediately told her that she did.

"What's wrong?" she demanded and moved into the room, closing the door behind her. "And don't tell me nothing. You told me you were concerned about Jackson, but it's more than that. Have the two of you been fighting?"

"Something like that," Chas said, sinking back into the chair she'd already warmed up.

Jodi sat next to her. "Is it because of your being here with us?" she asked. "Because if he needs you, Chas, we will manage just fine."

"I've felt all along that I needed to be *here*, which has made me wonder if he needs some space in order to deal with this. The problem is that he's taking way too much space. He won't hardly talk to me. He's depressed and struggling, but he doesn't want to talk to me about it."

"I take it this funeral was for someone close."

"Yeah," Chas said, and she was surprised by her own tears, "apparently she's someone he was once *very* close to. The problem is that he'd never told me about her; I'd never even heard her name."

"Okay, I think that would tick me off."

"I was proud of myself because I handled it well. I *didn't* get ticked off. I've been supportive and compassionate. But now that he's in Virginia, he's like a different person. It's almost like his old life just . . . sucked him away from me in a matter of hours. I just told him I deserved better than that. He told me I deserved better than *him*. What's that supposed to mean? If he's riddled with some kind of abstract guilt about living a worldly life before he met me, how am I supposed to convince him that it doesn't matter anymore? He's been baptized. It's all in the past. But if he's out there and he's depressed, the choices he makes now *do* matter."

"Did you tell him that?"

"No, it just came to me. But I think he knows; it's complicated, but . . . I'm not really worried about him doing something stupid as I am that he'll just . . ."

"What?"

"I don't know. He's been through a lot. I think deep down he's pretty vulnerable. I'm just . . . worried."

"Then maybe you should get on the next flight out and be with him."

Chas looked at Jodi and weighed that in her mind. She still felt strongly about staying; she believed it was right to let him handle this on his own. But she did say, "Let me pray about that and give it some thought."

"Okay," Jodi said. "In the meantime, I set aside a plate of breakfast for you. Come and eat. The worst thing a person can do when they're upset is not eat."

"I'll be there in a few minutes," Chas said. "There're some things I need to talk to Heavenly Father about first."

"Okay," Jodi said with a smile of understanding. They shared a hug and Jodi left her alone. Chas locked the door again and got down on her knees, asking if she *should* go to Virginia to be with her husband, asking if she really needed to be here at the inn. Logically, she knew her relationship with her husband was a much higher priority than anything she might accomplish here. But God knew what Jackson needed, and Chas needed personal revelation to know the best course. She prayed that Jackson would feel the comfort and guidance of the Spirit, and that he would remember all that was noteworthy in his life and take hold of it. She prayed that their goal of going to the temple together in fewer than two weeks would not be thwarted, but she expressed her commitment to helping Jackson get through whatever he needed, and in whatever time frame might be required.

Chas finished her prayer and left the office, relatively certain that she needed to stay here, keep praying, and find ways to help Jackson long distance. She didn't fully understand why, but it felt right. She concluded that if something changed, the Lord would surely let her know.

* * * * *

Jackson was glad to hear Shawn talking about everyday stuff, and was relieved that he didn't mention issues Jackson and Chas were dealing with. Shawn probably would have preferred to be left out of it, and thankfully he seemed fine with not talking about it.

Arriving at the Bureau office where Jackson had worked for many years felt surreal. The fact that Shawn needed to check him in and get him a visitor's badge was *very* strange. Going deeper into the building to the area where he'd worked enhanced the recent feeling of going back in time. Nothing had changed. It all looked the same, felt the same; it even smelled the same. It was Jackson who had changed.

Shawn technically had the day off, so he had no obligations on the job. He told Jackson that when he'd asked for the day off to attend Serena's funeral, he'd been told that if he didn't take some other vacation days right away, he was going to lose them. So he'd pretty much been told he had to take a week. Since his kids were in school and his wife had obligations, they hadn't been able to take full advantage of it. But he'd said more than once that he was glad he'd had some time off to spend with Jackson while he was there. Tomorrow he would be getting away for a long weekend with the family so that they could benefit from at least part of his time off. Today Jackson was glad to have Shawn around. He needed a distraction and he didn't want to be alone. But he didn't feel ready to go home yet, and while he knew he should talk to Chas about what was eating at him, he simply found it difficult.

A slow day at the office was a great means for distraction. Jackson enjoyed catching up with many coworkers and acquaintances. They laughed about funny moments from the past and caught up on life and families, completely avoiding discussion about the horrors that some of them had shared in years gone by. It was a part of the job, but it didn't come up and Jackson was fine with that. He went to lunch with a group of six who were enjoying Jackson's visit as an excuse to get out of the office and spend some time together. They ate at a nearby bar that served great sandwiches. Jackson ordered a ginger ale to drink and didn't feel out of place since everyone else except Shawn had to go back to work, so no one was drinking alcohol.

Near the end of the meal, someone said, "You know it's been about four and a half years since we lost Dave?"

A heavy silence followed the comment. Everyone here had known Dave well, and they'd all been severely affected by his senseless and tragic death. He'd been killed in the line of duty, but he wouldn't have been if someone within the Bureau hadn't been selling secrets to drug dealers. For Jackson, there were multiple negative experiences associated with this particular issue, and they were definitely the worst he'd dealt with in his work.

The timing of Dave's death brought on mixed emotions for him, however, and he said, "I met my wife right after that happened."

"Oh, that's right," one of them said. "You ran off to that bed-and-breakfast and never came back."

"I came back long enough to be kidnapped by drug lords," Jackson said.

"That happened after?" someone else asked.

Ekert stepped in and reminded those who had forgotten that Dave's death had preceded the undercover operation to take down the man responsible for selling huge amounts of drugs and paying off FBI agents in order to cover his tracks. They'd succeeded in bringing him down, but then Jackson's undercover identity had gotten him into a great deal of trouble. He'd been rescued on the brink of death, and the resulting physical recovery was nothing in contrast to healing from the PTSD. Jackson was amazed at how he'd healed enough that he didn't mind having his ordeal discussed in a casual setting. But then the conversation led to the last and final piece in this ugly puzzle.

"Did you hear about Myers?" someone asked Jackson.

He knew immediately what they meant. Myers had worked with everyone seated at this table; he'd been trusted and respected. But now he was in prison for his connections to organized crime, and he'd actually had a hand in the events they'd just been talking about. The betrayal felt by everyone who had worked with him was difficult to describe, but no one in the group had suffered more for Myers's indiscretions than Jackson. The hostage situation he'd endured likely wouldn't have happened if Myers had been doing what he was supposed to do. But Myers had caused other more recent problems for Jackson. Everyone present knew about that too. What they didn't know was that the information that had taken Myers down had come through Jackson. It was a complicated story that these people didn't need to know. But it was still validating for Jackson to listen to others share their feelings of betrayal and disgust that he had experienced himself. It felt good to be among peers who understood him that way, and he really enjoyed himself.

Back at the office, conversations became centered around current cases. Jackson listened while memories related to all that had been discussed over lunch began to create an overload in his brain. He realized that in his time away he'd become more sensitive to the horror of the criminal world that good people had to expose themselves to in order to protect and vindicate the innocent. Jackson was a husband and father now. Having children of his own made the depravity of some human beings feel all the more horrific. He simply couldn't believe the great lengths some people would go to for the sake of greed, or jealousy, or anger. He began to feel nauseous to the point that he wondered if there had been something wrong with his lunch. Others who had eaten the same thing seemed fine, but Jackson finally had to say, "It's been great, but I need to go."

Shawn stood up since he'd driven Jackson here, but Jackson said to him, "No, it's okay. I'll get a cab." He shook his friend's hand. "Thank you for everything. It's been good to see you."

"You're flying out tomorrow?" Shawn asked.

"Probably," Jackson said. He doubted he would leave the next day, but his urge to have some time alone was growing stronger. He said his good-byes to everyone else and hurried out of the building, handing in his visitor badge on the way out.

A strange headache settled over him while he rode in a cab to his hotel. He had been back in his room about half an hour when he started throwing up. Certain he either had food poisoning or some kind of bug, he was glad he didn't have a flight scheduled tomorrow because he'd probably have to cancel it. The headache worsened dramatically, but he couldn't take something to help it because he couldn't keep anything down. Resigned to a night of misery, and praying it wouldn't be longer, he laid down on the rug on the bathroom floor with a cold washrag over his face, wondering what he was doing here, wishing the earth would just swallow him now and get it over with.

* * * * *

Chas enjoyed her day with the ladies, intermittently popping in to see her kids and talk to Polly. She caught Polly up to speed on the issues with Jackson as far as it was appropriate to share marriage problems with a best friend. As always, Chas was careful not to speak ill of Jackson, but to simply express her own hurts and concerns. Since Polly had been Chas's friend for many years, she was more comfortable sharing the details of her feelings with her than she was with anyone else. Polly was supportive and encouraging, and she felt sure that Jackson would come home soon with new perspective—especially since Chas had been assertive enough to set him straight.

Chas tried to call Jackson but it went straight to voice mail. She gave him the benefit of the doubt in knowing that he was spending the day with Shawn at the office. She tried again early evening. He answered, but he sounded terrible.

"What's wrong?" she asked.

"I've either got the flu or food poisoning," he said and briefly told her his symptoms.

Chas expressed her concern for him, but he assured her that he would be fine. Not only was she worried about him being ill, she was disappointed over the fact that she couldn't possibly gauge if he was more like himself when he was too sick to talk even if he *were* himself.

"Should I come out there?" she asked.

"That would be a waste of time and money," he said. "I'm just going to hole up in this room until I feel better, and then I'll come home. At least this way you won't catch it."

"Are you sure?" she asked with a sigh.

"I am," he said, "but thank you. I need to go. My head is killing me."

"Can you take something?"

"I can't keep anything down."

"Right. You said that already. Well . . . if you change your mind . . ."

"I'll be fine," he said.

"I love you, Jackson."

"I love you too," he said.

In the silence she hoped that he might acknowledge their conflicts earlier and perhaps apologize. She wanted him to ask about the kids. He did neither, but she had to concede that he was miserable and she couldn't expect him to be thinking of anything but that.

"I'll talk to you tomorrow," she said and ended the call. She said a prayer for him, certain it was about the hundredth one she'd uttered since he'd left.

The pedicure party took place that evening after supper. Chas enjoyed herself as much as she enjoyed seeing everyone else having such a good time. And the foot soak and massage were heavenly! After the women from the salon left, the ladies all changed into their pajamas and gathered in the parlor for a late-evening chat. They continued with their detailed sharing of life's challenges and blessings, and it was looking like it would take all week. Chas wondered how a group like this could *really* catch up in less than a week. With so much history and so many years since they'd had a serious gathering, they certainly had a lot to talk about. Even though there was a great deal of conversation that took place around the craft and scrapbooking tables, and also over meals, this formal evening gathering seemed to be where the serious topics came up.

Marianne talked about how she'd given some serious thought—and prayer—to the insights and advice her friends had given her and she was determined to make some positive changes in her family, even though she knew it would be difficult. They all promised to be there for her via e-mail and phone as much as she needed, to cheer her on and help her keep a positive outlook.

Mia talked about the great career she enjoyed, her time-consuming Church calling, and her little dogs that kept her company and loved her unconditionally. She admitted that it was hard for her to look around and see other women with husbands and children, but she also said something the others had never heard her say before. She had always wanted a marriage and family, and she wasn't ready to give up. She insisted that even when she became too old to have children, she could still hope for a good marriage. But from listening to her friends' comments and their individual challenges, she had recognized that she had much to be grateful for and she wouldn't want to trade anyone's life with her own.

She could see that simply getting married was no guarantee for a happily ever after. She could see that marriage was hard work in most cases, and sometimes it caused more grief than joy after all the best that a person could do. She vowed to focus more on all that was positive and fulfilling in her life, and to make peace with being single. And if she *did* find a good man in the remaining years of her life, they would all share in her joy. They joked about how there had to be a great guy out there who might tragically lose his wife to illness or accident, and he would need Mia to bless his life and help raise his children.

Jodi mentioned that she was going to continue to be prayerful and patient about her husband becoming active in the Church, but in the meantime she was also going to focus more on all that was positive in her life. He was a good husband and father, and she knew her situation could be worse.

Tammy talked about her family and her part-time job in a specialty shop. She too expressed how much she had to be grateful for in her life. She had a nice home, a good husband, and kids that didn't give her too much trouble. But it was still evident from hearing her talk that her life wasn't perfect either. Her husband had some fairly serious health problems that were difficult for both of them, and they were working together to prepare for the possibility that he might not always be able to be the principal breadwinner.

Luci talked about how she'd completely made peace with her divorce, even though it had been a long, hard struggle. She'd reached a point where she felt a healthy indifference toward her ex-husband. His dysfunctional behavior was something she had learned to handle with as little contact as possible, and she had forgiven him for all of the grief he had caused her. She felt concerned about his influence on the children, especially since they were with him a lot more than they were with her. But she had faith that over time her children would come to see the truth of the situation, and they would always know that she loved them unconditionally, and she would always be there for them. She also shared a tender, spiritual experience wherein the Spirit had let her know that the Lord would help watch over her children and bring them back to her. This was her greatest source of peace during difficult times.

Chas noticed as the women were talking that Kristy remained more quiet than the others. She was the only one who hadn't shared anything about what was going on in her life. Chas felt concerned, and she sensed that the others did as well, but no one wanted to be too pushy. Kristy had been invited to share a few times, but she had steered away from it by saying things like, "Oh, my life is boring," or "I'd much rather hear what so and so has to say." Chas didn't want to see Kristy leave here without unburdening herself of whatever problem it was that she carried. It was evident just from looking at her that the burden was great, but she seemed reluctant to share it.

When they all declared that bedtime had arrived and exhaustion was overtaking them, Rachelle made them promise to help her the following evening. She mentioned that she needed some sound advice before she had to go back and face the fallout from her husband's bad behavior. The ladies all promised to have that conversation. Some of them joked that they were keeping a list of all the things she should or shouldn't do, based on their experiences in their own lives or the lives of people they'd been close to.

"And we haven't heard from Kristy yet," Luci said as they were walking toward the stairs in a little crowd.

"You can't keep avoiding us, you know," Tammy added.

Kristy chuckled tensely and said, "Like I said, my life is boring." She gracefully changed the subject once again, and they all went to their rooms to get some sleep.

Lying in bed, Chas mentally walked through the events that had occurred between her and Jackson since news had come of Serena's death. Following their conversation earlier, she had felt some relief in having spoken her mind, and in believing that he hadn't done anything he shouldn't have. But now that the busyness of the day had relented and she had only the stillness of night surrounding her, the reality of how quickly a good relationship could go bad settled in. For all of his assurances, for all that she believed he would stay true to her, she could not lie to herself and believe that his state of mind wasn't a cause for concern. And she had to concede that he was a man with a dark past that she hardly understood. He'd kept things from her. His intentions might have been good in doing so, but in the present circumstances, how could she not be concerned about his secretive nature? Did she really know him as well as she thought she did? Could she really be sure that he wouldn't yet succumb to temptations from his old life while he was in the midst of it? She felt somewhat better to think that his being ill and stuck in a hotel room might be good in that respect. But that wasn't likely to last long. And then what?

While Chas prayed and stewed and pondered, she felt strongly that she needed to address this. She needed to be assertive and forthright, not sit back and wait for him to handle it on his own. In her mind she could almost see an image of him drowning, unsure of his position in dark and swirling waters. She thought of his infantile state in gospel matters in contrast to her years of membership where she had learned much about contending with opposition and holding on to her faith. He needed her! He needed her to be proactive with this problem! She still held to her need to stay in Montana, but she wasn't just going to passively wait and hope for something to change. She knew exactly what she needed to do, and as soon as a reasonable hour of morning arrived, she would do it.

* * * * *

The moment that Chas knew Dr. Callahan's receptionist would be answering the phone, she dialed the number. When there was no answer she recalled that it was Saturday. Wondering what to do, she was relieved to realize that the doctor's cell phone number was written next to his printed office number on the business card she had. She called and got his voice mail, but she left a message explaining that she was Jackson Leeds's wife, and that his present behavior was reasonable cause for concern. She explained that her husband was out of state and didn't actually require an appointment. Rather, Chas just wanted to speak to him when he had a few minutes so that she might be better able to help her husband.

Five minutes later Dr. Callahan called her back. He was kind and listened attentively as Chas gave him the brief version of what was going on. She felt deeply grateful to be able to speak to a man in his profession who had come to personally care about Jackson.

"Do you have any advice?" she asked. "Am I handling this right?"

"Your idea to handle it in a proactive way is what I would advise. I think you need to call him on his behavior and insist that he needs to face up to what's bothering him. Given his history, I think it could be easy for him to regress if he doesn't talk it out and work it through."

"What do you mean by . . . 'given his history?' Obviously I know what he's been through, but explain the connection."

"His childhood was a nightmare. The biggest result of that for most human beings is little to no self-esteem at the core. Other traumas piled on since then can reinforce the false belief that he has little to no value. From what you're telling me, I suspect he's caught in a black hole, so to speak, between two worlds, two separate lives. He's made some dramatic changes in his life in not so many years. And he experienced some dramatic events in the midst of those changes. I'm guessing that this death of a former love, combined with returning to the setting of his old life, has probably left him in some kind of emotional limbo. Maybe some level of his psyche just needs to catch up and be able to connect the old Jackson to the new one."

"So, how do I help him?"

"You can't control his feelings or even his behavior. But you can draw boundaries with your own expectations. Does that make sense?"

"Yes."

"Confront him. Stay calm, but be firm. Let him know you love him. Let him know how this is affecting you. The very act of your doing this will let him know that you *do* love him. It takes love and concern to confront something like this. If he's being drawn into a place where he once felt very comfortable, your passiveness is more likely to feed his belief that you might prefer he stay in that place."

That thought horrified Chas. Could it really be so bad that he could just want to remain in this depressed and dormant state? She asked the doctor a few more questions and took in his advice. She thanked him for his time, and he expressed how much he'd come to care for Jackson. Before he hung up, he said, "If I don't hear from you or him by the middle of the day, I'm going to call him."

Chas felt some assurance from this. She knew that if she couldn't get through to Jackson, surely Dr. Callahan could.

Before she dialed Jackson's number, Chas knelt and prayed yet again for her husband, that he would know of her love for him, and of God's love for him, and that he would come home to her where they could surely work out anything if they could just face it together.

* * * * *

Jackson finally felt like his stomach had stopped its boxing match about midnight. An hour later he attempted taking some Tylenol with just a sip of water and was relieved when it stayed down. A short while later he was able to sleep. He woke up in the night with a stomachache but no nausea. His head hurt again, but it had been more than four hours so he took Tylenol again and went back to sleep. When he woke again, the sun was barely peering through the crack between the draperies. He went to the bathroom and took some more Tylenol. He felt hungry, but his stomach still hurt and he didn't want to eat. He wished he was home in his bed, where Chas would bring him Jell-O or warm broth. Then he thought of facing her in light of his recent behavior, and a smoldering of a different kind rumbled in his stomach.

It felt like some kind of ESP when his phone rang and it was her, as if she'd known he was thinking about her. And from her tone of voice when she said hello, she seemed to know that his thoughts were mixed and confused.

"How are you feeling?" she asked with genuine concern, but not enough to disguise the same edge that had been there yesterday when she had appropriately expressed her anger.

"Much better than last night," he said. "I think if I lay low today I'll be fine."

"We need to talk," she said with a firmness he couldn't interpret as anything other than a determination to talk here and now, whether he wanted to or not.

He pointed out what he considered was obvious. "I don't have anything to say, Chas."

"Then you're going to have to answer my questions." He neither protested nor agreed, so she pressed forward. "You're still depressed?"

"I'm not feeling terribly perky," he said, wishing it hadn't sounded so sarcastic.

"Why? Is it because of Serena's death?" He didn't comment and she clarified, "You did a one-eighty after you heard she was gone, so I'm having to assume that this dramatic change in your behavior is because of Serena. I'm trying very hard not to resort to petty jealousy here, Jackson. But I have no idea what I'm dealing with. Learning that you spoke foreign languages when I hadn't known about that threw me off a little. Learning that you feel this strongly for a woman whose name I'd never heard is hard for me to swallow. If I'm wrong, I need to know. What's the deal, Jackson? I just need you to be straight up and tell me. Did you just put your feelings for Serena into some kind of cold storage, and now that you're facing them you realize you *still* have feelings for her? Tell me the truth. I can handle it. I might not like it, but I think I could handle just about anything if you would just talk to me."

Again there was silence—a volatile kind of silence that made Chas want to scream. His silence implied volumes. The nausea it induced made her wonder if she could catch what he had through the phone.

"Okay, listen," she said. "You don't have to talk to me about Serena if you don't want to, but that doesn't mean you have to stop talking to me about *everything.*"

It occurred to Chas that if Jackson was completely preoccupied with Serena, then he wouldn't be able to share what was on his mind and would avoid talking about her. The thought was unsettling at best. She hurried to get to the point. "Maybe you should call Dr. Callahan."

"I really don't think it's necessary to bother him with this."

"He's a shrink and you're depressed. It's not a difficult equation, Jackson." He didn't comment, and she added, "He knows *your* brain better than anyone else, maybe even better than *you* do. Why don't you just call him." She paused. "Lucky for us, he's on call today even though it's Saturday. He's available this afternoon from one to three Montana time."

"You talked to him?"

"I did. And before you go scolding me, try to step back and consider how all of this looks from my point of view. It's making me crazy, Jackson. Maybe it's *me* that needs the shrink. Either way, I'm your wife and I'm not going to let you go on this way. Fix this problem and come home to me. If you don't know how to fix it, get some help. And no matter what, remember that . . ." Her determination to remain forthright and unemotional faltered, and her voice cracked. "I love you, Jackson. There's nothing you could do or say that would make me stop loving you. *Nothing!* Do you hear me?"

"I hear you," he said. "I love you too, Chas. I really do."

"Then come home to me," she said. She hung up before he could dilute her words with more strained silence. She cried for a few minutes, said a prayer, took a deep breath, and put the matter into God's hands—and Dr. Callahan's—enough to have faith that all would be well. She couldn't do anything more for the moment, so she spent some time with her children, gave Polly the update, and had a late breakfast with her new friends.

CHAPTER ELEVEN

Jackson spent the day staring at the ceiling, considering all that Chas had said, and wondering why it just made him feel more like *not* going home. What was wrong with him? He called room service and found out he could get some chicken broth and Jell-O. He got that down and didn't have any adverse reactions, so a while later he ordered some plain rice and more chicken broth. A few minutes after one o'clock Montana time, his phone rang. He groaned but he resisted the urge to not answer.

"My wife told me to call you," Jackson said into the phone.

"If you had, it would have saved me from having to call *you*," Dr. Callahan said. "What's going on, Jackson?"

"Get straight to the point, Doctor," Jackson said with sarcasm.

"I've got too much invested in you and your mental health to lose you to some wrestling match between the past and the present."

"Is that what it is?" Jackson asked.

"I'm just going by what Chas told me, and apparently she doesn't know much. Why don't *you* tell me what's going on?"

"How long have you got?" Jackson asked facetiously, wanting desperately to avoid this conversation. But he knew this man would not relent on such matters.

"As long as it takes," he said. "I can clear the rest of the day with an e-mail right now. Why don't you start with telling me why this woman's death has upset you so much."

"If I knew, I'd love to tell you." Jackson sighed loudly. "You're not going to let me get out of this, are you."

"You *are* in a different state, Jackson. You could hang up on me and not answer when I call. But I think a part of you is relieved that I called. You know you can't go on like this, but you don't know what to do about it."

"You're doing that thing—that almost psychic thing."

"I just know you, and I have a little experience with people being depressed and confused, blah, blah, blah. So, talk to me." Jackson didn't know where to begin, and Callahan added, "Start by telling me why you don't want to talk to your wife about this."

"I feel like I've let her down in too many ways to count. I'm not really sure why I didn't tell her about a lot of things from my past, but I didn't. Now she knows I had a serious relationship with this woman. I hurt her. I know I did. But there are a lot of things she still doesn't know."

"Let's look at this one concept at a time. First of all, you let your wife down. Because you didn't *tell* her about past relationships, or because you *had* past relationships?"

"Both."

"How could you have let her down when you didn't even know her? Let's keep the issues in their proper category here. I can understand why the past and present are getting muddled for you, and maybe that's part of the problem. Let's start by separating the two. Explain to me why you believe that past relationships have let her down."

"Chas was married . . . years ago. That's the only intimate relationship she's ever had. For me, it was immensely different."

"Okay," he said. "You took very separate paths to end up together. You've changed. You're a better man. Has she ever expressed criticism toward you for choices you made before you met her?"

"No."

"Then where is this coming from?"

Jackson hesitated. "I guess that's the million-dollar question."

"Lucky for you," Callahan said lightly, "my rates aren't that steep."

This actually made Jackson chuckle. Then he sighed, and then he started to talk—to really talk. In the end Callahan told him he wasn't nearly as messed up as he felt. It felt good to talk it out with someone who would hold no bias or be emotionally involved. Elliott and

Shawn had both known Serena, and Chas hadn't known anything—
which was part of the problem. Callahan suggested that Jackson give
himself the opportunity to officially say good-bye to his old city, his
old life, his old loves. And then he should go home and make a fresh
start. It sounded a little too simplistic to Jackson, and he couldn't say
that he really felt any better at this point. But Callahan said to give it
time and not be so hard on himself.

"Feelings are feelings and we need to just work through them,"
he said. "But they don't get felt if you're trying to ignore them or hide
from them."

"Okay," Jackson said.

"How are you feeling . . . the headache, sick thing?"

"Better. I guess we'll see how the day goes."

"What was going on when it came on?"

"What do you mean?"

"Where were you? What were you doing?" Jackson thought about
it but didn't answer. Callahan added, "You don't think it's possible
that you could make yourself sick? Sick with regret? Guilt?"

As Jackson realized where the doctor was going with this, he said,
"I was at the Bureau office listening to them talk about things they
deal with in their work that I used to be able to deal with. But I felt
nauseous. I thought it was something I ate."

"Maybe it was. Maybe it was a combination. The brain and
emotions have a huge impact on physical health. The biggest trigger
for a migraine for many people is stress, or even the letdown after
stress. The funeral was over; you had nowhere to go and nothing to
do but grieve. You were distracted by a day with the guys, but you
weren't *really* distracted. It's just a theory, Jackson, and it doesn't really
matter in the big picture. Just . . . get yourself out of that hotel room
as soon as you feel up to it and make your visit have some meaning.
Don't hide from what you're feeling. Just feel it. And let your wife
know what you're doing. If she knows that your staying there a few
more days has some purpose, I think she'll be just fine."

"Okay, thank you."

Jackson hung up the phone and sat for a long while just
pondering the conversation and his shrink's advice. After he'd showered he decided that he could be up to a leisurely stroll around the

botanical garden. It was a place he'd gone to frequently when his minimal spare time had allowed. Perhaps more important to what Dr. Callahan had told him to accomplish, it was a place where he'd gone with Serena. In fact, he'd first seen many of the sights of the city with her. Prior to spending time with her, he just didn't get out much. But she had taught him how to look at the world around him and see things he had never seen before.

Jackson drove to his destination and knew he wouldn't be walking around very long. It was too cold. Before he got out of the car he called Chas. She answered the phone quickly and he felt a sense of how much she loved him simply by her eagerness to hear from him in spite of his behavior.

"How are you feeling?" she asked. He could hear the chatter of women in the background, but it faded as Chas obviously moved to a more quiet place to talk.

"The headache is more mild. My stomach has settled, although I haven't eaten anything but rice and broth, so we'll see."

"How are you otherwise?" she asked with caution.

"I survived my conversation with Callahan."

"You called him?"

"No, he called me."

"And . . ."

"His advice was to stop hiding from my feelings; he said I need to feel them in order to deal with them. He said I should take a little time while I'm here to officially say good-bye to my old life; he said I should be proactive instead of just sitting around, wallowing in grief."

Chas took that in with a deep breath. It made so much sense, and already she felt a little better—provided that Jackson was going to *heed* the doctor's advice.

"How do you feel about that?"

"I think he's right. Sometimes I hate the way he's so blasted right." There was a mild edge of humor in his voice that deepened Chas's hope that he was making progress.

"He's been a great blessing in our lives," she pointed out.

"Yes, he has. I won't dispute that." He paused and added more softly, "I'm glad you called him, and . . . I'm sorry I've been such a rat. I don't know why you put up with it."

"I *don't* put up with it. But as long as I know you're trying to deal with this, I can be awfully patient."

"Yes, you're very good at that." He sighed again. "Anyway, I'm going to give myself a few days, if that's okay. That'll give you time to have fun with the ladies, and I won't be intruding or distracting you."

"Okay," she said, "although . . . I would be happy to have you come home anytime you want or need to. We have our own home, remember? They won't get in our way."

"I know, but . . . I think this is best. Maybe the timing is good."

"Maybe," she said.

"How's that going, by the way?" he asked, sounding more sincerely interested instead of just diplomatic.

"It's going well," she said. "When you get back I'll tell you all about it."

"I'll look forward to it." He then restored Chas's hope even more deeply when he asked, "How are those beautiful children of ours?"

Chas couldn't disguise her tears. "They're great," she said. "Polly and Elliott are taking very good care of them. I see them regularly, but they're not seeming to miss either of us very much."

"That's probably good. A little deflating, but good. And how are the babysitters surviving?"

"They're doing very well, actually. I thought they might need more rescuing than this by now. I think Elliott's treating this like 'Child Care 101.' He figures if he can get through the week and get a good grade, he'll be ready to have his own children."

"There's some logic to that," Jackson said. "He'll be a lot better prepared than I was."

"You've always been a good father," she said. "You were a natural."

Jackson let out a dubious chuckle, then a tense silence fell between them, reminding Chas that things were still far from normal between them. "I should go," he said.

"Okay. You take care."

"You too," he said. "I love you, Chas. Don't give up on me."

"I never would," she said.

"I know," Jackson said, but he felt sure that if she knew the whole truth about the kind of man he'd *really* been before he met her, she might not feel the same way. If she knew how he was *really* feeling right now, he could easily imagine her reneging on a lot of things. And he wouldn't blame her.

"I love you too," she added, and he ended the call.

He sat there for a few minutes before he bundled up and got out of the car to face his memories and the impact they'd had on his life.

* * * * *

Chas felt indescribably better with some evidence that Jackson was at least making an effort to move beyond this. Knowing he was in contact with Dr. Callahan also helped ease her concerns. She still felt worried, and she couldn't think too hard about where his stroll down memory lane might lead him. But for now, she had to put the matter into the Lord's hands, knowing she had done all she could do for the moment. She said a prayer on Jackson's behalf, then noticed that snow was falling—big, beautiful flakes that were coming down in abundance. Chas went back into the formal dining room where the ladies were gathered. As usual the drapes were closed, mostly because no one ever thought to open them.

"Hey, everybody," Chas said, "come here; I want to show you something."

They all followed her eagerly to the parlor, where Chas knew the view was much better with several windows where they could look out. The draperies were already open, and the effect of walking into the room made them all catch their breath. Chas loved watching them gather around the windows like children, delighted with the beauty and wonder of the storm. Mia seemed the most excited. She'd moved to San Diego years ago and she didn't see snow nearly as much as the others. They all agreed that the inn was a lovely place to be during a snowstorm, especially since they had nowhere to go. The coziness and security of their gathering was enhanced by the mood of the weather.

It was twenty minutes before they returned to the dining room, but they opened the drapes before they went back to their projects. This room had become the central point of activity and conversation throughout the week, except for mealtimes and when they gathered in the parlor each evening. They were all thoroughly enjoying the slow progression of passing around photos and reminiscing over them; scanning, printing and copying them for preservation while they never ran out of things to talk about. The craft projects had been set up in another room, but little by little most of that stuff had been moved here so they could all be in the same room while they worked on various projects.

Chas was especially entertained by a conversation that began with Tammy saying to Luci, "Remember the time I drove through the car wash in February, then when I got off work my car doors were frozen shut?" She laughed. "I had to call you because you were the only person that I knew would come and help me."

"Yeah," Luci said, "and we're out there *freezing* while we're trying to thaw out the car doors with a hair dryer and an extension cord."

The women all laughed and Tammy added, "And it took us about an hour to figure out that all the water had run down to the *bottom* of the door before it had frozen."

For more than an hour they shared hilarious stories that all began with *remember when*. There were all the kinds of things that often weren't funny at the time, but now that years had passed, these incidents had become hysterical. Chas could think of a few such moments with Polly.

Chas was glad that the humorous antics of the conversation seemed to be over before she had to leave. She didn't want to miss anything fun. It was her turn to have a massage and she went to the designated room in the inn to meet her appointment. She'd heard the others raving about how wonderful it was, and even Polly had experienced the pleasure yesterday while Chas had taken over with the kids. Chas had never had a professional massage before, but once the experience began, she became accustomed to the concept of true relaxation, and she allowed herself the luxury of thoroughly enjoying it.

As the massage was winding down, Chas started to think about Kristy. By the time she was dressed, she felt strongly that she should make some effort to speak to her privately. She was glad that having messy massage hair, accentuated by aromatic oil, had become socially acceptable here at the inn. She didn't want to take the time to shower right now.

Chas found the ladies in the dining room, mostly focused on finishing up some craft projects. She noticed right away that Kristy wasn't among them; everyone else was there. Chas went to Kristy's room after checking the list in the office to make certain she knew *which* door to knock on. Kristy answered, putting on a bright face. But Chas recognized the signs of strain and an effort to conceal it. It took her a moment to realize that she hadn't really thought about what to say.

"Is everything okay?' she asked, opting for the straightforward approach.

"Oh, sure," Kristy said with a convincing smile.

Chas took a long moment to weigh how hard she should push. Feeling like she should just go for it, she said, "I'm sure it's none of my business, but . . . I've sensed ever since you arrived that you were struggling . . . holding back. I can only say that I'm standing at your door because I felt like I was supposed to be here. I don't know if you'd feel comfortable talking to me or not. I can only offer to listen, and I can promise that I won't repeat anything that you don't want repeated. I just . . ." The correlation between this moment and her husband's present situation gave her some added confidence. "I just believe that when people don't talk about their troubles, it can eat them up inside. You don't have to talk to me, but you should talk to someone. Whatever might be going on, you've got some wonderful friends here who love you. I just don't think you should go home without sharing your burden . . . whatever it may be."

Once Chas got that out, she realized that Kristy had tears running down her face. She wiped them away but more came. Chas held her breath, wondering if Kristy would open up or simply apologize and politely ask Chas to leave.

"Come in," she said. Kristy closed the door, and they both sat down, but not before Kristy grabbed the box of tissues from the bedside table. "You're very perceptive." She sniffled and dabbed at her eyes. "Do you think the others know?"

"I suspect . . . that they suspect." Chas chuckled tensely at her choice of words. "I think everyone is concerned, but no one wants to be too pushy."

"Things were pretty good until about a year ago," Kristy admitted, and the flow of tears increased. "When it all hit the fan, I nearly called each of them at different times, but . . . I couldn't even imagine admitting to the problem; I wasn't sure I could even say it out loud. After some time passed, it just became easier not to talk about it . . . at all."

"Do you think they would be judgmental?"

Kristy shrugged. "I think they would all be kind and supportive, but what they might say and what they might think could be very different."

"You've heard them talking very openly about a great many challenges. None of their lives is perfect."

Kristy became so upset she couldn't speak. Chas slid her chair closer and put an arm around her. She crumbled into heaving sobs and Chas wondered if it was true that she hadn't talked to *anyone* about it—*at all*. She had no idea what the problem was, but it had obviously taken a great toll on Kristy. Chas just let her cry. Once Kristy got some composure, she apologized and expressed embarrassment.

"There's no need for that," Chas insisted. "I'm glad you feel like you can be yourself with me. I meant what I said: I would never break your confidence unless you wanted me to. Sometimes it's easier to talk to someone who doesn't know you as well. You don't have all those years of history with me, and you don't ever have to see me or talk to me again if you don't want to. But I'm glad to be a listening ear."

Chas wondered if she was being too pushy. But her instincts were telling her she needed to get Kristy to talk about whatever was weighing so heavily on her. She could definitely say the feeling had urgency attached to it. Perhaps if she returned home without sharing this burden, the situation—or the way it was affecting her—would cause further problems. She waited through thoughtful silence, wondering if Kristy would politely avoid the topic. But perhaps Chas could at least convince her to talk to her friends. When Kristy still said nothing, Chas proposed that very option. "Maybe you *shouldn't* be talking to me. Maybe you should talk to your friends. They really *do* care. And I really don't think they would be judgmental, in their thoughts or their words. I just want to help, Kristy, but I feel like I'm just babbling. Tell me what I can do."

"My oldest son is almost sixteen," Kristy said. "I have three other children. He was always an unusual child, but as a mother I thought unusual was good. I encouraged him to stand up for his individuality, to think for himself, to not be concerned with what others thought. I also taught him that the most important thing was to know that he was okay with God, that as long as he did what was right and kept the commandments, his differences from other people were okay."

"That makes perfect sense," Chas said when there was a long pause.

"I know that a lot of kids hit those teen years and the hormones kick in and they become difficult. At first it was just some belligerence, trying to get out of his chores, stuff like that. Then he didn't want to go to church. We insisted that until he was an adult he needed to live by the family rules, and that included going to church. He started shutting himself in his room more and more, and he started hanging out with different friends."

Chas listened and waited to hear that her son had gotten into drugs or something equally horrible. She couldn't imagine how terrifying it would be to see your child doing such self-destructive things.

"He was fourteen when his acting out really escalated. His father didn't handle it well." She let out a bitter chuckle. "I love my husband very much, but when it comes to dealing with an angry teenager, he does *not* handle it well. He just fed our son's anger with his own. I tried to talk to him. I tried to get him to go to some parenting classes with me, some counseling to help us know how to deal with this. He refused and kept saying the problem was not *ours.*"

Kristy took a deep breath and looked directly at Chas. "About a year ago we were having family home evening, and we always ask if anyone has anything they'd like to share with the family. That's when our son announced that he was . . . gay."

Chas managed to keep her gasp silent, and thankfully Kristy couldn't hear her inner turmoil. Kristy shook her head and squeezed her eyes shut. Chas wondered if this was the first time she'd said it out loud.

"I was too shocked to speak, but his father just started yelling at him. The younger children asked their brother what that meant and . . . he told them." Kristy shook her head again. "At family home evening." She wiped more tears. "Then my husband *really* got furious. I finally told him that he needed to be quiet and listen. Our son then informed us that he was tired of pretending to be something he wasn't, and he wasn't going to hide it any longer."

Chas noticed that Kristy hadn't used her son's name. She wondered if that was some kind of attempt to protect his privacy. Chas took her hand and encouraged her to go on.

"He declared that he was *not* going to go to church when God couldn't accept him for being who he was born to be. Later I learned that my husband was actually relieved that he wouldn't be going to church. He was afraid people might find out; he was embarrassed more than anything. All along, that's been the biggest difference in how we've handled this. I've been concerned about my son's well-being, wondering how I could help him. I've wanted him to know that no matter what, I love him—unconditionally—and I always will. But his father just . . . wants to write him off, makes it clear by his words and his actions that he's given up on him. My son doesn't even get *conditional* love from his father; he gets no love at all."

Kristy blew her nose, tossed a wad of tissues into a wastebasket, and pulled some more out of the box. "This whole issue with my son is a nightmare. I *never* imagined this as one of the possible challenges I could have with a child. It breaks my heart and it makes me sick. But I only have so much control, and . . . well . . . actually I have *no* control; not over that. I can give him consequences if he doesn't do his chores or gets bad grades. But I can't keep him from living this way. He's been bold about telling us he's sexually active, and he assures us that he's taking precautions to avoid getting any horrible diseases." Kristy sobbed. "I still can't believe it's real." She sobbed again. "I can't believe I'm telling you this."

"You need to tell *someone*," Chas said gently. "Have you told anyone else?"

Kristy shook her head. "I think some people suspect, but since our son doesn't hang out with the children of people we know, I don't think it's fully surfaced yet. But it will. I confess that the thought of people knowing is very difficult. I wonder what they'll think of my son; I don't want people to think he's a bad kid. And in all honesty I wonder if people will think I'm a bad mother; I wonder if they'll think I did something to cause this. I can honestly say that I did my best to raise him well. He was never abused. There's no logical reason for this." She chuckled and blew her nose. "Ironically, he's done better with his chores and his grades since he declared himself. It's my hope that eventually he'll be able to find his way around this. But whether he does or not, he needs to know that his mother loves him."

"I agree. I think a mother's love is a powerful force."

"My son understands that I love him even if I don't agree with the way he's living. But his father boldly declares his disapproval and disgust every time they cross paths. He's angry with me for being too easy on him. The reality is that our son's problem is destroying our marriage, and it's causing a great deal of confusion and contention among the other children. I've tried to help the others understand the right and wrong of the situation. I've taught them that Jesus would want us to love all people even if we don't like the things they do. Two of them seem to get it. The other is siding with his father in a way that's just not right. It's like my husband encourages one son to yell at and demean the other, just so he can have someone on his side."

"That is just horrible!" Chas said. "I can't imagine how you've even been functioning."

"I haven't," Kristy said. "I wasn't going to come here. I was going to think of some kind of excuse. Then I realized that if I didn't get out of that house I was going to really lose it. But I was determined to keep the problems to myself. I'm sure you're right about needing to share them. You're very kind to listen. I just don't know if the others really need to know."

"I'll respect your wishes, of course. But I disagree. I think they *do* need to know. This problem isn't going to solve itself quickly or easily, and you're going to need the support and strength of these women who care so much about you. They don't live in your ward or neighborhood. They're not personally affected by it. They can be objective. I've observed their different strengths, different insights. With six friends like that, you should always have at least *one* available to talk to during a time of crisis."

Kristy squeezed Chas's hand. "Seven friends, I think."

Chas smiled. "I would consider it an honor to be your friend, Kristy, and I hope you *will* keep in touch. I don't know that I can do anything to help, but I can always listen."

Kristy nodded and blew her nose again.

"May I ask . . ." Chas said, "how things are right now? When you left, weren't you worried about how your husband and son might behave in your absence?"

Kristy struggled for composure again. "Normally I would have, but our son isn't at home right now. He's . . ." Again she became too upset to speak, and Chas just waited patiently. "He's in the hospital; the psych ward. He . . . he slit his wrists."

"Good heavens!" Chas said. "Is he going to be okay?"

"Physically, yes. But he's a very confused young man. This happened after I'd made the decision to come here, and I considered backing out. But he reached a point where he was stable and I knew he would be there for a while. I've been able to call him every day. He's not saying much. I just . . . tell him I love him and that everything will be okay. He says that he knows I love him, but he's not so sure about the other. And I don't know what to say."

"I just can't imagine how hard this must be for you!" Chas could certainly understand now why Kristy was so thin, but she didn't comment.

Kristy's ongoing emotion certainly made a lot of sense, but now that she had apparently finished her story, Chas didn't know what to say. She searched inside herself for something to say that would be compassionate and wise.

"Kristy," she said gently, "no one can promise that your son will ever change his habits or his thinking in this life. I'm sure such things fall into the category of challenges that will never make sense in mortality. But those are the very things that make us realize the miracle of the Atonement. I believe that your son will have a chance in the next life to understand all of this and heal. I believe there is *always* reason for hope, Kristy, even if we can't logically see any reason for it in the here and now."

This made Kristy cry harder, but there was a little glimmer of something hopeful in her eyes. Again Chas wrapped an arm around her and let her get it out.

They were both startled by a knock at the door, and Jodi called, "Are you in there?"

"Yes," Kristy called back.

"You're missing the fun," Jodi said, but she didn't say anything about Chas; she likely assumed she'd slipped out to be with her kids, as she did occasionally.

"I know. I just . . . have a headache. I'll take something and be down in a while."

"Okay, well . . . let us know if you need anything."

"I will. Thank you," Kristy said, and Jodi left. Kristy walked into the bathroom. "At least I wasn't lying about the headache."

"All that crying will do it," Chas said.

Kristy swallowed some pills and came back to her chair. "You really think I should tell them?"

"I do," Chas said.

Kristy sighed deeply. "I need to think about it. Not tonight, though. Rachelle needs her time. She's going through some pretty tough things herself."

"Yes, she is. But so are you, and you are no less loved by these women than she is."

"I'll think about it," Kristy said. "Thanks for listening . . . and for caring. It feels like you *did* go to sixth grade with us."

"I wish I would have," Chas said. "When I lost my husband and baby, I could have used friends like you."

"What did you say?" Kristy asked, astonished.

Chas felt a little astonished herself. "I'm sorry. I just assumed that Jodi would have said something. It's been many years. I lost my first husband in a military training accident, and soon afterward our baby was born with a heart defect and she died."

"That's dreadful!" Kristy said.

"Yes, it was. And the years after that were very lonely. But now I've found a good man and we have two beautiful children. Life is good." Chas felt a little stab of heartache and concern as she thought of her husband, knowing that life wasn't as good as it had been last week. She could only hope and pray that it would get better—or at least back to normal. It felt appropriate to add, "Certainly not perfect, mind you, but good."

"You've been very kind," Kristy said. "I think I'll lie down for a while. I'll see you later."

"Okay," Chas said, and they shared a hug.

"Thank you . . . really. I think I needed somebody to prod it out of me. I'm glad to know I can trust you."

She said it in a way that seemed to be a reminder to Chas that she'd promised to keep her confidence. Chas assured her, "I'll not breathe a word, I promise."

Chas wandered outside for a few minutes and into the private entrance of her home while she pondered the things Kristy had shared with her. It was impossible for her to comprehend such heartache. For all the struggles in her own life, she didn't have to look far to see how much worse it could be. Even among this group of women, there was such a diversity and depth of trials. And Chas wouldn't trade places with any one of them. She said a little prayer that Kristy and her family would be okay, then she spent some time with her children, praying that their lives would be stable and praiseworthy.

CHAPTER TWELVE

Supper with the ladies was enjoyable, as always. Afterward they all seemed eager to gather for the usual evening chat session. They were barely seated when Rachelle said, "Okay, I feel the days passing and I'm terrified to go back. I really don't know how to handle this. I need some feedback . . . some advice. I need my friends; you can't let me down now."

"As if we would," Tammy said.

Mia said, "Tell us what concerns you most."

"I just . . . don't know how to face him. He's been staying somewhere else. I don't know if that means he's staying with another woman or not. Very little has happened, actually, but I know it has to be faced. He's so back and forth with his attitude that it's hard for me to know how I should handle it."

"Then you need to be prepared for every possibility," Luci said.

"What do you think he's most likely to do?" Marianne asked.

"I honestly don't know. Obviously I can't read him or predict his behavior nearly as well as I thought I could. I'm almost afraid that he'll do nothing, that he'll just be content with this . . . passive separation. No divorce means no child support or alimony, no attorneys, no hassles."

"But you can't live like that," Jodi said. "The very principle is intolerable!"

"I agree," Rachelle said. "But if that's what he's thinking, then it's up to *me* to file for divorce, and once that happens the battle will begin. It's the battle that scares me. Now that I realize I don't know him well at all, I'm afraid he could get ruthless in this."

"So, you've got to be ruthless too," Luci said. "I'm not saying you should be vindictive or vengeful. You simply need to be prepared to defend yourself." She leaned more toward Rachelle, and Chas realized that Luci's advice would be the most profound of any of the women in the room. She's the one who had been through an ugly divorce and had survived it. "I want to share something with you that made a huge difference when I was at the point of realizing divorce might be the only option. I'd tried everything. I felt like a failure. I'd always believed that marriage was supposed to be forever, but my husband wasn't holding up his end of the bargain. I simply had no choice. I prayed and prayed to be able to make peace with it, to absolutely know I was doing the right thing. While I was doing my daily scripture study, I came across the part in Nephi when the Lord commands him to take his people and separate from the Lamanites. I knew that the principle applied to me. Nephi and his people could not thrive and remain safe as long as they stayed with Laman and his people. And one of the first things that Nephi does following the separation is to make swords so that the people could defend themselves if the Lamanites attacked." She put her hand over Rachelle's. "*You* need to do what is best for the safety and well-being of yourself and your children. You're a righteous woman with a righteous need. You also need to prepare in every possible way to protect yourself, your home, your family from whatever attack might be thrown at you from an angry man who wants to just cover his own guilt and maintain his lifestyle."

Rachelle nodded and thought about it before she said, "But . . . what if he wants to work it out? What if he's sorry, and . . ."

"Would you forgive him and take him back if he was?"

"It would be hard, but I think I could. He would have to earn my trust, and . . . it would take time, but . . . I want to keep my family together if there's any possible way."

"Rachelle," Luci said gently, "it would be wonderful if he truly wanted to be forgiven and put his family back together. We all know you would never make the decision to divorce him unless you knew it was the Lord's will. But the Lord expects you to use your brain. You're an intelligent woman. Now . . . as hard as it is, I want you to really, truly, honestly consider this. Do you believe he *wants* to give up his other life, his habits, just to make you happy? He's lived this kind of life for as long as you've known him. What kind of willpower do you think it would take for a man to change that dramatically?"

Rachelle started to cry. It was evident that she knew the answer to those questions, and they were heartbreaking. Luci went on. "I suspect he might *tell* you he wants to work it out, so he can preserve appearances, or whatever it is that's important to him. If he does that, you tell him you need more than words, you need him to demonstrate that he wants to work it out. A man who is trying to win over a woman will do *anything* to make her happy. If that's not what you're seeing, then he's bluffing. Bottom line, you need to prepare yourself for both options. You need to consider what it would take for you to allow him to come back. Make a list so you know exactly what's important to you and what isn't. Beyond that, you need to take advantage of that attorney and be armed and ready to protect yourself. *Not* to be aggressive or obnoxious, but to do what it takes to protect you and your children. Does that make sense?"

"It does," Rachelle said. "It makes a lot of sense." But she looked even more distressed than when the conversation had begun. "I'm worried about facing him. It sounds so easy to say, 'I should tell him this,' and 'I need to expect that,' but the reality of actually standing up to him like that is terrifying."

"That's why you need to practice," Luci said and stood up, urging Rachelle to do the same. "You be Adolf and I'll be you."

"Adolf?"

"His name from now on for as long as he's not perfectly humble and penitent." The ladies laughed, but Luci was quite serious when she said, "I had to vent and cry to you guys so much when I was going through my divorce that I had to come up with a different name for mister-ex so my kids wouldn't hear me talking badly about their father."

"Oh, that's right," Jodi said. "You called him Fidel."

They all laughed harder and Mia said, "Evil dictators. That's clever."

"Well," Luci clarified, "it's not some attempt to be mean, but for me it helped distinguish between the good and bad traits of this man I had chosen to be the father of my children. It might be silly, but it worked for me."

"Okay," Rachelle said. "But why do I have to be Adolf?"

"Because you know him well enough to make a fair guess on how he's going to react. And I'm going to illustrate how a woman *should* handle this when she's tough and firm and doesn't allow her emotions to rule what she says."

"Okay, I'm ready," Rachelle said, folding her arms stiffly and scrunching up her neck.

The others laughed. Marianne said, "We need popcorn."

Luci dramatically pushed her hair away from her face, which evoked another chuckle before she got serious and said to Rachelle, "I realize I have no control over your choices or how you live your life, but I will not allow you to punish me simply because I'm the woman who's put up with it all these years."

"Hey, that was good!" Rachelle said.

"You're supposed to be Adolf," Luci said.

"Oh, right." She cleared her throat very deeply to sound more like a man. "You can't just throw me out of my own house and expect me to be happy about it."

"This is a home, a family dwelling. Your choices imply that you have no interest in being a part of this family. We've had family values established from the beginning. If you're not going to live by those, you're not welcome."

They went back and forth for nearly an hour with several scenarios. After Rachelle got the hang of it, they traded places. Luci did great at throwing out the lines an arrogant man might use in wanting to defend his wicked lifestyle. And Rachelle quickly improved on handling him. Sometimes the ladies watching applauded, sometimes they laughed. Chas noticed that Kristy didn't say much, but she wondered if she might be learning something in regard to her own challenges with her husband. She seemed a little more relaxed than she had previously, and Chas hoped their conversation had helped.

Chas felt her phone vibrate in her pocket and excused herself, relieved and grateful to have her husband call. He didn't have a lot to say, but he said it had been a better day and he would keep in touch. He asked about the kids and told her he loved her. Warmed by evidence of some progress, she returned to the parlor.

A while later they finally finished the role-playing practice with Luci saying, "And don't forget the broken record."

Rachelle said, "If you're going to talk to me like that, you can work it out with my attorney."

"That's right," Luci said.

Marianne imitated a scratched record and said, "Talk to my attorney, talk to my attorney, talk to my attorney."

They all laughed, then Chas suggested some late-night ice cream might be in order. While they were gathered in the dining room eating it, Rachelle admitted that she *did* feel stronger and better able to face whatever lay ahead. And she promised to keep everyone updated, as long as they promised to help get her through it. They all agreed wholeheartedly and unanimously.

It was nearly midnight before they all split up to go to their rooms and get some rest. Chas fell asleep with her thoughts mostly on Jackson, but they were intermixed with the tragedies going on in Rachelle's life, and also in Kristy's life. She was grateful beyond words to know that she could trust her husband, and also to know that if or when their children became old enough to assert themselves in challenging ways, Jackson would never treat them as badly as Kristy's husband had treated their son. She prayed that their children's problems would never venture into such difficult areas, but if they did, she knew her husband would stand by her in offering unconditional love, appropriately balanced with firmly upholding their standards.

Chas finally slept, but in a restless way with an awareness of drifting in and out of sleep. When she realized that Jackson was there beside her, she wondered how he had known which room to find her in. But she wrapped him in her arms and greeted him with a long, sweet kiss.

"Oh, I missed you!" she murmured and kissed him again, over and over.

"I missed you too," he whispered and held her close. "Chas," he said close to her ear, "there's something I have to tell you. It's not easy to say, but . . . I can't lie to you." She took the words in with a pounding heart and tried to ease farther away, but he was holding her too tightly. "I don't know how it happened. I was depressed and alone. She was just . . . there. One thing led to another, and . . . I'm so sorry, Chas. I never meant to hurt you—especially not like this."

Chas struggled to draw in breath, and when she did she started screaming at him, not caring who might overhear. She pushed him away and slapped him hard, then she came awake abruptly to find herself alone in the dark. It took her a long moment to accept that she'd only been dreaming, and the relief would have made her faint if she hadn't already been lying down. She knew in her heart that Jackson would never do that, he would never cheat on her under any circumstances. But hadn't Rachelle said that she'd believed the same about her own husband? Chas had to wonder if she was in some level of denial. Did she know Jackson as well as she thought she did? Obviously there was a great deal she didn't know about him! He *did* have a secretive nature about some things. And he had lived a worldly life for most of his life. Could depression entice him to do something that the Jackson she thought she knew would have never done?

Chas worked herself into such a frenzy that she had to get out of bed and pace the room. When she realized what she was doing, she forced herself to her knees beside the bed and prayed for peace and comfort and discernment until she finally relaxed and began to get sleepy. She crawled back into bed, certain that she *did* know Jackson, and that he would never hurt her that way. He just wouldn't! Thoroughly convinced of this, she fell asleep.

* * * * *

Jackson was awake early, having slept better than he had since he'd learned of Serena's death. He went out for an early-morning run that felt good to him in spite of the cold. He returned to his room to take a shower, focusing on the agenda he had planned for the next couple of days. He was going to visit some museums and historical sights; a couple that he'd gone to with Serena, and some he'd always wanted to see but never had. Since he intended to see them in that order, he was hoping that his memories of Serena could be replaced with new memories of this city that had been his home. And then he could return to his *real* home—the only place that had ever *really* felt like home to him.

Jackson was leaving his room when his phone rang. Assuming it would be Chas, he didn't look at the caller ID, then he heard a woman's voice that he didn't recognize.

"Hi, it's Lisa," she said. While he was trying to remember if he knew a Lisa, she added, "Serena's friend. We met at the funeral."

"Of course," Jackson said. Recalling the trouble he'd gotten into for talking to her in a bar, he was determined to keep this short. "Did you call those missionaries yet?"

"Not yet," she said. "I haven't gone home yet. I'm still in Norfolk. Are you still in the city?"

Jackson steeled himself to refuse to meet her anywhere for any reason. But he couldn't lie to her. "Yeah, I'm still here."

"I'm helping Serena's mother go through her things," she said, and Jackson stopped walking. "We've found some things that you should have."

"Um . . . I'm sure I took everything with me that mattered. Just . . . throw them away, or—"

"Listen," she said more quietly, "memories can be difficult when someone you cared about is gone, but her mother really thinks you should have these things. I think you left an impression on her. Just . . . take them . . . for her sake. If you want them thrown away, *you* can do it."

"Okay," he said. "Fair enough."

"Would you be able to come to Serena's apartment?"

"No," he said without even needing to think about it. Even if he could be assured that Lisa wouldn't be there alone, he couldn't get that close to his memories.

"Okay," she said as if she understood. "Then where can I meet you . . . just for a minute? It's just a shoe box with a few things."

Jackson agreed to meet her at a coffee shop he'd once haunted regularly that was within walking distance from Serena's place, which would make it easy for her. He drove straight there, imagining himself throwing the shoe box into the garbage, unopened. Lisa wasn't there when he arrived, so he bought a hot chocolate and a croissant and sat down to wait. Only then did he realize it was Sunday. Until he'd met Chas, Sunday had been just another day. It was one more reason to feel disoriented in comparing the old life to the new one, but he didn't bother pondering why he made a split-second decision to go ahead with his plans as opposed to doing the right thing and finding an LDS meetinghouse where he could attend church.

Jackson was only there a few minutes before Lisa came in, looked around, and saw him. He stood up as she approached, holding a box that didn't look at all like it had ever held shoes. It was nearly the same in size and shape, but it was printed with a dark blue paisley design, clearly made for holding keepsakes.

"Here you go," she said, passing it to him.

"Thank you," he said. "And . . . tell Serena's mother thank you for me."

"I'll do that," she said. For a moment there was an expectancy in her, as if she hoped he would invite her to join him. It would have been the polite thing to do, but Jackson didn't.

"I'm sure your help with Serena's things is very much appreciated," he said, moving toward the door. "That must be difficult for you to face."

"I'm glad to help her. It makes me feel like I'm doing something for Serena. Maybe it makes up a little for what I should have done for her before she died."

"I'm sure she understands," Jackson said.

Lisa smiled. "Maybe she does."

Jackson made a gracious exit and returned to his car. Holding the box in his hands, he was reminded of the box his sister had given him following their mother's death. It too had been filled with keepsakes. But his mother had put the things into the box before she'd died. Jackson felt then as he did now, a fear that opening the box would unleash some kind of monster. At a much later date he had finally explored the contents of the box his mother had left for him. It had been a healing experience, but only because he'd been ready. Right now he did *not* feel ready to open this one, and the idea of throwing it away came back to him, holding some appeal. It seemed a good metaphor to putting the past behind him. But out of respect for Serena he couldn't do that. If he *did* throw it away, he first needed to look at what was inside and know what he was getting rid of. That too struck him as a metaphor. Feeling suddenly chilled, he set the box in the passenger seat and started the car, determined to face his memories and move beyond them.

* * * * *

Chas awoke to a familiar sound, then she realized that it didn't mesh with knowing her husband was in Virginia. She went to the window and looked down to the parking lot of the inn to see Elliott on the ATV they owned; he was moving snow with the blade attached to the front of the machine.

"Oh, bless him!" she muttered, noting that the storm had ceased and the sky was clear. But the snow that had come down in the night was deep and heavy. By the time she showered and got downstairs, she met him as he was coming in the back door to put the key to the ATV away.

"You're a saint," she said, and he chuckled.

"Jackson asked me if I'd do snow duty if it stormed. It was no problem. Since it's Sunday, I assume you ladies will be going to church."

"Yes, we will," Chas said.

"Well, the snow is cleared and your vehicles have been cleaned off, so you're set."

"I'm going to have to give you a raise," she said. "Oh, wait!" She laughed. "You don't get paid."

"I owe you both," he said with a wink and took off his boots before he walked through the inn to get to the house. Chas followed to check on her kids. She spent a little while with them, then returned to the inn to share a quick breakfast with the ladies.

Right after they'd eaten, Chas asked Kristy privately if she'd made a decision about sharing her current struggles with her friends. Tonight was the last night the ladies would be staying at the inn. Time was running out.

"I do think they should know," Kristy said, and Chas felt relieved. "But I don't want to tell them." She put her hands on Chas's shoulders. "Will you do it for me?"

"What?"

"I'll be there; I just . . . don't want to say it. If you just get the momentum going for me, I think I can do it, but . . . would you do that for me?"

Chas took a deep breath. "If it will help, I'll do my best."

"Thank you," she said and hugged Chas.

A short while later the ladies all piled into the two SUVs for the short drive to the church building. Sitting together through all of the meetings was a warm and tender experience in itself. And Chas and Jodi enjoyed introducing their guests in Relief Society.

They returned to the inn and worked together to prepare a simple dinner. While they were eating, someone brought up the fact that they hadn't yet heard what was going on in Kristy's life, and they were looking forward to having her on the agenda that evening. Chas noticed that Kristy just smiled and didn't seem terribly concerned. Perhaps Chas being here meant something after all. Maybe Kristy had really needed her. If she could make a difference in this sweet woman's life, then her being here was worth it. She hoped that she still felt the same way when all was said and done with Jackson's current struggles. She would just be so glad when he came home to her.

* * * * *

Jackson returned to his hotel room, feeling like the day had been worthwhile. He was tired, but he'd seen some great sights while he'd been contending with his memories. He had gone back to places he'd visited with Serena, and he'd done his best to do as Callahan had suggested, to face the feelings and say good-bye. Tomorrow would be dedicated to going to new places, places that had no connection to her.

He tossed the box onto the top of the dresser and got ready for bed since it was already nearing that time and he was getting sleepy. While he was brushing his teeth, his mind went to that box as if it had been a command. He sat on the edge of the bed, staring at the box for several minutes, not sleepy anymore. He finally took a deep breath and opened it, thinking that if he knew what was in it, he wouldn't be haunted by throwing it away. He was startled to see a piece of notepaper on the top, on which was written, *For Jackson*—in Serena's handwriting. There was a separate note she'd also written that said, *Mom, When you're going through my things and you come across this box, I'd like you to get it to Jackson Leeds, if you can find him. Someone at the Bureau might know where he's living and you can ship it. Thanks, S.*

It took Jackson several minutes to digest the idea that these were not things Serena's mother had thought he should have. Serena herself had wanted him to have whatever was in here. He wondered how it might have felt to get the box in the mail, and how much worse it might have been if he'd not even heard of her death. He hadn't known she was sick, but at least he'd heard about her death in time to attend the funeral. He finally drew courage enough to look beneath the notes. He found photos of himself that she'd taken, and some photos of them together; one of those was in a frame. Looking at them felt strange and surreal, but somehow comforting as well. He found some ticket stubs from events they'd attended together, and some cards he had given to her. He indulged in some nostalgia while he examined each piece, then he moved on to a padded envelope. He picked it up to see that she'd written something on the outside.

Jackson, I've heard that you have children now. I thought you might get some good out of this. S.

Jackson opened the envelope, feeling a little nervous. He pulled out a white baby shirt, size twelve months. The old him would have never cared to notice the size of baby clothing. Unfolding the shirt, he could see that on the front, printed in dark blue it said, *FBI,* and underneath it in smaller letters, *Funny Babies, Inc.* He chuckled. When he'd been at the Bureau, they were often joking about other things that FBI could stand for, but this was one of the best. It seemed an odd thing for Serena to pass on to him, but it was easy to imagine his little Isabelle wearing it—only if he was able to come to terms with the irony. He stuffed the shirt back into the padded envelope and set it aside, catching his breath to see that the only thing left in the box was a white envelope with his name written on the outside. A letter? He'd longed to have one last conversation with Serena for the sake of closure. Apparently she'd found a way to speak her piece, but he felt sure that reading whatever she had to say would only make him feel more frustrated at not being able to express his own regrets.

He didn't want to read it. But he knew he'd never be able to sleep until he did. There was no point in going to bed and getting up again in a couple of hours to do what he could do right now. He picked up the envelope and turned it over in his hands a few times before he finally broke the seal and pulled out two sheets of elegant, high-quality paper, folded together. They were both filled with her handwriting. He felt nervous and unsteady. For a moment he wished that Chas was sitting here beside him, then he decided that would only make it more difficult. He took a deep breath and began to read.

Dear Jackson, If you're reading this then you must know I'm dead. I don't know if you've thought about me in the years since we parted, but I've thought about you. That doesn't mean I've been pining for you, so don't get all egotistical on me. I've just wondered how you were doing, and if the gossip I'd heard at the Bureau was really true. I hope it is. It's nice to think of you living a quiet life with a wife and kids. Ironically, when I found out I was going to die, I finally really made peace with the way things ended between us. I'm glad to know that you have someone, that you're happy, and that you're not going to be faced with losing someone you love. I genuinely hope that you are doing well, and I hope you're getting this box in the mail, and that you didn't waste any time or effort to come to my funeral. I'm certain it will be tedious, and I won't be there.

I've heard that dying people feel a need to unburden themselves, deathbed confessions and all that. I guess that's at least part of my purpose in writing this letter. It certainly would have been fine if you never knew what had happened, but since I was so good at keeping it a secret, no one knew but me. It doesn't seem right for me to go into the ground and take such a secret with me, so here goes. I was pregnant when you left.

Jackson lost his breath and couldn't get it back. He had to put his head between his knees and force himself to breathe to avoid hyperventilating. His memories of their parting were difficult at best. He'd regretted his behavior, regretted the way he'd handled it. To think that she was pregnant made him *sick*. The *true* picture, the *big* picture, rushed into his head. Random information and incidents all came together and made sense. And he felt like such a jerk. He felt more like a fool and an idiot than he'd ever felt in his life. Then his mind darted from the past to the present like a bullet train arriving at a destination with a screeching halt. Did this mean he had a child? Would she have really kept something like that from him? He recalled passing by her at the office on a regular basis, how they would dart their eyes away and not even acknowledge each other, like a couple of high school kids who weren't going steady anymore. Had she been wearing baggy clothes? Had she taken a lengthy vacation that he'd missed? Had she given birth to his baby and put it up for adoption? Or had she kept it and somehow managed to keep working and keep anyone from knowing? He could imagine others at the office knowing and not telling him; they would just call him a selfish jerk behind his back. But he had just read that no one knew but her. He had to wonder for a moment if she would have gotten an abortion, but he knew she wouldn't have. She'd been very outspoken about her pro-life views. She'd had a good friend who'd been adopted and she had strong feelings about giving every life a chance, even if it wasn't with the birth parents.

It took Jackson several minutes to accept the possibility that he had a child in this world that he'd not known about. He couldn't even imagine how to digest such a revelation. He didn't even know how to feel. His first reaction was anger toward Serena. He couldn't believe that she could *not* tell him something like this. After another few minutes, he realized he wasn't going to know the outcome until he finished reading the letter.

You're probably in shock right now, she wrote. "You think?" Jackson muttered back to the letter. *And you're probably angry with me for not telling you.* "So perceptive," he snapped with sarcasm; he felt like he was losing his mind. *You weren't terribly easy to talk to at the time. I assumed that eventually you would just figure it out and ask. I think a part of me believed a man shouldn't walk out of a woman's life after sharing what we'd shared without at least wondering if that was a possibility.*

Jackson had to stop reading again. His regrets were becoming insurmountable. He couldn't be angry with her and not acknowledge that he was angry with himself. She was right. He should have wondered, he should have noticed, he should have at least been kind enough to keep speaking to her after the breakup. He'd been so juvenile about the whole thing. He'd learned in recent years that every choice has a consequence, and he'd regretted many of the choices of his past. But he never would have imagined that such a consequence had been lurking in unknown closets.

I managed to keep it hidden rather well. No one figured it out. Not even my closest friends. I kept hoping that you would come back, that you would at least want to be friends again. I wouldn't have expected you to marry me, or even to take any kind of responsibility. I just wanted you to know, but I didn't know how to tell you, and the more time that passed, the easier it became to not say anything.

Jackson heard echoes of his own issues with not telling Chas things about his life and felt some empathy—if not hypocrisy—when he considered how angry he felt with Serena. He wondered if he had truly led her to believe that he wouldn't *want* to take any responsibility. Regardless of all the ridiculous aspects of their relationship, he never would have left her to be solely responsible for *his* child.

I had just made up my mind that I needed to tell you when the miscarriage happened.

Jackson exhaled sharply and again found it difficult to breathe for an entirely different reason. These minutes of wondering if he had an illegitimate child had been torturous. He wondered if she'd wanted him to sweat it out, just a little. He hung his head and willed his heart rate to return to normal, then he forged ahead, needing to have this experience come to an end.

I'd like to say that it wasn't a big deal, but I grieved over the loss of that baby for weeks. I think a piece of me died with that baby, or maybe it died when you left, but the baby had given me hope that we had something to build on. When I lost the baby, I realized that we never could have made it work. The reason I didn't tell you initially was the same reason I knew it couldn't have lasted. I didn't want you to stay because you felt obligated or duty bound. I wanted you to stay because you loved me. I think you did, or maybe I'd just like to think you did. You never said it, but I'd like to believe that you felt it.

Looking back, I know that I changed when I realized I was pregnant. My attitude shifted, and I've wondered since if that's what made you leave. I know you had commitment issues, even though you didn't let me into your life or your heart enough for me to understand why. Maybe you sensed my homing instinct kicking in and you felt stifled or threatened. I don't know for certain why you left me, and it really doesn't matter anymore. I want you to know that my broken heart healed a long time ago. I was genuinely pleased to hear you'd found someone. I saw her when Veese and Ekert brought her to the Bureau and took her to your office. I have nothing but admiration for her. My hat is off to the woman who could get inside your heart.

I wish you every happiness, and I would plead with you to not hold on to any grief over me or what happened between us. I had a good life, and now I'm ready to let it go, although there is a little piece of you in my heart that will go with me to the grave. Serena.

Jackson hadn't shed a tear since the news of Serena's death, but he did then. He couldn't be sure if his tears were for her life being cut short, or for the sorrow she'd experienced years ago when he had broken her heart—once when he left her, and again when he'd left her alone to deal with the grief of losing their baby. *A baby.* He didn't have to deal with learning he had a child out there somewhere, but he couldn't help wondering how it would have felt if that were the case. How would his life have been different? Would she have kept the child and raised it with or without him? Or would she have put it up for adoption, given the likelihood that a marriage between them would have very little chance of succeeding? He could only speculate, but every scenario showed him a heartbreaking, gut-wrenching possibility that he had difficulty contending with.

Suddenly exhausted in the deepest sense, Jackson knew he needed sleep, but the churning of his mind and emotions would never allow him to relax. He knew he should call Chas before he went to sleep, but he just couldn't talk to her about this yet, and he didn't want to have another conversation that involved trying to evade her questions about how he was doing. He turned off his phone, took a *whole* sleeping pill, and went to bed, hoping his drug-induced slumber would postpone the necessity of facing something that he wondered how he would ever face.

* * * * *

Evening seemed to come too soon when all of the ladies were expressing their disappointment at having the week come to an end. The final pajama gab session began with Tammy announcing, "Okay, Kristy, you've avoided saying hardly anything all week. We want to know what's going on in your life. It could be a decade or more before we can be together like this again. We need a good catch-up."

"I've sensed that something's wrong," Mia said, "but I don't think any of us wanted to be pushy."

"Oh, yes we do!" Marianne said, and they all laughed. "Seriously though, we need to know what's going on."

"I must admit," Kristy said, "things have been rough. We've been having some problems for about a year, and I really haven't wanted to talk to anyone about it. If you must know, I was determined to not say a word." They all looked astonished but kept quiet, waiting for an explanation. "But Chas talked me out of it." They exchanged a smile. "And since I've already told her everything, and . . . it's hard for me to talk about . . . she's agreed to help me out."

Kristy nodded toward Chas, who said, "I'm glad to help, but you need to correct me if I get something wrong." She said to the others, "She assures me that if I can get the worst out and get some momentum going, she'll be okay talking about it." Chas cleared her throat and did her best to repeat the story Kristy had told her, glancing occasionally at her to see if she was doing okay. The ladies were horrified regarding the problems, but showed nothing but perfect compassion and love toward Kristy. When one of them started to cry tears of warm empathy, the others quickly joined and they were all crying. After the tears had started, Kristy seemed fine and was able to finish the story herself and answer their questions.

"So, now what?" Jodi asked her when they seemed to have heard the whole story.

"I'm afraid that he'll try it again," Kristy admitted tearfully. "I don't know if I could live with the guilt."

"Guilt? What have you got to feel guilty for?"

"Because . . . a part of me has to admit that I think life would be better for him on the other side of the veil. He doesn't know how to solve this problem; *I* don't know how to solve this problem. See how messed up I am? But, honestly, whether it's right or not, whether it makes sense or not, I can understand why my son would rather be dead." She became too emotional to speak for a minute, then managed to say, "His father has actually told him . . . that he would prefer having him dead than have to deal with something like this." The ladies were all astonished. "How can I counteract that? How can I convince my son that living would be better under the circumstances? I don't know what to say to him. And sometimes . . . when this help-lessness overtakes me . . . I confess that . . ." Again she became very upset, but the others waited patiently for her to go on. "I've been tempted . . . to do the same."

"What are you saying?" Tammy demanded gently. "That you've been suicidal?"

Kristy nodded, unable to say anything except, "A little."

The ladies *really* rallied around Kristy then, full of kind advice and unconditional love. They assured her that they would be there for her, no matter what. A couple of them offered to fly to her home and stay there for a few days if a friend was ever needed there. By the end of the evening Kristy had agreed that *she* was going to start seeing a counselor, even if her husband wouldn't go. It had been offered in relation to her son's hospital stay, and she was going to go for it. At least then she could gain some skills and get professional advice for how to best help navigate her family through this crisis.

"You need to take good care of yourself," Tammy said to Kristy, then she added to the group, "We all do. And part of that includes taking the time to enlist the support of friends in our lives. If you isolate yourself, your life is more likely to get out of balance."

"It's like that oxygen mask thing on an airplane," Luci said. "If you're not breathing, you're not in a position to do any good for anybody. I don't think I could function if I couldn't just talk to a friend and decompress from the problems. It's the way God made women; we need friends."

"I think it's part of the divine purpose of Relief Society," Marianne said.

"I agree," Jodi said. "Women need to talk to women. When we feel heard and understood, it's easier to face whatever we have to face."

A sense of calm and hopefulness settled over the entire group. Chas felt grateful to see Kristy so open with the others, and to see the deepening of bonds between them. Having had a little part in helping Kristy come to this point, she felt like she actually belonged. Jodi smiled at her from across the room, and the feeling deepened. All in all, it had been a good week at the Dickensian Inn.

CHAPTER THIRTEEN

While the conversation in the parlor was winding down, Chas realized that she'd had her phone in her pocket, certain Jackson would call and she would have to excuse herself to talk to him. She'd left him two messages earlier, so the ball was in his court. When she realized it was nearly midnight on the East Coast and he hadn't called, she felt disheartened and freshly concerned. She tried to call him even though it was late, but the phone went straight to voice mail. Would he really have just turned it off and gone to bed without listening to her messages? Or had he listened to them and chosen not to call her? She just didn't know what to think. She reminded herself that she had a great deal of evidence that husbands could be much worse, but that didn't excuse the obvious problems going on with hers.

Chas prayed for Jackson while she was brushing her teeth, then she knelt by the bed and prayed more formally. She kept praying as she climbed into bed, and while she was trying to fall asleep. Her prayers merged into tears and back to prayers again that finally lulled her into sleep, holding the hope in her heart that her husband would get beyond whatever had cut him off from her, that he would come home to her and they could start over.

* * * * *

Jackson woke up feeling like he had a hangover. It took him a minute to be absolutely certain that he *hadn't* been drinking. When he recalled the events that had preceded his taking that sleeping pill, the idea of a good stiff drink was more tempting than it had been in a very long time. He thought of Chas and groaned. With every fiber of his being, he dreaded talking to her. Realizing how wrong it was to feel that way about his wife, he truly began to wonder if these feelings were somehow fate's way of letting him know that Chas truly was better off without him. Maybe he'd been wrong to ever make her a part of his life to begin with. Perhaps it was best if he just stayed away. He could recognize the absurdity of his own thoughts, but at the same time there was a logic to it that seemed to ease some of his confusion. The idea of never facing her with the reality of who he really was had a certain kind of calming effect on him.

Jackson looked once more at the contents of the box Serena had left for him. He read through the letter again, feeling like a stranger to himself. The baby shirt took on a whole new meaning, and he wondered when she might have purchased it. He finally put the box into his suitcase, unable to stew over its contents any further.

While Jackson showered, the temptation for a drink subsided into the lesser temptation to have a strong cup of coffee. Instead he took some Tylenol for his headache and sat on the edge of the bed, holding his phone, afraid to turn it on. When he did, he found messages from Chas, sounding more concerned than angry. He knew he should call her, but his inability to do so felt crippling. Instead he dialed the office of Dr. Callahan, glancing at the clock as he tried to calculate the time in Montana. He'd slept late, so he was okay. But since the doctor had been on call on Saturday, he wondered if he would be available on a Monday morning. He left a message for the doctor, who was in a counseling session, something that gave Jackson enough time to get a quick breakfast in the hotel restaurant. Chas tried to call him once, and he ignored the call, overcome with guilt as he did so—but not enough guilt to answer the phone. When Callahan called back, Jackson answered saying, "I'm losing my mind."

"If I find it, I'll let you know."

"Always a comedian," Jackson said.

"Not always."

Jackson told him a brief version of the new twist in his attempts to face the past and deal with it. Callahan listened, offered some insights, then said, "Call your wife, Jackson. You're confused and you're upset, but you're going to need *marriage* counseling if you don't share what you're going through with your wife. Call her now, and start with an apology. Doctor's orders."

"Okay," Jackson said.

"Call me if you need to talk it through some more. Call my cell phone; leave a message if I don't answer it. I'll get back to you as soon as possible."

"Thank you," Jackson said, but it took him ten minutes after hanging up to gather enough courage to call Chas. He was helped along by imagining how much better it would be if he actually called her instead of waiting for her to have to try calling him again.

"I'm sorry," he said as soon as she answered. "I turned the phone off."

"Why?"

"I . . . needed some time."

"You could *tell* me you need some time, Jackson, instead of leaving me to wonder if you've been hurt, or . . ."

"Or what?"

"Or . . . going off the deep end. You have no idea where a woman's imagination can go if she believes her husband could go off the deep end."

"Like what?" he demanded.

"Just . . . tell me what's wrong. You sound worse than you did when you were ill."

"Maybe uncovering memories wasn't such a good idea," he said. "Maybe we both would have been better off if I'd never come back here." He thought of receiving that box in the mail if he *hadn't* come back, and knew he never would have escaped the way he was feeling. But at the moment he would have preferred to. "How can you get closure when you've opened an ugly can of worms?"

"What are you talking about?" she asked.

"I can't talk about it, Chas; not yet. Maybe not ever."

"You think we can just . . . go forward with you keeping *more* secrets from me?"

"Not likely," he said, and she wondered what *that* was supposed to mean. Before she could ask he said, "I don't deserve you, Chas. I'm not sure I ever did. I don't know what ever made me believe that I could be what you need me to be . . . that I could be what you deserve."

"I don't know what's going on, Jackson, but what you're saying is crazy. You can't possibly believe that."

"Oh, I do!" he insisted. "Is this what you mean by going off the deep end?"

"Maybe."

"I'm just telling you how I feel."

"But why, Jackson? I don't understand. You've always been a good husband, a good father. Unless you've done something since you arrived in Virginia that I don't know about, you can't possibly believe that things have changed so much in less than a week."

"Nothing's changed, Chas; I was just in denial."

Chas began to feel panicked. It was getting easier to believe that her imagination hadn't been so out of proportion.

"So . . . what are you saying, Jackson? Has all your reminiscing just . . . what . . . made you want to go back to that world and stay there?"

"No! Not even close! It's made me *sick!* Seeing who I used to be has made me wonder how I got through those years at all."

"But you did get through them," she said. "You're a different man."

"Maybe not as much as I thought," he said, and Chas didn't know how to argue with this. She really had no idea where this was coming from.

"Maybe you should stop talking in generalities and tell me what's happened since we talked last that's got you so upset."

"What would you say if I told you I had a child before I met you?"

Chas had to put a hand over her mouth to keep herself from making any sounds that might alert him to her shock. She quickly gathered a steady voice and asked, "Is this hypothetical, or are you trying to tell me that—"

"Just answer the question."

Chas thought about it and answered firmly, "Your having a child would be much easier to deal with than finding out that you *knew* you had a child and you didn't tell me."

"Well, I didn't know."

"You *do* have a child?" she asked, astonished at the possibility.

"No," he said, and she wondered what the point to this conversation might be. "But I found out that Serena was pregnant when I left her."

Chas didn't even try to hold back an audible gasp. "What happened to the baby?"

"She told me she miscarried."

"She *told* you?"

"She left some things for me that her mother passed along. There was a letter in the box; a deathbed confession, basically."

"Why didn't she tell you she was pregnant?"

"Because . . . she didn't want me to stay for the wrong reasons; she didn't want me to feel obligated or duty bound." His voice dripped with sarcastic self-recrimination. "I'm assuming that since we worked in the same building, she was prepared to lie to me and tell me the baby wasn't mine. I wouldn't have believed her. But I wonder what I would have done. The thought makes me *sick*, Chas. It makes me *sick.*"

"I can understand why this is hard for you," she said, "and I'm sure you need some time to adjust to something like this and accept it. But it still doesn't change who you are now."

"Are you telling me that you're really okay with all of this?"

"At least you're talking to me. That's worth a great deal, in my opinion. I'm not saying it's easy, but you're my husband and I love you. I'm not going to let your past life rattle me that much. As long as you remain the man I know you to be in your present life, I can live with whatever happened before then."

He made no comment, and she attempted to get him talking again. "You really loved her, didn't you."

"I *did* love her, Chas; I did! But I never told her that. I was an emotional wreck, and I was too immature to take responsibility for her or the kind of relationship we were having. I was in my thirties and I was an idiot."

"Would you have married her if you had known?"

"I don't know," he said. "She was more antimarriage than I was. We both came from bad homes. I think we both believed that marriage was an inevitable collision course. But I would have stood by her. I would have taken responsibility for the child. I would have tried to be some kind of a half-decent father."

"Because you're a good man."

His one-syllable laugh was bitter. "Do you hear what you're saying? Do you hear what *I'm* saying? I shouldn't have been sharing that kind of relationship with her *at all*. I wasn't prepared to be a father. I couldn't even commit myself to a woman I loved."

Chas wanted assurance that his feelings for Serena were all past tense, but she knew that wasn't the point of this conversation. She could deal with her own feelings of jealousy after he came to terms with whatever was eating at him right now.

"I don't know what to say, Jackson. I don't know how to convince you that it's in the past." She sighed and softened her voice. "Come home to me, Jackson. I need you; we all need you. Surely we can work this out better face-to-face."

"The inn is a little crowded," he said, using the first excuse of avoidance he could come up with.

"The ladies are going home this afternoon," she said. "Come home."

Jackson was silent far too long.

"Please come home," she said.

"I just . . . need a little more time, Chas."

"Time to what?" she asked, allowing her frustration to show in her voice.

"I'll call you later."

"Will you?" she demanded. "Or will you turn off your phone and ignore me?"

"I'll call you," he said, "and I'll leave my phone on. I promise."

"Okay," she said, trying to trust him on that. "I love you."

"I love you too, Chas," he said, and she could only hope that he could hold on to that love until she could be with him again and help him through this—whatever *this* might be.

* * * * *

The mood was more somber among the ladies as they did finishing touches on projects, gathered their things, and packed their bags. Everything was pretty much ready to go by the time they sat down to share lunch, their last meal together at the inn. They talked more of the future than the past, committing to keep in touch, and to be there for each other across the miles. Those who were struggling recounted the goals they had set and got a fresh cheer of encouragement from the others. When they had finished eating but were still at the table visiting, Chas slipped out and came back with a box.

"I have a little going-away gift for each of you, compliments of the Dickensian Inn." Everyone oohed and aahed dramatically. "Jodi helped me, but I will completely take credit for the idea." They all applauded. Chas lifted one of the seven identical pieces out of the box to show them, and they all got tears in their eyes. Chas figured the pictures spoke for themselves, so she just passed them around and watched while they all examined the three photos closely. The frame was long, with three ovals. On the left was a photo of the seven girls at a sleeping party in the sixth grade. On the right was a photo of the seven young women at high-school graduation. In the middle was a photo taken of the seven ladies on the porch of the Dickensian Inn when they had first arrived. Across the bottom of the frame it said, *The pleasure of a generous friendship is the steadiest joy in the world.* —*Charles Dickens*

Once they had all gotten a good look at the treasured souvenir of this getaway, they stood up and took turns hugging Chas and thanking her for her friendship, and for all she had done to make their stay so pleasant and charming. Then they started hugging each other and saying preliminary good-byes, even though they didn't have to leave for an hour, and they would all be together for a few minutes at the airport.

After they had cleaned up lunch, the ladies all went to their rooms to finish packing, then they set out for the airport in two vehicles, just as they'd arrived a week earlier. Once again they were blessed with fair weather during the drive, but this time Chas felt completely comfortable with the women in the car, and she knew she was going to miss them.

At the airport Jodi and Chas shared their final hugs with everyone at the curb where the luggage was dropped off. They didn't figure it was worth parking and paying a fee when the ladies would need to hurry and check in and get through security. When Chas and Jodi were left alone by their vehicles, they hugged each other, then drove back to Anaconda.

The inn felt eerily quiet to Chas in spite of knowing that the maids had arrived and they were upstairs stripping beds and cleaning the rooms. Since they had two couples coming in this evening, everything needed to be put in order. But the maids would be doing the work. Chas only had two objectives: to take over Polly's job with her home and children, and to talk to her husband. The first wouldn't be a problem.

Polly hung around for a while to visit with Chas since Elliott was working and the children were down for their naps. Chas thanked Polly several times before Polly went to the office of the inn to see if there was anything urgent that needed her attention. She'd kept up a little every day, so the work wasn't terribly far behind.

Since the children were asleep and the house was relatively clean, Chas sat on the couch and dialed Jackson's number, holding her breath until he picked up.

"See, I answered it," he said.

"I'm very impressed. What are you doing?"

"Looking at the ocean."

"Is it beautiful?"

"It's gray; everything is gray."

"The sky is blue here; brilliant blue. Come home and we'll go for a walk."

"It's too cold."

"Then we'll stay inside by the fire," Chas said. "Please come home."

"I just need some time," he said.

"Okay," Chas gave in, not wanting to be the proverbial nag. "Anything you want to talk about?"

"Not at the moment, but thank you."

Chas told him the ladies had left, and she told him a little bit about the things they'd done, omitting any discussion of their problems. He listened and made an occasional comment, but he was still far from himself. When the baby woke up Chas reluctantly ended the call, but Jackson promised to call before he went to bed. Now that Chas didn't have the distraction of seven women to spend time with, she felt her husband's absence all the more keenly. But as much as she missed him, it was his emotional state more than his absence that troubled her. She prayed that he would come to his senses and come home to her soon.

* * * * *

Jackson returned to his hotel room feeling depressed and confused. He wondered if he'd made any progress whatsoever. He'd visited all of the old haunts and some new ones. He'd taken Callahan's advice and formally said good-bye to his old home and his old life. But he still felt stuck. As he turned on the light and locked the deadbolt, it occurred to him that in his emotional state his prayers had been sporadic at best. He'd almost felt ashamed to talk to God about this, as if He didn't already know *everything* about Jackson's past life. He realized now what should have been obvious all along. He wasn't going to solve *any* problem without God's help. The change of thinking felt so dramatic that he had to believe Chas was praying for him. Of course she would be. She'd prayed for him before they'd even met face-to-face.

He then recalled that he'd packed his scriptures, but he'd not even gotten them out of the suitcase. He opened it to get them out and saw the box Serena had given him. But he also saw the copy of *Great Expectations* he'd thrown in because he'd been reading it at home. It hadn't been so long since he'd read it, which was when he'd been in the psych ward being treated for PTSD. But he'd read it quickly then, and his mind had been somewhat foggy. Before then he'd not read it since his youth. The book had left a huge impression on him, and reading Dickens's novels had changed his life at a young age. And many years later, because of his personal fondness for Dickens, he had chosen the Dickensian Inn over all other bed-and-breakfast inns in obscure towns. And there he had found Chas.

Jackson made himself comfortable and picked up the scriptures. He read a couple of chapters, then set them aside to pick up the novel. He quickly found where he'd left off and became absorbed in the unique nuances of Dickens's voice and his powerful use of nineteenth-century language. He lost himself entirely in the tumultuous life of Pip, the young man struggling to make his way through mystery and unforeseeable hazards.

The ringing of the phone startled him. He picked it up and heard, "You were going to call me before you went to bed."

"I haven't gone to bed," he said.

"But it's late there."

"Yes, but . . . I'm reading."

"What?" she asked, intrigued.

"Great Expectations."

"Ah, yes." Chas was pleased. She'd far rather have him hanging out with Dickens than leaving her to wonder if he was hanging out in a bar or something. "You were reading it before you left. And how is Pip?"

"In a pickle, as always."

"Yes, he usually is," she said. He didn't comment and she added, "Anything else going on?"

"Nope."

Chas resisted the urge to ask when he was coming home. He knew she wanted him to. He might appreciate not having her bring it up in every single conversation.

"I miss you," she said. "It's awfully quiet here."

"I'll be home soon," he said.

"Good," Chas said and avoided asking when. But she had a feeling that getting her husband to come back to her wasn't going to be easy.

* * * * *

The following day Jackson became so caught up in *Great Expectations* that the hours passed with little awareness beyond his need to eat. He spoke to Chas twice, but they didn't have a lot to say to each other, and it felt more awkward than anything. When he finally became too sleepy to read any longer, he was struck with some guilt for not having read anything from the scriptures. He vowed to do that first thing in the morning and went to sleep without having to take a sleeping pill. He woke up feeling excited to finish the novel today, and he chose not to think about anything else in his life—past or present. But before he started, he did spend half an hour studying the Book of Mormon. Chas called just as he was finishing 2 Nephi.

"Still reading?" she asked, and in those two words he recognized a strained effort to sound indifferent to his absence from home, and patience with his reticence toward her.

"Yes," he said.

"How *is* Mr. Dickens?"

"I assume he's fine. I'm actually reading Nephi's work at the moment."

"Oh, good," she said, as if knowing he'd not abandoned the scriptures gave her some hope that he might not abandon her.

Jackson examined the situation and realized that he was well aware of exactly how she felt, and he needed to stop pretending that he wasn't. He knew he was to blame for her present heartache, and he knew he should do something about it. But that was going to take some thought. For the moment he tried to ease the strain a little by saying, "I love you, Chas; I really do. I'm sorry this has been so difficult for you."

"I love you too, Jackson," she said, the strain in her voice turning quickly to evidence that she was crying. "Just . . . come home."

"I will," he said.

"When?" she asked, more with pleading than anger.

"Soon," was all he could say. "Soon, I promise."

Following a long pause where he could feel the possibility of an argument brewing, she simply said, "Okay. When you decide to come back to your family, we will be here waiting. You call me later. I don't want to interrupt whatever it is that you're doing."

She hung up quickly and he suspected she'd started crying uncontrollably the second she did.

"You're such a jerk," Jackson said to himself. He thoughtfully considered what to do to solve this problem. He couldn't come up with anything that didn't feel too hard to handle, so he set aside the phone and the scriptures and became quickly lost in the ongoing adventures of Pip. Jackson knew how the story ended, but he still felt deeply anxious to see how everything was going to work out. He felt a little bit the same about his own situation, except that he wasn't entirely certain *how* it would turn out in the end. Reading fiction was safer than dealing with his own conflicts. It was too bad Mr. Dickens wasn't available to write him out of this mess.

* * * * *

Chas felt completely drained of hope as she reflected on the inter-action she'd had with her husband since he'd left for Virginia. She prayed for what seemed the millionth time that his heart would be comforted, that he would find peace, and that he would come home to his family—not necessarily in that order. She felt sure that he could get through this much easier and more productively if they were living under the same roof, but she was completely helpless in knowing what to do or say to make that happen. She considered the possibility that if he wasn't going to come home, she should go to him. She'd prayed about doing that days ago and she'd known it wasn't right, but maybe now it *was* right. It seemed so pointless though, and so unnec-essary. In the end, she knew she needed to stay here and wait. But the waiting felt torturous. She'd cleaned and organized in between caring for her children, trying to keep herself busy and occupied. But that was getting old, and everything was just about as clean and orderly as it could get with babies to take care of. She'd talked all of her feel-ings through with Polly, grateful for a friend who would listen, help her with perspective, and never break confidence or pass judgment. Jackson was like a brother to Polly, and the relationship between Jackson and Elliott was similar. They were as good as family. They were both concerned but felt equally helpless. Elliott had talked to Jackson a couple of times while Jackson had been in Virginia, but Jackson had been distant and not very talkative with Elliott either.

Chas felt like she had to do something, anything, to be proactive about solving this problem. She finally settled comfortably on at least calling Dr. Callahan for advice. She left a message and didn't get a call back for a few hours.

"Sorry for the delay," he said when he called back. "I was with a patient who needed some extra time and care."

"I could never complain about that. You holed up for a couple of days with Jackson, as I recall."

"It was a great learning experience for both of us," Callahan said with typical humility. "Is he still giving you grief?"

"He's still hiding in Virginia and not being very communica-tive, if that's what you mean. I'm trying to be patient, but I'm having a hard time understanding what's going on here. I was hoping you could give me some insights that wouldn't break your doctor-patient confidentiality."

"I think I can do that. Jackson's never had a problem with my talking to you about our conversations. In fact, the last time we talked I asked him if he was okay with my talking to you. He told me that he was. I don't think he has a problem with your knowing what's going on; his problem is simply not being able to talk about it."

"Okay," Chas said, trying not to feel offended that her husband didn't feel comfortable telling her things that he could tell his shrink. But then, she'd often told him that he needed to talk things through, even if it wasn't with her.

"I think that what he's feeling is a lot more complicated than just Serena's death. He made some pretty drastic changes in his life in a very few years. And those years weren't easy in many respects. I'm guessing that he's not just grieving over the death of a past love, but he's grieving over his past life. Even if he would never want to go back, he might just have to mourn over it. I don't think it's any reflection on his level of happiness or satisfaction in his present life. I just think that a man sometimes has to stop and take account of where he's been. I think he's methodically shut himself off from the past; he's compartmentalized certain times of his life, or certain incidents, not wanting to really think about them because it's stirred uncomfortable feelings or memories. We're talking about a man who didn't speak to his mother for twenty-six years with the hope that it would block out his painful childhood. Speaking of which, if you consider the kind of home he came from— the abuse, the alcoholism—his behavior isn't surprising. The man you got to know when you met him was the best of everything he'd become through more than four decades of his life's experiences. But the worst of him based on those experiences exists in there as well. I believe he's always had good intentions; he's always wanted to be better than his father, he's wanted to accomplish good things in this world."

"And he has."

"Yes, he certainly has. But his most defining years were spent in a home with a violent, drunken father and a depressed, unloving mother. He's healed amazingly well from those events, *but* the deepest core of Jackson Leeds is based in poor self-esteem."

"I don't understand."

"Have you ever heard him say that he doesn't deserve you?"

Chas's heart quickened. "Yes. More this last week than ever before."

"In the simplest terms, Chas, when a man is raised by a parent figure who demeans and belittles him, it damages the core belief of being a valuable human being. Jackson is capable of changing the behaviors caused by that belief—which he has done. But he may never fully heal from that belief. When tough things happen, a person reverts to that core belief. If you were raised with a healthy self-esteem, then problems can throw you off, but you have the confidence of being able to get through them and conquer them because you see yourself as a valuable person. I think he's stuck in a place of being overcome by the mistakes of his past that seem to be a validation of what his father taught him to be."

Chas felt almost sick to her stomach as she took in the truth of what she was hearing. "That all makes sense," she said. "But how can I help him?"

"The same way you've always helped him. You love him no matter what, and you let him work it out. My guess is that he'll come back to you in every respect; he's just the kind of guy that has to get lost inside himself once in a while."

"You really think so? You think it's just temporary?"

"Yes," Callahan said with no hesitation. "That doesn't mean you shouldn't keep calling him on his behavior. He's a husband and father, and he needs to come back and take responsibility for his family. If this goes on much longer, I think reminding him of that is something that might appeal to his sense of duty at the very least and bring him home."

"Okay," she said again.

"Would you forgive him if he cheated on you?" the doctor asked.

"What?" Chas asked, shocked by the question.

"He started drinking again at one time and you forgave him. Would you forgive him if he cheated on you?"

She had to ponder the question carefully, balancing the impact something like that would have on her marriage—and her life—with her deepest values. "Yes," she said, "but it would be hard."

"Hard, but possible."

"Yes. However, let me clarify that staying married to a man who had cheated on me would depend on *his* attitude. He would have to work very hard to demonstrate his commitment to me, to never doing it again; he would have to earn my trust. But yes, I would forgive him."

"That was a very good answer, Chas. Now, why don't you call him and tell him that."

"Why? I don't understand. *Has* he cheated on me?"

"As of the last time I talked to him, no."

"Then why should I tell him that?"

"If he's weighed down by guilt over a relationship that happened before he met you, maybe it would be good for him to realize that even if it happened now you could forgive him. Therefore, having it happen a long time ago, when it wasn't a betrayal to you because he didn't even know you, it might be easier for him to connect the dots. Is that making sense?"

"I think so."

"Well, I hope that helps," the doctor said. "I've got to run but I'll be available later if you need me, or if he does. Just leave a message."

"I can't thank you enough," Chas said. She knew they would be billed for his time on the phone with them as much as if they went in for a counseling appointment. But he knew what he was doing, and he genuinely cared. He was truly a great blessing in their lives, and the price paid for such sound help and advice was worth it. She thought of the money that people spend on things in this world that are of little or no consequence, and the overall tendency to avoid paying for help with the things that really mattered. She knew she would give up a great deal of her worldly belongings to get Jackson whatever help he needed to get through this.

Chas gave herself some time to let Dr. Callahan's words sink in before she called her husband. She considered how to open the conversation and tell him what the doctor had suggested, but she just couldn't put the words together in her mind. Throughout the afternoon she pondered the doctor's insights, and they settled into her with a chilling accuracy. He understood Jackson well. She just hoped that understanding the problem would help them solve it.

CHAPTER FOURTEEN

By evening Chas still couldn't come up with the right words, and she figured that would certainly be defined as a stupor of thought. Apparently it wasn't the right time to tell Jackson these things. Recalling that she'd told him quite plainly she would wait for *him* to call *her*, she was further convinced that she should leave the ball in his court and let some time pass.

Polly and Elliott stopped by to see how she was doing, and they both ended up playing with the children for a long while. Chas suspected that they missed the children and they'd just wanted an excuse to see them. And she was fine with that. She felt distracted and concerned for her husband; having someone else help with the children was a blessing.

They stayed and helped put the children to bed. When the house was quiet, the three of them sat down together in the common room.

"Any word from Jackson?" Polly asked.

"Nope," Chas said and looked down.

"I'm not sure of everything that's going on," Elliott said, "and I don't need to know; I don't *want* to know any more than what either of you want to share . . . only if it might help. But there's something I would like to say . . . something I think you should know."

"I'm all ears," Chas said, eager for anything that might help her understand the situation.

"I realize that Jackson's lifestyle was much different from yours, and I know this difference of values has been difficult for him to come to terms with in some ways. But you should know . . . in the world that he lived in . . . before he came here . . . he was the strong one; he was considered the good guy. It wasn't uncommon for single men to be promiscuous and to be more than willing to brag about it. Jackson was disgusted by that kind of thing. Granted, he wasn't interested in marriage, but he wasn't interested in flings or one-night stands either. He was careful. He was respectful. If he ever heard anyone say something degrading or demoralizing to or about any woman, he would tell them to shut up. More than once I saw him defend a waitress—no one he knew—because some drunk guy would say something crude to her. There were a few guys we worked with who went to strip clubs all the time. Jackson never went to those kind of places. Sometimes they teased him, but he just shrugged it off. I asked him once why he didn't go with them."

Polly glared at him, and he added quickly, "*I* never went to those places. I just wanted to know why *he* didn't go. I wondered if it was for the same reasons."

"And what were those?" Polly asked, pretending to be more offended than she was.

"Truthfully, I thought it was embarrassing. That's all. I wasn't raised with strict rules about such things. It wouldn't have gone against anything I believed at the time. Just the thought of going into a place like that was embarrassing."

"And what did Jackson say?" Polly asked. "What were *his* reasons?"

"He said it was an insult to humankind. He said that whether it was men or women up there degrading themselves, it was a pathetic insult and he wanted nothing to do with it."

Chas sighed. It sounded so much like him. And she missed him so much!

"Anyway," Elliott continued, "he didn't care what anyone thought. He cared about doing the right thing. Even if his definition of 'the right thing' was different from yours, he was still a good man."

"I know that, Elliott; I do. The problem is that *he* doesn't seem to know it. And I don't know how to convince him."

They talked for a while longer, then Polly and Elliott left so that Chas could get some sleep. She wasn't surprised that Jackson hadn't called, but it still broke her heart and she cried herself to sleep.

* * * * *

Jackson finished reading *Great Expectations* much sooner than he'd anticipated. He realized the book had a thick section of commentary at the back, which made the story appear to be longer. Feeling out of sorts with nowhere to hide, he attempted to read the commentary, but it bored him out of his mind. He picked up the nearby scriptures and opened up to where he'd left off, at the beginning of the book of Jacob. He was reading passively, his mind still wrapped up in the story of Pip, when a verse jumped off the page and into his heart, cutting him deeply, leaving a wound of guilt that stung and burned. *Ye have broken the hearts of your tender wives, and lost the confidence of your children, because of your bad examples before them; and the sobbings of their hearts ascend up to God against you.*

Jackson slammed the book closed, as if he could hide his guilt. He picked up the novel again, longing to go back to the escape that it had given him. He reread the last page, relishing again the contentment it had created in him not so many minutes ago. The effect was now tainted by an awareness of his own guilt in the way he had been self-ishly clinging to his petty confusion and sorrow, completely oblivious to how this was affecting his family. Then something warm began to tingle inside of him when he reread that last, final sentence.

I took her hand in mine, and we went out of the ruined place; and, as the morning mists had risen long ago when I first left the forge, so, the evening mists were rising now, and in all the broad expanse of tranquil light they showed to me, I saw the shadow of no parting from her.

In a flash in his mind, Jackson saw the forge as the life he'd lived before Chas, and the ruined place the city he'd left behind. And most of all he saw himself with Chas and their children, surrounded by a tranquil light that exemplified all the light she had ushered into his life, and the hope they shared of making that life better. His confusion and sorrow did not relent. He knew he had much to figure out and come to terms with. But for the first time since he'd come here, he could fully see and feel the reality of what Chas had been trying to tell him: he would be better able to solve these problems at home, with her. And with any luck she would forgive him for being such a fool.

* * * * *

Chas woke up a little after one, wishing she could find her husband sleeping beside her. She got up to use the bathroom, and she checked on the children to find them breathing evenly with gentle sleep. She returned to her bed and prayed amidst her pondering of concern for her husband. A year ago he had been preparing for his baptism, glowing with enthusiasm to have the gospel a part of his life. They had quickly made plans to go to the temple together as soon as the year-long waiting period was over. Now that day was almost here, and Chas felt brokenhearted to consider the possibility that their going to the temple together might be postponed. In Jackson's present state of mind—for whatever reason—she doubted he would feel good about going. And they couldn't go until they both felt completely ready. Trying to force it or rush it would defeat the purpose, and it might cause more issues for him in the long run with his deep sense of feeling so unworthy.

While Chas was lying there in the dark, searching for something to hold on to, something to hope for, she recalled suddenly the remarkable dream she'd had only a week or two before news of Serena's death had turned everything upside down. She found great comfort in considering its message from where she was now. It seemed to her that she and Jackson had been foreordained to do the temple work for their deceased ancestors, and that angels would be with them in that work. Surely those angels would be with him now and help bring him home to her! Surely with time all would be well, and she would be wise to not be so impatient, to trust in the Lord and allow Him to guide Jackson along in His own time and in His own way.

Chas felt better but not sleepy, so she focused on imagining what it would be like to have her husband back again—both physically and emotionally. It was a moment she longed for and looked forward to. Beyond that, she could see in her mind the image of her and Jackson kneeling at a temple altar. It was easy to imagine, since she had seen it clearly in her dream, and the vivid memory of it was further evidence of the dream's validity. Surely everything would be all right!

* * * * *

Since Jackson hadn't bothered to call Chas and tell her he was on his way home, he didn't see any point in calling to say that his connecting flight had been delayed and he was stuck in an airport somewhere between purgatory and home. He didn't even know for sure what city he was in. He didn't care. He just wanted to be home. His impulsive decision to get home as quickly as possible had forced him to take a flight with a layover, and now it was working against him. His aggravation and impatience over the wasted time made him feel like a hypocrite when he'd wasted so many days away from home for no reason that he could define. He didn't know if Chas could ever forgive him for being such a fool, but he'd never know until he faced her. He needed her, needed to be with her. He needed her reason, her strength, her courage. He needed her love. He knew that no matter how badly he had let her down, she would always love him. Her love was the force that lured him home.

It was past midnight when he finally set foot in Montana. By the time he got his car out of long-term parking and started home, he knew his family was all sleeping soundly. He turned on his phone but didn't find a message from Chas. She'd said she would wait to hear from him. Apparently she was keeping her promise. He just prayed that she would hear him out rather than *throw* him out.

When Jackson finally arrived at the Dickensian Inn, he just sat in his car and looked up at the third-floor eaves of the Victorian mansion he loved so dearly. Torn between being too tired to sit there and too tired to move, he finally forced himself out of the car and through the back door of the inn. He'd decided that coming in that way would cause less noise and be less likely to wake Chas. He wanted to just slip into bed and sleep, knowing she was there. They could face the fallout in the morning.

* * * * *

Chas had just crawled back into bed after using the bathroom *again,* when she distinctly heard a noise downstairs. Was it possible that she actually had an intruder? Or could it be that her husband had finally come home—without bothering to let her know? She couldn't decide which was more likely, but both possibilities sent her heart pounding. She hurried to do something her husband had taught her to do, something she'd hoped she would never actually *have* to do. She knew exactly how to find the gun in the dark, even though it was high on a closet shelf. And she knew exactly where to find the clip that was stored in a different place for safety's sake, especially with children in the house. She snapped the clip into the gun and felt her way into the hall and to the top of the stairs. Her pulse raced, and her palms became clammy when she saw the shadow of a man standing in the common room below.

With the gun concealed in the folds of her nightgown, she flipped on the light, exhaling sharply to see her husband look up at her. She was so glad to see him she could hardly breathe. The shock, combined with the rush of adrenaline that had put a loaded gun into her hands in seconds, made her feel a little concerned about passing out. She leaned against the wall for support, willing her heart to slow down. Their eyes met with echoes of silent questions and expectation. He looked weary, not unlike when he'd been struggling through his PTSD. But the love in his eyes was evident. She wanted to be in his arms, but she couldn't move, and he just stood there as if he might be afflicted with the same problem. She figured that a little conversation could buy her some time and allow her to be more steady on her feet.

"My husband owns a gun and I know how to use it," she said, mildly facetious. "Give me one good reason not to."

"Because that gun belongs to me," he said.

"Oh," she said with more sarcasm than humor, "that explains why you look so familiar. From our phone conversations—or the lack of them—I was thinking you'd been replaced by an impostor."

He offered no response except the guilt that was reflected in his eyes. Chas finally felt calm enough to make it down the stairs, and she took hold of the handrail, hurrying as fast as she could manage. She stopped in front of him for just a moment and looked into his eyes before she wrapped her arms around his neck, still holding the gun in her right hand. He responded immediately with a smothering embrace, as if he might have melted into oblivion if he'd gone another minute without holding her close.

Jackson took in the reality that Chas was holding him so tightly that he could hardly breathe. He returned her embrace with all the desperation he was feeling, wishing he could feel like he actually deserved to be holding her this way.

"I love you," he murmured and pulled back just enough to look into her eyes.

"I love you too," she said, then pulled back farther. "Maybe you should take this."

She held up the gun, and Jackson was a little startled. "Whoa," he said and chuckled, taking it carefully from her.

"I didn't know whether or not you were an intruder," she said. "You taught me well."

"I should be careful to stay on your good side," he said and dropped the clip from the gun, setting them both down nearby.

"What are you doing here?" she asked, pressing a hand to his face.

"I live here," he said.

"I mean . . . I didn't expect you. I didn't know you were coming."

"I was supposed to get here at supper time, and I was going to surprise you. Then one of my flights got delayed, and . . . it doesn't matter. I'm sorry if I scared you."

"You didn't scare me . . . not tonight at least."

The silence forced him to acknowledge the comment. He'd scared her. He'd scared himself. He was hoping to save this until morning, but it had to be faced.

"I'm *so* sorry, Chas . . . for everything." He was shocked at the emotion in his own voice; or perhaps he shouldn't have been. "I've been such a fool. I was so stupid. I can only pray that you'll be able to forgive me. Oh, Chas . . . if you can't forgive me, I just don't know how I'll . . ."

She took a bold step back and her eyes went flinty. "What exactly do you need to be forgiven for, Jackson?" Her demanding tone contradicted the tears that came in quick abundance. He was so stunned that he didn't know how to answer. "I need to know. And I need to know now. What happened that made you . . . slink back here in the middle of the night . . . begging forgiveness?"

"I did not intend to arrive in the middle of the night," he said, entirely avoiding the point.

"But you feel the need to beg for forgiveness. You tell me what happened, and you tell me now! And *then* I'll decide if forgiveness is an option. You don't talk to me, then you do, then you don't. And I've spent the week realizing that I don't know you nearly as well as I thought I did. I'd still like to believe that you would never lie to me."

"I wouldn't."

"Then what happened?" she insisted, but he still didn't know how to answer. "Did you drink while you were away . . . at all? Since we last talked about it?"

"No!"

"Since the day I found you drinking before you went in the hospital, have you consumed any alcohol at all?"

"No."

"Have you been looking at porn?"

His voice rose in astonishment. "No! Of course not!"

"Since you and I met, have you ever behaved inappropriately with another woman, to any degree?"

"No, Chas. I would never betray you in that way; never!"

Chas believed him and let out a deep sigh. "Then everything else is manageable, Jackson. As long as you remain faithful and you're honest with me, there is nothing we can't overcome."

"Are you sure?" he asked.

"Is there something else you need to tell me?" she asked, wondering what could have gone wrong that she might not have foreseen. Jackson glanced at the unloaded gun and she said, "You're afraid I would shoot you if I knew what you know?"

He sat down at one end of the couch, and she sat at the other, folding one foot up beneath her to turn directly toward him. She watched him lean his forearms on his thighs and press his fingers together. Her nervousness increased at the evidence of his own uneasiness.

"No one was more stunned than I was at how news of Serena's death affected me. I've been trying to . . . figure it out, to understand what's wrong with me. I was . . . wandering around the city . . . trying to deal with the memories. I was holed up in a stupid hotel room, wondering why I'd done so many stupid things in my life. I was wondering why I couldn't have been more of what you deserved. I was wondering why I had been so blessed when I'd done so little to deserve it."

"Get to the point," she said. "You're scaring me."

Jackson looked down and let out a guilty sigh and she wondered what else he might have done that she hadn't heard about yet. He looked back up and said with a broken voice, "I seriously considered not coming back, Chas." She gasped softly, then put a hand over her mouth.

"It was like . . . every bad choice I'd made came back to haunt me with so much force that I felt like it would swallow me," he continued. "I finally realized that whatever might be going on, I needed you to help me solve it. Staying away could never be the right choice. It occurred to me that if you had ever, for any reason, considering leaving me, I would have been . . . devastated. And I felt so horrible. Just the fact that I even pondered abandoning you that way feels like . . . I betrayed you."

"Okay," she said. "But you only thought about it; you didn't do it. We just need to understand why you felt that way so it won't happen again. We need to talk about it, not ignore it."

He nodded in agreement, and Chas picked up on the obvious. "What else? Are there other offenses you've been thinking about committing against me?"

"No, but . . ."

"But?"

"I cannot begin to express my regret for all the stupid things I did before I met you."

She pointed out the obvious. "It was before you met me."

"I know, but . . . before you met *me* you only had one intimate relationship, and that was with your husband. It's like . . . you were loyal to me even though I was in your future. When I think about that, I feel so grateful. I know you must feel the opposite when you think about my past. I feel like I betrayed you, Chas; I feel like I cheated you out of something precious."

"Listen to me carefully, Jackson," she said. Since this wasn't the first time these feelings had come up, she felt well prepared to say what needed to be said. "Knowing you had intimate relationships before you met me is a little unsettling, but it is nothing that requires forgiveness from me. All of that is between you and God, and you settled with Him when you were baptized."

Jackson hung his head. "I'm not so sure I did."

"What does that mean?"

"When I told the bishop about my past, it was pretty much the same as what I told you."

"But he knew—like I knew—that it had been at least a few years before you and I were married that anything inappropriate had happened. Right?"

"Yes."

"It's in the past, Jackson. The only thing keeping it in the present is your wallowing in it. But maybe you could *stop* wallowing in it if you actually faced up to it. I think you worked very hard to put away all of those things and not look at them. I think that's why Serena's death knocked you so flat, because you'd never stopped to consider how you *did* feel about her and the part she played in your life. I know you weren't married to her, but I can still see her as something of an ex-wife, and I can live with that. Before we ever became romantically involved, you told me that you respected my need to save intimacy for marriage, and you wished that such a thought had even occurred to you. I knew what you meant. And how can you be judged for something that had never even occurred to you? I think you're blowing this way out of proportion. What I want to know is *why*. I want to understand where all of this doubt and concern is coming from. Whatever is going on inside of you, it's my problem as much as it's yours. I'm your wife; neither of us should be taking those vows lightly. In my opinion, there is only one issue here that you should be asking me to forgive you for."

"What?" he asked, looking at her as if she might have a magic answer to solve every problem.

"You won't talk to me," she said with careful enunciation. "If you had talked to me a long time ago about your past, this would have been a little problem instead of a big one. If you had talked to me about what you were feeling this week, it would have brought us closer together and not further apart. I have never done or said anything to make you not trust me, Jackson. I have never been judgmental or critical of your past, or even the present. I deserve to have you talk to me. I don't need to know everything, and there are some things I don't *want* to know. But I'd like to know the basics of your life before the Dickensian Inn. You've told me nothing about serving in the Marines except that you served in the Marines. The same about the FBI. What I know I've mostly learned from your friends who worked with you. Or there's the occasional revelation that you speak foreign languages. If you want my opinion on how you can get over all these feelings pulling you toward the past, I think you should allow it to become a part of who you are instead of trying to hide from it. And I think that sharing it with me could help that happen. Does that make sense?"

"Yes," he said.

"And?"

"And . . . I'll work on it."

"Okay," she said. "Then there's only one more thing I have to say."

"What?"

"I want to be with you forever, Jackson; nothing else matters. Nothing!"

He looked surprised but showed a hint of a smile. Chas slid across the couch, took his face into her hands and kissed him the way a wife should kiss her husband after a lengthy absence. She kissed him as if he'd been off to war; maybe he had. He responded in much the same way, and eased her fully into his arms.

"Is there anything else you need to tell me?" she murmured.

"I love you. I was a fool to think I could ever live without you."

"Yes, you were," she said and kissed him again.

Jackson pulled away long enough to stand up, take her hand, and pull her to her feet.

"It's the middle of the night," he said, picking up the gun and the clip to put them away. "We can talk some more tomorrow."

He followed her up the stairs and put the weapon and ammunition in their separate hiding places while Chas went into the bathroom. Now that he'd made peace with his wife, the next most important thing lured him down the hall. He peeked into the rooms of his children and saw them sleeping soundly. He leaned over each of their cribs, carefully touching their wispy hair and listening to them breathe. He hoped and prayed that he could be the father they deserved. Just being in the same room with his beautiful babies felt like a miracle. He turned off the hall light and returned to the bedroom where he found Chas in the bed, her eyes closed. He went in the bathroom to brush his teeth and get ready for bed. Going back into the bedroom, he felt the need to just look at his wife the way he'd looked at his children. He got into bed but left the lamp on, tired but not sleepy. He touched her face and her eyes opened.

"It's good to be home," he said.

"I'll second that." She touched his face in return. He kissed her the same way she'd kissed him downstairs, and her arms came around him. He reached for the lamp and turned it off, not interested in anything at the moment but basking in the reality that Chas was the most important person in the world, and she loved him. Everything else was negotiable.

* * * * *

Jackson woke to daylight and rolled over to see Chas watching him. He breathed in the relief of being with her, and the healing influence of her love for him.

"I'm so sorry," she said.

"For what?" he asked, touching her face.

"If we're going to confess our thoughts, I must say that there were moments when I really wondered if you had cheated on me."

"I would never do that to you, Chas."

"I know that, and I think a part of me never doubted that. But I did anyway. So, I'm sorry. I'm sorry for . . . jumping to conclusions, for thinking the worst. You deserve better than that from me. It's just that . . . I'd been listening to this woman . . . this friend of Jodi's, talking about how her husband had been cheating on her. And then . . . when Elliott told me what Ekert had said, and . . . well . . . you weren't very forthcoming on the phone. You sounded like you felt guilty, and I thought that's why you didn't want to talk to me. I can see now that I just . . . put it together all wrong, and I'm sorry for that."

Jackson kissed her. "I *should* have talked to you about what I was feeling, about what was going on." He shook his head. "Still . . . I can't believe that you thought I had done that. I can't imagine how much that must have hurt you."

Tears in her eyes verified the truth of what he was saying. He kissed her again and she said, "There is nothing more important to me than being with you forever—and everything that goes along with that." She sniffled and added, "There were moments when I really thought I was going to lose you."

"Never," he said.

"But you told me you'd considered not coming back. *Did* I nearly lose you, Jackson?"

"It was temporary insanity, Chas. It wouldn't have taken me long to realize that I need you . . . and you need me."

"I *do* need you, Jackson. We all need you."

"I know that, Chas; I do. I will never leave you. I promise. And again, I'm sorry."

Chas smiled and touched her nose to his. "You're back now. Everything will be okay."

He smiled in return and kissed her.

* * * * *

The first day that Jackson was home, Chas felt as if heaven surrounded her. Watching him care for and play with their children filled her with a gratitude for the simple joys of life that she could never take for granted. He settled quickly back into catching up on the office work and maintenance of the inn that he considered his responsibilities. But a few days after Jackson had returned from Virginia, Chas had to accept that something was still not right. He was more somber and often deep in thought, reminding her of the time following his mother's death. More than once she told him that she was available to talk anytime he felt the need. He thanked her, but she wondered if he ever would.

As the date of their temple sealing drew closer, Chas began to feel an urgency. She didn't want this experience of a lifetime to be marred by any unspoken feelings or issues between them. When the moment felt right, she took his hand and said with gentle firmness, "Jackson, I know you're having a hard time. And I know that for some reason you don't want to talk about it, but I want you to know that you *can* share these feelings with me. You really can. I've said it before but I need to say it again. I'm not going to judge you *or* your past. I am committed to you for life . . . for eternity . . . and when I made that commitment, I knew you had a complicated past. I just want you to know that you can talk to me. And . . . if you really feel like you *can't* talk to me about it, then talk to someone. Go see Dr. Callahan, or talk to Elliott, or . . . someone."

Jackson heard Chas's words and allowed them to settle into his spirit. He wrapped her in his arms and said close to her ear, "I'm sorry I've made this so difficult for you."

"You don't need to apologize," she muttered. "I just want you to make peace with this." She looked up at him. "I want you to make peace with your past so that we can go to the temple with only the future before us." His eyes darted down uncomfortably and she asked, "What?"

Jackson eased away from her. "I wonder if . . . we should postpone . . . the temple."

"What?" she said in a completely different tone.

"We can still go to DC and have our little vacation, but . . . I don't know if I'm ready, Chas. You're right. I *do* need to make peace with my past. I don't want it to be an issue between us, but . . . I'm just not sure it's realistic for me to be able to do that . . . now."

Chas wasn't terribly surprised to hear what he was saying, and she knew it was good to have it voiced between them, but she still couldn't hold back the hot tears that gathered in her eyes, then fell. "We've been counting days, Jackson. We've agreed that there is nothing more important than this."

"Yes, that's true. That's why I can't take it lightly."

"The past is washed away, Jackson. It's not an issue in regard to your worthiness. This should *not* keep you from taking such an important step."

Jackson looked away and put his hands on his hips. "I don't know how to make you understand, Chas. I just know that I need some time."

Chas swallowed hard and tried to feel compassion rather than frustration. But all she could feel was that she was upset. She opted to hurry from the room rather than let him see her dissolve into tears. A little while later she heard him leave the house, and she assumed he'd gone out to the garage to work on one of his ongoing projects. When hours passed and he hadn't come back in, she began to feel concerned. She was about to go and look for him when the phone rang and the caller ID reported that it was her husband's cell phone.

"I'm sorry," he said as soon as she'd answered. "I needed some fresh air, and then . . . I just needed to go for a drive. I didn't intend to be gone so long, especially when I didn't tell you I was leaving. I just . . . need some time to sort my thoughts."

"Okay," she said, hoping this would be a good thing. She tried not to react emotionally to his declaration for needing time. At least he wasn't in Virginia. "I appreciate the call," she said. "Are you coming home soon?"

"I . . . don't know," he said. "Please don't worry."

"Okay," she said again, not finding any means of protest. "Be careful."

"Of course," he said, then a long moment of silence preceded him saying, "I love you, Chas. It's going to be okay. I just need a little time; that's all."

"Okay," she said still again, but couldn't disguise the emotion that had crept into her voice. "I love you too."

Chas thought he would surely be back for supper, but he wasn't. She was certain he'd make it back to help tuck the children into bed, but they were sound asleep and he still hadn't shown up. She fell asleep praying for him, and woke up to see on the clock that it was after two and her husband still wasn't there. After lying there consumed with worry for half an hour she realized she had a headache and went down to the kitchen in search of the bottle of Tylenol. She flipped on the light switch at the bottom of the stairs, and gasped to see Jackson sitting at one end of the couch in the common room. Apparently he'd been there in the dark for a long while.

"Why are you awake?" he asked.

"How do you think I could sleep?"

"I told you not to worry."

"And if it were the other way around?" she asked, and he sighed.

Chas weighed her options. She could go back to bed and try to sleep, at least knowing that he was home and safe. She could try to get him to talk. Both seemed futile, so she just stood there. When the silence became unbearable, she followed through on the original goal to get some Tylenol. She swallowed the pills and took a long drink of water.

"You okay?" she asked, pausing on her way to the stairs.

Their eyes met and she held her breath, hoping that all of his time away with his thoughts might have produced some good results. She saw more than heard him sigh before he said, "I love you, Chas, and I want to be with you forever. I just . . . need you to be patient with me. I'm working on it; I really am."

Chas felt comforted and strengthened by his sincere appeal. "Okay," she said and held out her hand. "Let's get some sleep."

He rose and took her hand and they walked up the stairs together, going into each of the children's rooms to make certain they were okay before they went to bed. Holding Jackson close, Chas counted her blessings—foremost having him there with her. Having him home and knowing that he was trying, she could be patient for a long time. But oh, how she wanted to know that he was hers forever!

CHAPTER FIFTEEN

Chas was surprised by the idea that came to her mind, and the clarity with which it came. Before Jackson had a chance to fall asleep, she said, "Can I tell you something?"

"Of course," he said, reaching for her hand beneath the covers.

"It might sound strange, but I just feel like I need to say it. I want you to know that . . . if you *did* cheat on me . . . I . . ."

Jackson abruptly turned on the lamp on the bedside table so he could see her face. "What are you saying? Do you think I *did*? Do you think I'm just keeping it from you?"

"No! Of course not!"

"Do you believe I told you the truth when I said I didn't do anything wrong?"

"Yes, I believe you. I'm just . . . trying to make a point. *If* you had, I want you to know that I would forgive you."

"You're saying that if I told you . . . right now . . . that I had committed adultery, you would forgive me?"

"It would be more horrible than I could possibly imagine," she said with tears that added sincerity to her words. "But I would forgive you. I need to clarify that whether or not our marriage could survive something like that would depend on many different factors, and developing trust again would be a challenge, to say the least. But I want you to know . . . I *need* you to know . . . I would never stop loving you, and I *would* forgive you."

Jackson looked at her thoughtfully for a full minute, then said, "Do you think by saying that, I'll burst forth with a confession? I can't confess something I didn't do."

"No!" she insisted and actually laughed at the absurdity of their crossed wires. "I *know* you don't have anything to confess. I'm just trying to make a point."

"And what point is that, exactly?"

"If it's possible for me to forgive you for such a thing, and you know I would love you regardless, why would you believe that I couldn't forgive you for something that happened years before I met you?"

"Is that what you think the problem is?"

"I don't know. You tell me. *Is* that what the problem is?"

Jackson thought about it and had to admit, "I don't know; maybe."

"Then just . . . think about what I said."

"Okay," he said and turned off the lamp, but it was a long while before he slept. Could it be possible that Chas was right? Did a part of him believe that Chas couldn't forgive him—or love him as much as she claimed—considering all that he'd done? Had his thinking become so distorted? Yes! He *knew* it had become distorted. He just wasn't sure why, or what to do about it. With any luck an answer would present itself soon. He wanted life to go back to normal. He wanted to feel the perfect happiness he'd felt before this had gotten into his head and thrown him off balance.

The following morning Jackson analyzed his feelings while he shoveled a fresh snowfall from the walks. He kept thinking while he used the ATV with the snow blade to clear the parking lot and driveway. He felt every bit as confused as he had when he'd flown to Virginia. He didn't know how to fix it, but he knew he wanted to. Once the snow was all removed he went in and called Callahan's office to get an appointment. He was glad the good doctor could get him in that afternoon. Chas seemed pleased to hear where he was going. She gave him a kiss for good luck, and another one for good measure, and he told her that she was so good to him that he didn't deserve her.

"Now *that,*" she said, "is the root of the problem."

"Yes, it is!" he agreed firmly. "I *don't* deserve you. That *is* the problem."

"No," she said. "That's not what I meant. The problem is that you believe you don't deserve me. *We* deserve to be together and be happy, and *you* need to accept that."

During the drive to Butte, Jackson considered what Chas had said, and when his appointment with Dr. Callahan began, Jackson was surprised when the doctor asked him why he didn't feel like he deserved to live a good life.

"Have you been talking to my wife?" Jackson asked.

"Yes, actually. But I only explained to her why you *might* feel like you didn't deserve to have a good life."

"If you already know, then why are you asking me?"

"I want to know what *you* think."

"I think I'm seriously messed up and I need a shrink."

"I think that you're not nearly as messed up as you think you are. Considering your roots, you're doing pretty well. But I think we should talk about how your roots might be affecting levels of your beliefs and thinking of which you're not even consciously aware."

"I'm listening," Jackson said.

Callahan explained some basic psychological principles that applied to someone growing up in an abusive home. Jackson related surprisingly well to those principles. He felt validated as feelings that hadn't made sense suddenly had a definition. But Callahan's only suggested solution was simply that Jackson had to correct his thinking and beliefs, one hour at a time, as his life progressed.

"Each time you hear your brain trying to tell you that you don't deserve Chas or the life you have with her, you need to talk back and remind yourself of all the reasons you *do* deserve it. Then be humble and grateful and do your best to take good care of your family and make them happy. Each act you do to make your life what you want it to be will help dispel the myth that you don't deserve a good life. Does that make sense?"

"It does," Jackson said and sighed.

"What else?" Callahan asked.

"I'm just . . . having trouble letting go of certain things from the past . . . things that have come up recently."

"So, let's talk about it," he said, and they reviewed the concept they'd discussed on the phone, about saying good-bye to the past so that the present could be more fully embraced. They talked about ways that Jackson could complete that process, but in the end there were no easy solutions. He simply had to face up to some things that he was very much in the habit of trying to ignore.

Through the drive home, Jackson contemplated all he had been told and all he had been feeling. He knew in his heart what he needed to do. He didn't know why it felt so hard for him, but difficult or not, he had to do it.

That evening he avoided talking to Chas about his appointment with Callahan other than saying, "I believe it was productive. He gave me a lot to think about." They shared supper and he took charge of the children while she cleaned up the kitchen.

After the children were in bed, he told Chas he would be in the inn, which he pointed out facetiously was still "home" since it was technically the other side of their house. A part of him hoped she would come looking for him, while another part of him preferred that she didn't, and then he could put it off a little longer. Tonight was better, however, since they had no guests at the inn, and there was no concern about strangers passing by on their way in or out.

Jackson built a fire in the fireplace of the formal dining room and made himself comfortable on the couch that faced it. When Chas walked into the room he felt more relieved than disappointed, but he also felt nervous. He prayed that this would go well, and that the results would be what the doctor had suggested they might be.

"What are you doing?" she asked, and he noticed she was carrying two baby monitors, one for each child.

"Just . . . pondering," he said.

"Why here?"

"I wanted to sit by the fire," he said. A fireplace was something their home didn't have. With the lovely fireplace in the inn, they hadn't felt it was worth the extra expense. "I was hoping you would join me."

"Were you?" she asked, setting the monitors down.

"If you're asking if I want to spend time with you, the answer is yes. If you're asking if I want to have a conversation that I know we need to have, the answer is 'not really, but I know it needs to be done.' In both cases, I'm glad you're here."

"But you didn't actually invite me to join you."

"I could hope to put off the conversation. But I knew you would find me." He reached for her hand. She took it and sat beside him, sitting sideways on the couch to face him. "You have a way of always finding me when I'm lost."

"I love you."

"I know. If not for that, I truly *would* be lost."

"So, what did you want to talk about?" she asked.

He looked toward the fire. "Would it be all right if . . . I tell you about Serena?"

Chas almost slumped with relief. "Of course," she said, squeezing his hand with reassurance.

It took Jackson a minute to be able to actually begin, and he had to remind himself that he had no reason not to trust Chas, no reason to believe that any of this would change the way she felt about him.

"She worked at the Bureau," he began, still looking at the fire. "She had a desk job, dealt with case records. One year she decided to invite some of us over for Thanksgiving. We had nowhere else to go. Until I came here, it was one of the best Thanksgivings I'd ever had. I barely knew her then. But she was kind and thoughtful. After that she found excuses to continue to have some of us over. It was always a group of us. She gave us a place to go. I didn't know her any better than a handful of other people we worked with. But I liked her; I respected her. And then . . ." He hesitated and almost grimaced. He shifted in his seat and let go of Chas's hand to lean his forearms on his thighs. "There was a shooting incident. It was cut and dried. There was no investigation or problem. It was very clear that I'd had no choice. It was either him or me. The problem was that he'd *wanted* me to shoot him. I'd just talked him out of holding a gun to his own head, then he shot me instead."

"He *shot* you?"

"Yeah, but I was wearing a vest."

"Bullet-proof, you mean."

"That's right. It knocked me flat and I was awfully sore where the bullet hit me. I pulled my trigger about the same time, I think." He sighed and shook his head. "My supervisor called it suicide by FBI agent. But it haunted me." He leaned back and rubbed a hand over his face. "I was given some days of administrative leave, and I was required to get some counseling and the standard psych evaluation before I could go back to work. I was upset. I didn't want to be alone. Serena had opened her home to me and others like me, so I went to her door. That was the beginning of our spending time together exclusively. I don't even remember how it evolved into something romantic; it just did. I do remember that it was the first time in years that I didn't feel alone, that I felt like someone really understood me, really cared. In fact, I think she was the first true friend I'd ever had."

When he didn't say anything for more than a minute, Chas said, "Why is this so hard for you to talk about with me?"

He turned to look at her. "I lied to you, Chas. I told you I'd only had brief and meaningless relationships. I hardly knew you at the time. It didn't seem to matter. I didn't want—or feel the need—to explain. But when our relationship became more serious, I *should* have explained. My relationship with Serena was neither brief nor meaningless. We didn't actually *live* together, but that's only a technicality in light of the fact that we both kept our own apartments. We usually spent the night together at one place or the other. I loved her, Chas; I really loved her."

"And I loved Martin; you know that."

"But you were *married* to him, Chas. There's a *huge* difference."

"In some ways, yes. As far as the emotional relationship you shared, it's not different. You've told me many times that you just . . . didn't know any better. You can't hold yourself accountable for a decision made in ignorance. But even if you *had* known it was wrong, it still wouldn't matter. Not now, not after all we've been through, all the changes you've made in your life. You're a different man now. I'm not hurt or offended by your relationship with her. I'm just . . ."

"What?"

"I'm just wondering why it ended."

He looked away again. "Because I was a fool. Of course, I can look back now and know that it wasn't the right path for my life. But at the time . . . what we had was good. I don't know that it could have lasted a lifetime, but . . . I wasn't even willing to consider the possibility. She started hinting about taking our relationship more seriously. And it scared me, plain and simple. My home life had been so horrid that I was certain any effort I made toward having a family of my own would be a disaster." He shook his head. "And now I realize she was pregnant. Of course, she would have wanted our relationship to become more serious. We were going to have a baby."

"But she didn't tell you," Chas said. "Don't you think if you'd known it would have made a difference?"

"I'd like to think so, but truthfully, I might have been even more of a disappointment to her if I'd known. It's hard to say. I was so unkind to her. I told her she was ruining what we had by putting pressure on me. That was not part of the bargain in our relationship. I told her it wasn't personal; I just couldn't handle any implication of long-term commitment. But it *was* personal. I know I hurt her. And nothing was ever the same after that. We just . . . drifted apart. We avoided even making eye contact when we passed in the office." He shook his head again. "I was just such a jerk." He let out a bitter chuckle. "I always had it in the back of my mind that I would call her up one day and tell her that it wasn't her fault; I wanted to apologize for hurting her, for being so unfair. If I had known she had cancer, I might have been able to do that. As it is . . . I've lost that chance."

"Why don't you write her a letter?" Chas suggested. "Even if it's more for you than for her, it would give you a chance to say all the things you wanted to say. And if the Lord thinks it's important for her to know the things you feel, I'm certain He can find a way for her to know."

Jackson felt strangely comforted by the idea and believed it was a good one. "I'll work on that," he said. But he knew this conversation was far from over.

Jackson picked up the box he'd left on the coffee table and set it on Chas's lap. Together they looked at the pictures and other mementos. Together they read the letter Serena had written to him. Partway through it she said, "She was there when I came to the office? She saw me?"

"That's what it says."

"It must have been hard for her . . . to know there was someone in your life, and to have me there."

"I have no idea," Jackson said. "I'm ashamed to say that it didn't even occur to me when I asked Veese and Ekert to bring you there."

"It's just so ironic," Chas said and read on. She showed no signs of jealousy or any other negativity. In fact, she shed a few tears that she claimed were a combination of sadness on behalf of Serena's untimely death, and compassion for Jackson's grief. She laughed over the baby shirt and insisted that they were going to use it as Serena had suggested. When Jackson protested, she told him it would be good for him to change his memories associated with it. Once he saw one of his children wearing it, he might come to see Serena more as just a cluster of memories—and he could choose to focus on the positive ones. Again he was touched by her wisdom and insight, and when he felt the tension over Serena easing between them, he regretted not talking to her sooner. When they were finished sharing the contents of the box, Jackson put everything back in the box but the baby shirt, put the lid on the box, and tossed the entire thing into the fireplace.

"What are you doing?" Chas protested.

"I don't need these things to hold on to the memories," Jackson said. "I need a way to make me feel like it's truly behind me, and this is it."

"Is *this* why you wanted to sit by the fire?"

"Very perceptive," he said and squatted down to watch the box catch fire. The box and its contents burned quickly and disintegrated into the hot embers already on the grate. Jackson returned to the couch to sit by his wife.

"You look sad," he said.

"I was just wondering what would have happened if you *had* married Serena."

"I would be a widower," he said, "except that we likely would have divorced long before she got sick."

"Maybe not," she said. "Maybe the two of you would have made it work. She sounds like an amazing woman."

Jackson took her hand. "Let me clarify something, Chas. Serena *was* an amazing woman. She was there when I needed something solid to keep me from drifting off the deep end. She was kind and compassionate and giving. She had a lot of love to give. But there was the flip side that I haven't told you about. She liked to drink more than I did. She was careful and discreet, but it was a weekly ritual for her. She thought it was good psychology for a person to devote one night a week to getting just drunk enough to get rid of all of the stress from the previous week. She reserved Friday nights for the purpose, spent Saturdays laying around and getting past the hangover, and Sundays she would do her grocery shopping and errands before starting another work week. I'm ashamed to say my lifestyle was compatible to hers at the time, except that I held my liquor better, and I was the one who made sure she didn't do anything stupid while she was drinking. I have a hard time believing she would have changed those habits for the sake of a baby. Even if she let it go during pregnancy, I wonder what kind of mother she would have been. Those things don't matter now, Chas. The point is that I believe God knew I needed her at the time. I was in a place where I couldn't have connected with someone like you, even if our paths had crossed. But when the time was right, God brought me here. *You* are the love of my life, Chas. I don't know why I have been so blessed to have such amazing changes in my life, but I'm grateful for those blessings. I don't fully understand all that's happened and why, but I do know that it never would have worked long term for me and Serena."

Chas nodded as if she understood, but Jackson knew this wasn't over yet. He tightened his hold on her hand and said, "Serena is only one episode of my life, Chas. There were twenty-six years between Julie—after which I joined the Marines—and meeting you. We need to talk about those years. I can't hope to tell you every important aspect of those years in one conversation, but I need to tell you the highlights. I don't ever want a name or a situation to come up again that blindsides you. I want you to know a little bit about the women I was close to during those years, and I want you to help me put those experiences away properly instead of hiding from them."

"Okay," she said with no hesitation or reticence. Her willingness to have this conversation for *his* benefit touched him deeply. He knew it couldn't be pleasant for her, and he suspected some women would respond by exhibiting jealousy or anger.

They talked for nearly three hours before they finally left the fireplace with a few dying embers and went back into their home. Together they checked on the babies, prayed together, and fell asleep in each other's arms. Jackson still didn't feel entirely comfortable with the past or how to deal with it, but he did feel better. He had nothing to hide from Chas; the secrets had been spilled and she still loved him. Now if he could just make peace with all of this within himself.

* * * * *

Jackson followed Chas's advice and wrote Serena a long letter. It was difficult at first, but once he got some momentum, he was able to clear his head of every thought and feeling he would have wanted to share with her. Knowing she wouldn't actually read the letter, he was able to cleanse his feelings more fully than he might have otherwise. After he wrote it, he read it through and decided he would like Chas to read it as well. She did and cried a little bit. She told him she thought it was a beautiful letter, and that if she were Serena it would give her a great deal of peace and comfort. Jackson then took Chas with him into the formal dining room of the inn where he struck a match and lit the letter on fire before he tossed it onto the cold grate. He held Chas's hand while they watched it burn, then he hugged her tightly.

"Be patient with me," he murmured, certain that for all the progress he'd made, this wasn't over yet. But he *was* making progress.

* * * * *

As the days on the calendar were crossed off approaching their scheduled trip to Washington, Chas became painfully aware that Jackson was avoiding any discussion of going to the temple together. She resisted bringing it up, feeling that it would be best to allow him to come to terms with this on his own. On the other hand, time was easing closer. She didn't want their trip to Washington, DC, to be just a vacation. She wanted the temple to be the highlight of that visit, just as they'd planned all along.

Chas knew that Jackson had appointments with both the bishop and the stake president on Sunday, but each time she thought about reminding him, something held her back. She feared that if he remembered the appointments he would call and cancel them. If she brought it up at the last minute, his sense of responsibility would not allow him to back out and leave these men wondering where he was. Her hope was that a conversation with the bishop—a man he knew and trusted—might help him get over this obscure belief that he wasn't worthy to attend the temple. She knew she was deliberately manipulating the situation, but she was also willing to admit that to Jackson when the time was right.

When Sunday morning came, Chas still said nothing about the appointments. She sensed that Jackson didn't want to go church, which concerned her more deeply than she could even express. But he went and she was grateful. After church, Chas had dinner all ready in the slow-cooker, and they were able to eat fifteen minutes after they got home. When Jackson stood up to help clear the table, she said, "You have an appointment with the bishop . . . and the stake president afterward."

"When?" he asked, alarmed.

"You need to leave in five minutes."

"What for?" he asked, setting the dishes in his hands back down.

"I can't believe you even need to ask. Hello! 'Houston, we have a problem.'"

"*What* are you talking about?" he demanded and sat down again.

"It's from *Apollo 13,* when there was an explosion and they—"

"I know where the quote came from, Chas; I have no idea how you think it relates to my having these appointments."

Chas leaned over the table and looked at him fiercely. Everything that she'd been feeling and had tried to hold back in order to handle the situation delicately just came gushing out. "Do you know how many times you have said to me that our getting to the temple together was the most important thing to you? You were counting the months, then the weeks. You've said over and over that being sealed to your wife—and your children—for eternity was more precious than anything else you could have in this life. *You* scheduled these appointments, Jackson, right before you went to Virginia and lost your mind. I've been patient, gracious, kind, forgiving, and loving. I've figured that nagging and manipulating would accomplish nothing. But now is the turning point in this situation, Jackson. If we put this off, it will become easier to keep putting it off. If we're going to go to the temple when we planned to go, you need to get your recommend today. These appointments need to be kept."

"You could have said something before right now."

"I knew if I did you would cancel them."

"So you *are* manipulating me."

"You bet I am," she said with no apology. "Whether you come out of these appointments with a recommend or not, you need to talk to these men about what's going on in your life. You probably should have talked to the bishop a long time ago. Dr. Callahan has a great deal of knowledge and skill, and he's helped you immensely. But he doesn't have the spiritual knowledge or the proper keys of authority to help you with the most important aspects of healing. You know all of this. You've been here before for different reasons."

Jackson heard everything she was saying and couldn't find a way to dispute or counter any of it. He could only say, "I don't know if I can do it, Chas."

"Do what?"

"Talk to them about this; go to the temple; any of it."

"I agree that you really have to be ready, Jackson; I don't want you to do it just to do it. And if waiting is best, I will wait with you. But don't wait for the wrong reasons. From my perspective, *nothing* has changed in your life except your perception. You haven't committed any sins or made any mistakes since your *last* appointment with the bishop. You have nothing in your life that should hold you back."

"I haven't handled the situation very well; I haven't been a terribly good husband through all of this."

"Do you hear yourself? You were depressed, Jackson; I think you still are. You didn't cheat on me, or start drinking again; you didn't even yell at me. You're a good man, and you should not be holding yourself back from this simply because you're struggling to come to terms with things inside of you that have us both confused and frustrated. Go talk to these good men. Just do it. They might have something to say that will help you. If they don't feel like you're ready to go to the temple, I will respect that. Frankly, I'm not prone to trust *your* judgment on that at the moment."

Tears finally crept into her calm tirade. "I've been counting the weeks and the days, Jackson. Don't cheat *me* out of this. If there's a *good* reason to wait, we'll work on resolving it together. But I'm not going to put it off without getting some proper guidance to help us work toward it in the right way."

Jackson just stared at her, not knowing what to say and feeling helpless to soothe the obvious pain he had caused. It was apparent she'd been holding back in that regard. If nothing else, he'd just been slapped in the face with how very difficult this had been for her. He'd had hints and he'd suspected. But the tears on her face now enhanced the anguish showing in her eyes. He was surprised at the thought that came to his mind. During a difficult time when he'd been dealing with his PTSD, a friend had told him that he was like Sydney Carton in *A Tale of Two Cities,* for reasons that had been obscure to Jackson. Sydney had gone to the guillotine so that the woman he loved could be happy. He'd always loved that story. At the age of eighteen it had changed his life. And in that moment its concept touched something in his heart. He *would* put his head in a guillotine if it would preserve Chas's happiness. If he was willing to die for her, why was it so difficult to take these simple steps that she was asking him to take? He knew the answer. Having put his life on the line many times for the sake of duty, the thought of dying was easier than facing his inner demons. But she needed him. He was responsible for her—and not just for providing for her needs. She'd been running this inn and making a living for herself just fine before he came along. What she really needed from him was entirely spiritual and emotional. And he needed to muster up the courage to do the right thing. He knew that his temptation to be angry with her for not giving him the opportunity to cancel these appointments was childish and selfish. She'd had nothing but his best interests at heart; she always had.

"Well then," he said, coming to his feet. "I guess I'd better get to the church." He shook his head. "No wonder you fed me so quickly and didn't give me time to change my clothes." He looked at her sideways. "How clever of you!"

"Just go," she said.

He kissed her quickly and left.

Jackson had to wait when he arrived at the church. He sat outside the bishop's office just long enough for his nerves to completely overtake him. He felt nauseous at the very thought of telling the bishop everything that he knew he needed to tell him. His blanket confessions prior to baptism didn't feel like enough now. He felt certain the temple recommend would be delayed. But at least he could look his wife in the eye and tell her that he'd taken this step.

When the door to the bishop's office opened, Jackson's heart beat as hard as if he'd been going into a hostage situation with his weapon drawn. The couple that the bishop had been talking to left, and

Jackson rose to greet him. Jackson noted with some chagrin that there was no one else waiting. He was hoping this might go quickly if the bishop had other appointments to keep.

Bishop Wegg greeted him kindly, seeming genuinely pleased to see him. Not only was this the man who had helped Jackson prepare for baptism, he'd also married Chas and Jackson, and he'd conducted the funeral for Chas's grandmother. He'd been there through a number of significant steps—and challenges—in their lives. Jackson just hoped this step wouldn't diminish the bishop's opinion of him too much.

Once they were both seated, the bishop said, "So, it's finally time to get that temple recommend. You must be getting pretty excited."

"Actually," Jackson drawled, "I'm not sure I'm ready to take this step."

The bishop's concern was immediately evident. "What's going on?" he asked, leaning his forearms on the desk.

Jackson did his best to explain it briefly, emphasizing the fact that he'd omitted a great deal in his confessions prior to baptism, and pointing out that he wasn't nearly as worthy of the blessings of the gospel as he had led himself to believe. The bishop asked some specific questions about the issues of Jackson's past that troubled him, and Jackson gave him specific answers. The conversation made him sick, but he knew he needed to get through it. He knew he couldn't progress without being completely honest. He owed Chas that much, at the very least.

"Are there any other issues you feel the need to talk about?" the bishop asked when Jackson didn't seem to have anything else to say. At that point, Jackson hoped there *wasn't* anyone else waiting to see the bishop. This had certainly taken a while. He felt sure his appointment with the stake president should have already happened and he was late. But that appointment was probably pointless under the circumstances.

"No, I think I've covered it," Jackson said.

"Okay, there's something I'd like you to think about."

"I would welcome any advice you have," Jackson said.

"For all that Latter-day Saints are taught to strive for perfection, it's something we can only strive for while we're in this mortal existence. Mistakes and setbacks are a part of our earthly experience.

The questions that are asked as part of the temple recommend interview establish the minimum requirements of worthiness to attend the temple. Beyond that, people who attend the temple are at every possible degree of spirituality in their lives. There are angry people in the temple. There are depressed people, dysfunctional people, grieving people. As long as these people meet the minimum requirements of worthiness, the temple is exactly where they should be. The temple is where we gain strength and receive healing. The temple is where we're taught and retaught the things that will bring us closer to our Savior. Do you understand what I'm saying?"

"I do," Jackson said, steeling himself for a gentle lecture on the things he needed to do in order to make himself worthy to take his wife to the temple. Instead, the bishop opened a book on his desk and picked up a pen. "What are you doing?" Jackson asked.

"After we go through this list of questions, I'm going to give you a temple recommend—unless there's something that you haven't told me about."

"No, but . . ." Jackson felt alarmed, certain the bishop hadn't been listening, or he'd misunderstood.

"Is it all right with you if we just go through these questions?"

"Of course," Jackson said. He answered them thoughtfully and firmly, waiting for something to come up that would emphasize how *unworthy* he was to take this step. When the bishop asked him if he had a testimony of Jesus Christ, Jackson felt compelled to elaborate, and surprised by his own emotion in sharing his personal knowledge of the healing power of the Savior in his life. He concluded and struggled to get his composure, then he realized the bishop was writing in the book.

"What are you doing?" Jackson asked again.

"I'm giving you a temple recommend," he said. He looked Jackson in the eye and added, "I have no reason to think that you haven't been completely honest with me, and I have no reason to believe that you aren't entirely worthy to go to the temple."

Jackson's emotion rushed back. He couldn't speak due to his efforts to keep from crying like a baby. When the bishop asked him some questions in order to write down accurate information, he couldn't conceal his emotional state.

The bishop looked at him and said, "I hope this is joy you're feeling."

"Yes," Jackson managed, "and . . . confusion. With everything I've been feeling, I just don't understand how it could be this simple."

The bishop reached for his scriptures and quickly found a particular page while he was saying, "I've found that the answer to every question can be found somewhere in the scriptures. We just need to have them open in front of us enough to allow the Spirit to guide us to those answers."

"Well, I haven't been doing so well at that lately," Jackson said, thinking that might make him renege on his decision to give the recommend.

"Studying the scriptures helps keep us close to the Spirit," the bishop said, "but it wasn't on that list of questions." Jackson couldn't argue with that. The bishop passed the book across the desk and said, "Could you read just the first sentence of verse eleven."

Jackson took the book, noting it was open to 2 Nephi, chapter two. He cleared his throat and swallowed the lump that was there, relieved that he now felt more composed. "'For it must needs be, that there is an opposition in all things.'"

"Okay, that's all," the bishop said. "I know that you've had the gospel in your life for a very short time. It takes time to learn the principles and doctrines that affect our lives. It can be hard to recognize what's happening around us when we don't understand those principles and doctrines. I hope you can take my word for it when I tell you that with my years of experience in living the gospel, there is no good thing that happens without Satan opposing it in every possible way. Look again at the sentence you just read. It doesn't say opposition in *some* things; it says *all* things. It doesn't say there *might* be opposition. It says there *must needs be* opposition. It's part of the plan, and it's necessary to face the opposition in order to prove ourselves throughout this earth life. Over time and with practice, you will learn to recognize the voice of the Lord more readily, and you will also come to recognize the workings of Satan when he's trying to hold you back. Depression, discouragement, unwarranted guilt are all among his tools. It's important for us to be able to separate what's real and true from the adversary's attempts to confuse and discourage us. If you've genuinely made a mistake, then the remorse you feel will prompt you to put your life in order. When your life *is* in order, feelings of guilt and discouragement do *not* come from your Father in Heaven. When you hear false messages in your head, you need to recognize them for what they are and correct your thinking."

Jackson felt chilled as the concept perfectly coincided with advice Dr. Callahan had given him. The bishop concluded by saying, "It's my opinion that Satan does not want you to go the temple. He loathes the temple above all else in this world because it gives us strength to keep him at bay. He saw you in a vulnerable situation and took advantage of it. Now you can chalk it up to having learned something, and you can move forward."

CHAPTER SIXTEEN

Jackson was stunned as he left the bishop's office with that precious piece of paper in his hand. The bishop had called the stake office to let them know Jackson had been delayed but he was on his way. The stake president had agreed to wait so there would be no delay in Jackson being able to get to the temple. Jackson had to drive to Butte for this appointment, but the time on the road allowed him opportunity to think about his conversation with the bishop and to become accustomed to this new perspective. He arrived at the stake center only half an hour behind his originally scheduled time.

Jackson's interview with this good man was more brief, but in essence he told Jackson the same things. After he signed off on the recommend, he asked Jackson if he would like a priesthood blessing. The request took Jackson off guard, but he easily agreed. He wasn't going to turn down any offer for divine assistance. The blessing reaffirmed everything these two good men had told him, and the warmth that filled Jackson verified the truth of what he was hearing. His Heavenly Father loved him and was pleased with the changes he'd made in his life. The past was forgiven. The blessings of taking his family to the temple would be innumerable.

Through the drive home, Jackson became more comfortable with the shift in his thinking—and in his heart. He cried a few tears that seemed to fully cleanse the past out of him, then he focused on returning home to the woman who loved him. He was determined to dedicate his life to deserving the love that she gave him.

* * * * *

Chas tried to keep herself distracted while Jackson was gone, and not think too hard about what the results might be. She knew that he had to drive to Butte and back, on top of the time for the actual interviews. In her opinion, lengthy interviews were a good sign. She just hoped his sense of responsibility in meeting the appointments had prevailed, and that he hadn't ditched them. For all she knew, he could just be taking a long drive and getting more depressed. She felt tempted to call his cell phone, but if he was in an interview he'd have it turned off anyway. All in all, she felt it was best to do what she'd had to do a lot lately: she said a prayer and waited.

Chas heard the chime ring that indicated someone had come through the door of the inn. They were expecting a couple to check in, so she wasn't surprised. She left Isabelle in a playpen and Charles playing with some toys in an area that was completely baby-proofed. She knew they would be safe for the short time it would take her to check in their guests. She took a baby monitor with her so she could hear if one of them started to cry.

Chas entered the main hall of the inn to see a young couple removing their coats and brushing snow out of their hair. She hadn't realized it was snowing, but added a quick addition to her prayer that Jackson would be safe during his drive home. She greeted their guests and took care of the technicalities in just a few minutes. She led them to their room on the second floor while she told them about the amenities of the inn, and how they would need to use a key she was giving them to get in and out of the outside door at night, since it remained locked. Once they were settled, Chas went downstairs to lock that door and make the inn ready for nighttime. She came into the hall to see Jackson taking off his coat and brushing the snow out of his hair. It was so much like the first night he'd come here that she had to stop and catch her breath. A sense of déjà-vu overcame her so intensely that she could only stand there and look at him, trying to connect the present to the past.

On that night, there had been a power outage; the storm had been terrible. She'd called the cell phone of her expected guest to help him with directions. When he'd arrived she had stepped out on the porch with a lantern to meet him. He'd stepped through the door and brushed the snow out of his hair. There was a moment when their eyes had first met that she never would have noticed at the time as anything significant. But she remembered that moment clearly, and now she knew that two spirits had come together, having finally found their way to a meeting that was meant to be. He looked up now, more than four years later, and their eyes met again. The way he just stood there and stared made her wonder if he was feeling the same sense of déjà-vu.

"Wow, that's weird," he said after at least a minute of silence.

"What?" she asked.

"Coming in like that . . . out of the storm . . . and seeing you there. It almost felt like . . . the first time . . ."

"Yeah, I was thinking the same thing," she said.

"Except you came out on the porch . . . with a lantern."

Chas heard the baby jabbering on the monitor in her pocket, reminding her that she couldn't stand there in the hall all night. "Why did you come in this way?" she asked, stepping past him to lock the door.

"Less wind and snow from this side," he said.

Chas turned to find him still staring at her. "What?" she asked with a little laugh. There was something warm and open in his eyes that she hadn't seen there for a while, and it made her heart quicken. He smiled and took hold of her chin before he bent to kiss her. He laughed softly and kissed her again.

"What?" she asked again, looking into his eyes as if they could answer all her questions.

With her peripheral vision she saw him hold up a piece of paper. She turned to look at it just as he said, "Houston, we have liftoff."

Chas realized he was holding a temple recommend. She laughed and threw her arms around his neck. He wrapped her tightly in his arms, and she started to cry.

"I'm so sorry I made this so difficult," he muttered close to her ear.

"It's all right now," she said. "Everything's going to be all right."

"Yes, it is," he said, lifting her feet off the floor.

More baby noises came through the monitor, and they both laughed. He set her down and turned off the main lights while she locked up the office. They walked hand in hand from the inn into the house, locking the door in between. Jackson greeted his children with a relaxed demeanor that Chas hadn't seen since he'd gone to Virginia. When he caught her staring at him, she said, "You're back."

"Yes, I believe I am," he said and kissed her while he was holding Isabelle. He put the baby down to play and they sat close together on the couch, where he held her hand and told her all about his visits with the bishop and stake president, and the understanding he'd gained of all that had happened and why. He told her he was looking forward to studying *all* of 2 Nephi chapter two, and other related scriptures, so that he could more fully grasp the implication of these things in his life, and how to be better prepared to handle Satan's fiery darts in the future.

Chas took in what her husband was saying, along with his changed countenance, and she found it impossible to contain her overflowing joy.

* * * * *

Everything became crazy as Jackson and Chas worked to get ready to take their trip to Washington. Polly would be left in charge of the inn, something she had proven over and over to be capable of handling. Elliott would be staying there with her and helping with anything that needed a man's hand. Polly and Elliott didn't fully understand the implications of what this temple thing meant to Chas and Jackson, but they were fully supportive.

The drive to the airport and the flight proved to be an adventure with a two-year-old and a baby who was learning to crawl. But they arrived in Washington safely and were soon in a rented vehicle on their way to the hotel where they had reservations. Jackson took a detour to see a few sights first, if only from a distance. They followed the directions on the GPS to the address of the LDS temple, and they both caught their breath as it seemed to appear out of nowhere, magnificent and shining in the sunlight.

"I'm so glad we didn't postpone," Jackson said, reaching for Chas's hand.

With the glisten of tears in her eyes, she said, "Me too!"

The following day they went together through those temple doors. Chas was weepy before they even got there, overcome with joy at having reached such a joyous day. Long before she'd married Jackson, when he'd had no interest in religion, she had dreamt of this day. But she never could have imagined the rocky paths they would take to get here, and she hadn't really pictured children being involved. They turned the children over to sweet temple workers dressed in white, knowing they would be well cared for until they were brought to the sealing room at the appropriate time. Chas had prayed very hard that the children would be well behaved during the two or more hours they needed to wait, and especially while they were in the sealing room for this unique experience that neither of them were old enough to remember. But to their parents, it would be a once-in-a-lifetime moment.

Chas's prayers were answered and her expectations exceeded as the sealing of her family took place. The children looked so beautiful in white! And Jackson had never looked happier or more at peace. He kept looking at her with stark love and admiration showing in his eyes. She had never felt more loved.

After the ceremony was completed and eternity was made official for their little family, Jackson asked a stranger on the temple grounds to take a couple of pictures of them. From the little screen on the digital camera they could see that the pictures were perfect. The best ones would be enlarged and framed and enjoy a prominent place in their home. It was surely the most important day of any of their lives.

The remainder of their time in the nation's capital felt as much like a honeymoon as it could feel with two children around. They were surprisingly cooperative through most of their sightseeing as Jackson and Chas took in the historical significance of the city. For all that Jackson disagreed with certain aspects of current politics, he was deeply patriotic. Chas having lost her husband while he was serving in the military had given them something in common when they'd first come together. Now, they shared a deep love of their country, their religion, their family, and each other. All things combined, it made for a splendid life.

* * * * *

A week or so after the family returned home from Washington, Jodi stopped by to visit Chas, and they enjoyed catching up on a number

of things. After sharing much good news with each other while the
children napped, Chas took the baby monitors with her and found
Jackson in the office of the inn.

"Was that Jodi I saw coming and going?" Jackson asked. One
window had a perfect view of the little front yard of the attached
house.

"Yes, we had a good visit. She gave me the update on the ladies."

"Anything good?" he asked. Chas had told him all about her
experiences with these amazing women when they'd had lots of time
to talk during their vacation. Most of all she'd enjoyed sharing with
him all the wonderful things she'd learned about relationships that
she hoped would help in her own life. She'd also come to appreciate
the value of true friendship, and was grateful to have good friends in
her own life.

"Yes, actually," she said. "Mia, who never married, has started
dating a widower, and she really likes him."

"Ooh," Jackson said.

"Marianne, the one who has been in denial over her bad marriage
for years, has given her husband an ultimatum and he's agreed to go
to counseling while they have a temporary separation to see if he's
capable of being a decent husband and father." She smiled at Jackson.
"He could learn a thing or two from you."

He gave her a sidelong glance, and she continued. "Rachelle—
she's the one whose husband has been leading the double life all these
years—has determined that she has no choice but to divorce him,
because it's evident he's not going to change. But she's doing well with
the adjustment, and she's handling the situation with a great attitude."

"That's great . . . that she's handling it well, I mean. One day the
guy is going to wake up and realize what he lost."

"Yeah, it's pretty sad," Chas said. "But I'm glad Rachelle is doing
well. She's always tried to be a good person; she deserves to be happy."

"Yes, she does."

"And," Chas said with aplomb, "Kristy is actually doing very well."
She knew Jackson didn't need any reminder of Kristy's situation; she
was the one Chas had talked about the most, the one Chas had
become closest to. In fact, she and Kristy had talked on the phone a

few times since she'd returned home. It looked as though they would continue to be friends, and Chas was great with that. "Kristy and her husband are going to counseling that's affiliated with the facility where their son is staying for the time being. He's still struggling but he's not suicidal anymore. It's going to be tough, but it seems her husband has finally gotten on board and realized that he needs to change his attitudes if they're going to have any hope at all of helping him. So, all in all, it's good news."

"That *is* good news," Jackson said.

"Which reminds me," Chas went on. "There's something I've been thinking about that I wanted to bring up."

"Okay," Jackson said, leaning toward her. "You know that thing about people coming to our inn to find healing and peace?"

"Yes," Jackson drawled, intrigued.

"Well . . . a person who only stays one night, or even two, isn't likely to experience any great impact. Obviously people have been led here for longer visits, like . . ."

"Like me?"

"Yes, like you." She smiled. "But I was going to say . . . like Brian and Melinda. Your sister and nephew are family, of course, but their being here through tough times made a big difference in their lives."

"Yes, I'm sure it did. It was good to be in a position to help them."

"I also think we left an impression on Artem."

"Ah, yes. Mr. Tarasov."

"He stayed for weeks, and he was here through some pretty eventful stuff. But it was because of our influence that he spent all that time in Salt Lake City. His letters have been very sweet. I really think that with time he *will* join the Church."

"Yes, I think he will," Jackson said. "What a sweet man."

"And this thing with Jodi and her friends worked out really well . . . in the long run. I'm so glad we were able to provide the inn for them. In spite of my own personal . . . stresses at the time, I'm glad I was involved. I think it taught me something about who I am and what I'm capable of. I never believed that I could make a difference to people in crisis in such a personal way, but I did, and it felt good."

"You made a difference to *me* when *I* was in crisis."

"Yes, but I was in love with you; still am."

"So you were biased," he said lightly.

"Maybe."

More seriously he said, "But you have also helped perfect strangers, many times."

"Like who? Besides Jodi and her friends?"

"Cortney," he said with caution.

Chas groaned. "What did I do to help Cortney? She ended up dead."

"She ended up dead because she made poor choices that involved her associations with organized crime. But when I think of Cortney being here for those months before that horrible day when we lost her, the first thing that always comes to mind was how kind you were to her. You have a loving heart, Chas; just like that little wall-hanging in the hall, with the quote from *David Copperfield*. It reminds me of you each time I pass it. I know exactly what it says. *A loving heart was better and stronger than wisdom.* It reminds me so much of you. It's not that you aren't wise, because you are. You're *very* wise, but I think you know how to put love in its proper place. It's always more important than anything else. That's what Christ taught above all else, and you live your life like that. You always have. I think Granny taught you that. She was so much the same way. She could just reach out and love someone . . . without even trying." His chin quivered slightly as he smiled, and his eyes sparkled with memories of Chas's grandmother. "She didn't even know me, but she was so kind, and she taught me such powerful principles in simple conversation. She had a great impact on my life, and I didn't know her all that long before she passed away."

He took Chas's hand. "The thing is . . . I think you need to realize that you have that same gift, that same ability. You *have* made a difference in people's lives, and I think you will continue to do so. If this is to be a place of refuge for people who are struggling, it will be your influence as the innkeeper that will have the most impact. An old Victorian house itself isn't going to change lives. Although this old Victorian house has a great spirit about it."

"I won't dispute that," Chas said, and paused to ponder everything he'd said in light of her original purpose in opening this conversation.

"Okay, so . . . I've been thinking that maybe we should take this . . . purpose for our inn more seriously. Obviously we need to trust that God will guide people here who need to be here. But . . . maybe we need to help it along a little; encourage the opportunity, so to speak."

"Yes," he said, intrigued.

"Our biggest source of advertising is our website. Our second is word of mouth. So if we look at the first one, we know that people do Internet searches and they find our website. I think our website needs to have a very visible notation on the home page that indicates this is a great place for lengthy getaways: pleasant, peaceful atmosphere, accommodating staff, discounts on weekly or even monthly rates. So let's say that someone is in a crisis, needs to get away, has a feeling they should look online, they Google and find us, and when they see that—which is something they aren't likely to see on sites for other bed-and-breakfast inns—they may be drawn here."

"That is an amazing and inspired idea!" Jackson said and had to laugh just because it felt so good.

"Definitely inspired," she said and hurried to move on. "Now, if our second-best source of advertising is word of mouth, then we need to have something posted in the dining room, and perhaps some high-quality brochure or flyer that we leave in the rooms to indicate the same thing. People will stay here, tell people that it's that kind of place, or come back themselves for longer stays when they feel like they need to."

"I think I would be thrilled to take care of both of those things right away."

"I was hoping you'd say that, because I hate the computer stuff, and the getting-stuff-printed thing. I'm glad you came along and took those things over—among many other tasks I hate."

"A pleasure, Mrs. Leeds," he said and kissed her. He smiled and added, "You're a genius, you know."

"Because I was smart enough to marry you?"

"Because you were wise enough to teach me the greatest lessons of life, and because you loved me enough to make me believe that I could be the man you deserve."

Chas smiled at him and said, "You want to know what's amazing and incredible?"

"What?" he asked, smiling back. "I'm going to be with you forever, Jackson Leeds."

"That *is* amazing and incredible," Jackson said. They stared at each other for a long moment, and he shared a thought that occurred to him. "Did I tell you what I read in *Great Expectations* that really touched me . . . while I was in Virginia?"

"No," she said in a tone that implied her chagrin at him keeping things from her.

Jackson stood up and grabbed a copy of the novel from one of the shelves in the office where they had Dickens novels and paraphernalia for sale. He quickly found the last page and said, "This is how it ends . . . when Pip and Estella are finally together." He cleared his throat and read aloud. *"I took her hand in mine, and we went out of the ruined place; and, as the morning mists had risen long ago when I first left the forge, so, the evening mists were rising now, and in all the broad expanse of tranquil light they showed to me, I saw the shadow of no parting from her.'"*

"It's beautiful," Chas said, but she wasn't sure why it had left such an impression on Jackson. She became entranced as he explained that he had seen metaphorical images in his mind when he'd read it, that he'd seen the forge as the life he'd lived before Chas, and the ruined place as the city he'd left behind. And most of all he saw himself with Chas and their children, surrounded by a tranquil light that exemplified all the light she had ushered into his life, and the hope they shared of making that life better. Chas couldn't hold back tears as he concluded with a tender appreciation for knowing they would be together forever.

"You know," Chas said, "in Dickens's original ending of that book, he *didn't* have them end up together. If I remember correctly, the publisher asked him to change it; they wanted a happy ending." Jackson made a contemplative noise, and Chas added, "I remember when I read about that, thinking how the different endings were indicative of the choices we make in life. The outcome is a result of what we choose." She stood up and leaned over to kiss him. "I'm glad you chose to be with me forever."

"Best thing I ever did," he said and pulled her onto his lap, kissing her again.

* * * * *

A little while after Chas had gone back into the house since the children were waking up, Jackson heard the outside door of the inn open and close and looked up from his desk to see a nice-looking, well-dressed young man enter the doorway of the office. His confident air was contradicted by a mild nervousness.

"Agent Leeds?" he asked.

"Not anymore," Jackson said.

The young man's nervousness relented a little when he smiled. "You haven't changed." Before Jackson could ask how this young man knew him, he went on, "I have, I know. I didn't expect you to recognize me. You change a lot more in twelve years when you started out at age eleven."

Jackson stood and moved around the desk while he put pieces together in his mind. This had something to do with an FBI issue that had happened twelve years ago regarding an eleven-year-old boy. A memory began to stir just as this young man stepped forward and held out his hand. "Michael Westcott," he said, shaking Jackson's hand firmly. Then he put his hands into the pockets of his expensive jeans. "It's been a long time, and I know it left a deeper impression on me than it would on you. Trust me when I tell you that I will never forget your face. You killed the man who was going to kill *me.*"

It all came back to Jackson in a rush. "You were kidnapped for ransom. They said they'd give you up when they got the money."

"But I'd seen their faces. They were going to kill me anyway. Then you came out of nowhere. You told him to drop the gun—the one he had pointed at my head—but he just put the barrel to my forehead while he was trying to drag me out of the room. He was going to use me as a hostage to get away, which meant that he would just kill me later." Michael glanced down and chuckled tensely. "To say I was terrified would be such a gross understatement." He looked up again. "But I was terrified. And you were so calm, so cool. You just . . . pulled the trigger and I was free."

"That calm and cool thing was just part of the job, Michael. An agent had to be that way. It didn't mean it was easy."

"I know that; I do. I saw it in your eyes. But you did what had to be done. You saved my life." He chuckled again. "Then you held me while I cried like a baby, and you stayed with me every second until you delivered me safely to my parents."

"Oh, that was a great moment," Jackson said.

The silence almost became awkward before Michael said, "I talked to Agent Ekert; he told me where to find you. I hope it's okay."

"Of course it's okay," Jackson said and motioned him to a chair. Jackson sat down next to him rather than on the other side of the desk.

"I guess I've just reached a point in life where I've had the need to take an accounting of where I am before I can really figure out where I'm going. It just felt right to let you know that I think of you every day of my life. Now that I'm an adult and can look at what happened, it just didn't seem right to not offer you a formal thank-you. And it just didn't seem like the kind of thing that could be done over the phone or with a card."

"I was just doing my job," Jackson said.

"No, I think it was more than that. I talked to Agent Ekert. He told me that you always drove your team hard and rough, especially when a life was at stake. He told me some agents would have given up, but you didn't. And he told me you were smart, that you could think like the criminals, you could figure them out. He said I probably *would* have died if it hadn't been for you."

Jackson didn't know what to say. He'd prided himself on being the best agent he was capable of being, and he'd found fulfillment in working hard and pushing a case until there was nothing left to push. But he had still considered it his job. He felt humbled, and even gratified, to recall how the Westcott incident had worked out. But he didn't feel like he could take so much credit.

"You know what, kid? Whether any of us realized it at the time or not, I think your life was more in God's hands than mine. Looking back, I can see that He guided my mind and my instincts so I could do my job well. But the outcome wasn't always as good as it was with you."

"I know that too. Sometimes I wonder why it *was* so good for me."

"Because it wasn't your time to go. Now it's up to you to make something of your life that's worthy of surviving something like that."

Michael's eyes widened and sparkled. "How did you know?"

"Know what?"

"That's *exactly* what I've been thinking, but I'm not sure that *anything* I'm capable of doing is worthy of surviving something like that."

"I'm sure there are all kinds of things you can do."

"I do *not* have my dad's business skills. He tells me I'm only good at spending money. And maybe he's right. But my parents certainly have money for me to spend. My dad with all his fast boats and hot cars. My mother and her shopping sprees. It's hard to take advice from them on *not* spending money. But then it was their flashy money that nearly got me killed. Nobody wants to steal a kid they can't get a good ransom for. Sometimes I think my parents keep handing me money to ease their guilt for that. I've tried college a few different times and I always bail. My mother makes excuses for me, saying that anyone who went through what I did as a child would surely have issues."

"Maybe she's right," Jackson said.

"Or maybe it's just an excuse." Michael seemed to catch himself, and he chuckled tensely. "I have *no* idea why I am talking to you about this stuff. You don't even know me; not really."

"I'm the one who saved your life," Jackson said. "You think we didn't bond while you were crying like a baby? And you don't know how hard it was for me *not* to cry. I just kept wondering what it would have been like to get there and find you already dead. I haven't thought about you as much as you've thought about me, but I've certainly wondered how your life went after that. The memory of bringing you safely out of that ordeal is one that makes me smile. And you don't get a whole lot of those memories in the FBI."

Michael nodded and bit his lip, clearly trying to hold back emotion that he was embarrassed to show.

"Let me tell you something, Michael. Since the last time we saw each other, I've been on the other side of this." Michael's eyes widened. "I was held hostage in South America for a few weeks. It took a long time and a lot of therapy to recover."

"Is that why you retired?" Michael asked.

"I'd been ready to retire when it happened. I was just going to do this one last case."

"Do you wish you had retired earlier?"

"I used to."

"Used to?"

"Until I realized that if I hadn't been there, someone else would have gone in my place. Someone like Agent Ekert."

"So you saved him, too."

"I had no control over it. I was just doing my job and ended up in the wrong place at the wrong time."

"Instead of someone else."

"Maybe it's what I needed," Jackson said. "Now that I've come through it and stopped having nightmares, I can't imagine *not* having that as a part of who I am. I'm a better, stronger person because of it."

Michael chuckled. "I wish I could say the same about me."

"Can't you?"

"I feel like it's damaged me."

"And I felt that way too."

"I've already gone through years of therapy for this," Michael said.

"Maybe they're not telling you the right things. Maybe you should talk to someone who's been through it, instead of someone who has read about it in a textbook."

"I didn't realize I was coming to you for advice."

"Maybe that's why you felt so strongly about coming to see me. Maybe God knew that my personal convictions were something you needed to hear."

"You really think God works that way? My parents always took me to church on Sundays—unless there was something better to do. But I never heard anything there that made me feel like God really cared about me."

"He does," Jackson said firmly. "He sent me to save your life, didn't He?" He paused and their eyes met firmly. "And now you're here."

"So, what would your advice be for someone who has been traumatized from a hostage situation?"

"Forgive."

"What?" Michael asked. Then he leaned back as abruptly as if he'd been slapped.

"You might think you have a right to be angry with the people who did this to you. Anger is certainly something you have to work through. But eventually you have to let it go. Holding onto to *any* negative feelings towards those people is like carrying around a backpack full of rocks. You get so used to carrying it that you don't even feel it anymore, but it's weighing you down and holding you back. I resisted forgiving. I argued with my therapist about it. I argued with my wife about it. But in the end, it's what healed me. And I also had to accept that I not only needed to forgive my captors, I had to forgive my father."

Again Michael winced. "For what?"

"That's personal," he said. "But maybe you should at least stop and ask yourself if you're holding a grudge against your father for being *that* rich."

Silence preceded Michael saying, "Okay, you've given me some things to think about."

"For me it was a spiritual matter. You need to find those things inside yourself in your own way. But trust me when I tell you that if you don't forgive, you'll carry it for the rest of your life."

More silence. "And what other advice would you give me?"

"To get outside yourself. Instead of spending so much energy wondering what's wrong with you, take a look at what's wrong with the world and do something to make it a little better."

"Like how?" Michael asked, as if the concept had never crossed his mind.

"You've got money, you've got time, and I bet you flew into Butte in a private jet."

"Yeah, so?"

Jackson leaned a little closer. "Have you ever considered how many people in a third-world country could be supported for a year with the cost of a hot car?"

Michael looked intrigued but said, "I wouldn't know where to start."

"A man with your resources ought to be able to find all kinds of philanthropic opportunities, if you just start digging."

Michael's silence was now accentuated by the sparkle in his eyes. Jackson could feel his mind spinning, venturing into new places, new possibilities. Jackson let him think for a minute, then he said, "Puts a new twist on wondering why you didn't die twelve years ago, doesn't it."

"Yeah, I think it does," Michael said and glanced around, his expression indicating that his mind had shifted gears. "This is a nice place."

"Yes, it is. I love it here."

Michael looked at him. "I don't want to offend you, but . . . is there anything I can do to help you, or your family?"

"I'm not offended, but no. Thank you. We're doing fine. Take my advice seriously. You could do nothing better for me than that."

"Okay, I'll do it," he said with conviction. Perhaps in his mind, doing it to repay the debt of having his life saved would actually make him follow through, rather than just thinking about doing it.

"Are you hungry?" Jackson asked. "I can put together a pretty great sandwich without much effort."

"No, thank you," Michael said, coming to his feet. Again he offered his hand. "You've been very kind . . . now, and back then."

"It was truly a pleasure . . . now *and* then. Keep in touch, kid. I'd love to hear what you're up to. You can always find me through the website for the inn." He picked up a business card from the desk and handed it to him.

"I'm sure you'll hear from me."

"Good. I'll look forward to it. And tell your parents hello for me."

"I'll do that. My mother talks about you occasionally."

Jackson walked outside with Michael, who surprised him with a quick hug before he got into his rented car and drove away. Jackson stood there for a minute, pondering such an unexpected encounter. He went back through the inn and into his home, where he found Chas picking up toys.

"You would never believe who was just here," he said.

She smiled and plopped onto the couch. "Tell me," she said eagerly.

Jackson sat beside her and took her hand. "You know that blessing? How the inn will be a place where people will find healing and peace?"

"Didn't we have this conversation just a while ago?"

"Yeah, but now there's a new twist. I'm wondering if that qualifies for certain people who just stop in for half an hour."

Chas's eyes filled with intrigue. Jackson started at the beginning.

About the Author

Anita Stansfield began writing at the age of sixteen, and her first novel was published sixteen years later. Her novels range from historical to contemporary and cover a wide gamut of social and emotional issues that explore the human experience through memorable characters and unpredictable plots. She has received many awards, including a special award for pioneering new ground in LDS fiction, and the Lifetime Achievement Award from the Whitney Academy for LDS Literature. Anita is the mother of five, and has one adorable grandson. Her husband, Vince, is her greatest hero.

To receive regular updates from Anita, go to anitastansfield.com and subscribe.